We hope yo'

THE TWO-WEEK WAIT

Lucy J Lewis

The Book Guild Ltd

First published in Great Britain in 2021 by
The Book Guild Ltd
9 Priory Business Park
Wistow Road, Kibworth
Leicestershire, LE8 0RX
Freephone: 0800 999 2982
www.bookguild.co.uk
Email: info@bookguild.co.uk
Twitter: @bookguild

Typeset in 12pt Adobe Jenson Pro

Printed and bound by CPI Group (UK) Ltd, Croydon, CR0 4YY

ISBN 978 1913551 438

British Library Cataloguing in Publication Data.
A catalogue record for this book is available from the British Library.

To Mom and Dad, for everything...

Part One

Part One

Monday 1st February
Day 1 of TWW

"Thank you for a delicious lunch," said Annie, hugging her sister goodbye.

"Kids, come on now." A small boy followed by a small girl followed by a tiddly toddler appeared from out of the sitting room, the toddler dragging a holey blanket along the varnished wooden floorboards. He had bright red cheeks and a thumb firmly ensconced in his mouth.

"Fin, Izzy, get your shoes on," said Annie. "And you, pick up your blanket, Benny."

"I've found a small rabbit," said Keith, coming out of the kitchen clutching a floppy, furry toy.

"It's mine," said Izzy.

"If anyone has left anything else," said Annie, "it has to stay. Now come on, you lot, let's leave Jane and Keith in peace." She gave Jane a hurried hug, waved to Keith and in a whirl of shoes, coats and blankets, was gone, her ducklings trotting along behind.

"Phew," said Jane quietly, shutting the door and breathing in the restored sense of calm.

"That was fun," said Keith.

"Tiring," said Jane.

"OPCs always are tiring," said Keith. OPCs being other people's children, which, in the case of Jane and Keith, was all children.

"Boiled egg?" Jane moved into the kitchen and opened the dishwasher, ready to unload the plates from lunch.

It was standard procedure nowadays for Jane and Keith to 'get on' with life after spending time with OPCs, to keep busy, move on to the next thing, not to dwell on the enormous void in their own lives, made all the hollower after hosting a houseful of small people wreaking havoc.

"I'll most probably just have a chicken sandwich, if there's any chicken left from lunch?" said Keith, sweeping the crumbs from a squashed digestive biscuit off the table and into his hands.

"There's quite a lot. Annie didn't have much – not quite got her appetite back after that bout of flu."

"I suppose you catch everything when you have young kids," said Keith. "In the firing line and all that."

"Well, we wouldn't know, would we?" said Jane, suddenly straightening and turning her back on Keith, pretending to busy herself at the sink.

"Benny's adorable, though, isn't he?" Keith continued, refusing to get sucked in. "And Izzy. Fin is quite reserved, like Pete."

"He's got a wicked sense of humour, though," said Jane, recovering herself and sidling up to Keith.

"Though not as funny as you."

She nestled her head in Keith's neck and kissed him.

"Oh, so you're going to be nice now, are you?" said Keith, stroking Jane's back.

"Why wouldn't I be?" said Jane.

4

"Haven't I served my purpose for this month?"

"Oh, you mean? Yes," said Jane. "You're totally pointless to me now. May as well go and make yourself useful pottering in your shed or hanging pictures."

"I'd love a shed to potter in."

"You've got a garage."

"Yes, but a shed, it just sounds so…"

"Manly?"

"I was going to say peaceful, but manly works." Keith lifted Jane's head so that she was looking into his deep, brown eyes. "Are you OK?" he said.

"I will be," Jane said. "Just give me an hour or two."

"It's not that Annie means to be cruel – it's just she has no idea what it's like," said Keith. "What did she say, exactly?"

"Oh, the same sort of stuff she's been saying for nearly twenty years. 'When you and Keith eventually get around to having kids'… Like it's something we're purposefully putting off while we live our own rich, full lives."

"It's better like that, though, isn't it? You'd hate her to pity you and steer clear of the topic completely, I know you would."

"Yes, but it still hurts."

Jane made no secret of the fact that she and Keith had been trying for a baby for not far off twenty years, ever since they got married in their early twenties.

"It's only because you don't show her how upset it makes you feel," said Keith. "She has no idea."

"That's because she just needs to look at a male genital and she's pregnant. Anyway, I don't want to be the sourpuss older sister, all judgemental. It's great she can have kids and as a consequence we can have nephews and a niece. I am sure they will bring us great pleasure."

"When they are old enough to have broader conversations than, 'Who has the smelliest bum?'"

"Oh, come on, isn't that your main topic of conversation at work?"

Jane broke away from Keith and went to drop an egg in the boiling water. "Time it for me, would you, please? Two and a half minutes."

"Sooo," said Keith, glancing at his watch as instructed. "How are you going to spend the next two weeks… of waiting?" He opened the fridge to retrieve the leftover chicken.

"I've got some ideas," said Jane, tucking a wayward brown curl back behind her ear. "I might try and crochet a new blanket for Benny."

"Yes, Grandma, you could indeed, or… you could always go on a road trip."

"Where would I go?"

"It's years since you went to Bristol."

"Not much of a road trip, that's only, what? Sixty miles down the M5? Anyway, why would I want to go there?"

"Oh, just, well, stuff."

Jane spun around to face her husband, a look of suspicion in her deep green eyes. "What sort of stuff?"

"It's just, well, there's this golden retriever—"

"What are you saying, Keith?"

"It's my colleague's aunt – her dog has given birth to a litter of five puppies and she is looking for owners."

"You are kidding me, right?"

"I'm not, Janey," said Keith. "Come on, let's do it. Let's get a puppy."

Jane, who was not one for vast displays of emotion, gave a small leap, losing one of her slippers in mid-air, and clapped her hands. "How cute are they, Keith?"

Keith got his phone from his pocket and began scrolling down his emails.

"About that cute," he said, showing Jane a photo of five rolled-up balls of fluff.

"That is so cute."

"This photo was taken about six weeks ago. I spoke to Sue the other day. She still has one available. Ready to collect in three days," said Keith.

"But…" Jane's smile dropped away from her face as her delicate features plunged into seriousness. "What if I get pregnant? We couldn't have a dog *and* a baby. That would be a nightmare."

Keith shifted on his feet and said nothing.

"No, Keith. Don't do that. Are you giving up on me?"

"No, Janey, I'm not. It's just… we've waited so long. Life on hold. I want to move on."

"That sounds like giving up."

Jane's heart was hammering in her chest. Too many emotions soaring through her normally calm, composed self. She picked up a glass, filled it with cold water from the tap and took three rapid sips, attempting to maintain her composure. This had never happened before, Keith giving up on the hope that had sustained them their whole married life. It was Keith who kept Jane going through years and years of disappointment, Keith who pushed for IVF the first time and subsequently worked nights and weekends to afford the second round. He couldn't be giving up on the dream, not now. Surely, not now.

"Look, Janey, I'm in for the long haul on this fertility ride, you know I am. But it's just, I can't bear you being sad."

"I'm not sad."

"That's not true."

"OK, I am sad, but that doesn't mean I'm not happy. I'm happy because I have you and my friends and family and my life, it's just, well, yes, of course, I want to be a mum. That's what I want more than anything but, look, I'm just not sure I'm ready to give up, not yet. I still feel there's a baby waiting to be made in this rickety old body of mine."

"You mean in that gorgeous, sexy body of yours," said Keith.

"No, wait, Keith. Not yet," said Jane, extrapolating Keith's hands that had sensed an opportunity and made a rapid beeline for her slim waist. "Are you sad? Is this what all this is about?"

"I'm happy and sad, like you are," said Keith. "Of course I am. I have to go to work and smile politely as I hear yet more and more horrendous sounding birth stories, or cover for people leaving early for school assemblies, parents' evenings. It devastates me, but I don't want our lack of a baby to define our whole lives. We can do great things."

"Like go on road trips to Bristol."

"Tempted?"

"You know I am. OK, let's make a deal. We sweat it out for two more weeks, only two more measly weeks. If I get my period this time around, we get a dog. How about that?"

"Sounds perfect. We'll put our puppy plans on ice."

"And in the meantime, I'll learn to crochet. A pair of woolly crocheted underpants would really suit you, Mr Smelly Bum."

"Mrs Smelly Bum."

"Oh, Ke-eith..."

"What?"

"You were meant to be timing my egg."

"I am. That's fifteen minutes, three seconds. I think you'll find it's ready."

Later that evening, Jane went onto the TWW forum and created a new chat. It was not the first time she had started a chat on the same topic. In fact, it was close to the twentieth time, but it always brought her comfort, knowing that she was not alone and that with her vast experience of trying to conceive, she might actually be able to offer some helpful tips and insights:

Jane@closetoTWWentyyearsandcounting
Monday 1st February
    "ANYONE ELSE STARTING THEIR TWO-WEEK WAIT?? SHALL WE WAIT IT OUT TOGETHER?"

Hi all. The big wait starts today, anyone fancy sitting it out with me?

Monday 1st February

Day 1 of TWW

It was only 9.30pm, but Becks was gagging to be out of the wine bar; the atmosphere was suddenly stifling. "I'm sorry," she said, pushing back her chair and blowing kisses in the general direction of her friends, who in turn were looking at her, a mix of concern and, yes, she could see it, loud and clear, pity in their eyes.

"It's Mikey, he's needed back at work. This whole new promotion thing. He's indispensable to the entire police force, apparently." She threw her arms up in faux despair before zipping her phone into her top pocket.

"But this is your night out, Becks," said Angela. "You live for your nights out."

"Things change," Becks said, placing a £10 note, her share of the drinks, on the table. "Life doesn't stand still. We all know that." She caught Susan's eye and quickly looked away. "I'll be in touch in a day or so. I've really gotta get back for Hector."

She gave a taut wave, turned and strode across the tiled floor, spine straight, arms by her side. She could sense eyes burning into her back. They knew she was lying about Mike, but she just had to get out of there. "Hold it together, Becks."

It was only when halfway up Ricksan Hill that she let rip with the second half of the sob. The first half had slipped out, accidentally, when Susan broke the 'happy' news.

"So pleased for you," Becks had said, hiding her (half) sob in an overly enthusiastic hug. "Best news ever. You must be so thrilled."

Bullshit, bullshit, bullshit. Worst news ever – at the very least up there – in the worst news stakes. It was meant to be her, Becks, mother of Hector, announcing the happy news that number two was on its way. She had pictured herself making the announcement enough times – not as many as she had pictured actually being pregnant, but not far off. How dare it be Susan? 'Susan Smugs', 'Smuggy, Smuggy Susan'. Susan didn't even want another baby, or so she said…

"We're happy as we are…" Becks said out loud, mimicking Susan's voice. "Happy, happy, happy…"

Another sob burst forth, which Becks attempted to hide behind her clenched fist. People were passing her by: joggers, relaxed couples holding hands, laughing youths dressed to thrill, immune to the bitter February chill, lining up outside the Bronx Club, all set to dance their way into the early hours. *And here I am*, thought Becks, *going home early, sober… and barren.*

She pulled the black jacket hood over her head and stomped up the hill. Normally, she would bemoan the fact that out of all her friends, her house, two miles from the high street, was the furthest out of town, but right now, when she was so hot and bothered, the walk was a good opportunity to calm down. And she needed to calm down before she got home to Mike. The last thing she wanted was for him to see how much Susan's news had riled her.

She had managed to contain herself in front of him when both Angela and Judy had revealed their baby bumps, and again with Jacks, but for some reason, it was Susan getting pregnant that had hit her the hardest. Susan, mother of Frankie – who, aged three (same age as Hector), was already able to spell his name and recognise the word 'butterfly'. Susan, with her stylish townhouse and curvy frame, who effortlessly glided through life.

Becks decided she wouldn't even break the news to Mike, not tonight at least. She was pretty certain he lusted over Susan's big (motherly) breasts, at the best of times, so the less said the better.

"Huh, you're early," Mike said as Becks walked into the sitting room. He made a half-hearted attempt at shifting his large frame from its outstretched position on the sofa.

"Can't you turn it down?" said Becks, more irritably than she intended, lifting Mike's legs up to sit beside him.

"Only two minutes left and we're leading 2-1."

Becks gave an over-exaggerated yawn and rested her feet on the coffee table. "You could have cleared up your plate at least."

"I was going to, but you're early."

"Still, the whole place stinks of curry."

"You like curry."

"Not when it's stagnating."

"Chill out, Becks. What's got into you?"

"Nothing."

"Oh, is it Angela again? What did she say *this* time?"

"No, it's not Angela. It's no one. I'm just tired." Becks scraped her blonde highlighted mid-length hair into a loose ponytail.

"Then go to bed." There was a cheer from the telly. "Go on, my boy," Mike cried, jumping forward.

"It's OK, I'll wait for you," said Becks, taking a sip from Mike's beer can and settling into the sofa. "Any sound from Hector?"

"Don't think so."

"Don't think so. That's solid parenting."

"Oy, oy, oy, don't come in and start nit-picking."

"I'm not, it's just you're always—"

"Always what…?" Mike gave a roar and a moan. "…Oooh, so close."

"It doesn't matter. Just watch your football."

Becks took a deep breath. Caaaalm. It wasn't Mike's fault that Susan was pregnant, hardly fair to take it out on him, but, Josh, Susan's husband, he would never leave the remnants of his curry lying all over the place. He most probably didn't even eat curry, more likely grilled fish or vegan sausages.

"Stop it, Becks," said Mike suddenly, causing Becks to jump.

"Stop what?"

"Stop stewing."

"I'm not stewing."

"You are, I can see you are. What the hell's got into you?"

Becks stopped twitching the frayed thread on her sleeve and looked directly at Mike. "Susan's pregnant." The words spilled out in a small voice and hung in the air as Mike, half an eye on the telly, processed the news.

"Oh, I get it… you're mad because… hold on a minute… yesssssss, beautiful, beautiful, fucking beautiful, Gomez – you genius. Did you see that? Goal in the last thirty seconds? Goooo, my lad."

Mike jumped up with a fist pump. "Three-one, three-one, three-one," he chanted, hopping around the room.

"Yeah, whatever, Mike," said Becks when the ads came on. "Are we going to bed or not?"

"Looking for a bit of action?" said Mike, eyes glistening, previous conversation forgotten.

"Er, no. What's the point? Window's passed."

"There's always a point," said Mike, grabbing Becks and pulling her into his arms.

"There really isn't, Mike," said Becks pushing away. She didn't like the judgemental way that Mike, who was so well toned by doing sod-all exercise, squeezed her squidgy love handles.

"I'm not going to get pregnant, so what's the point?" she said, folding her arms across her chest.

"Stop obsessing about getting pregnant."

"I'm not obsessing."

"Yes, you are. Can't you just be happy with what we've got?"

"No."

"You've already got a son. Isn't that enough for you?"

"No, Mike, I want another, not only for me, for Hector as well."

"He doesn't care."

"He will, one day."

"He'd most probably rather have a mother that's not miserable all the time."

"Oh, just fuck off, Mike. You don't understand anything."

"I understand a spoilt cow when I see one."

"Screw you."

"Yeah, dream on." Mike stormed out of the sitting room and grabbed his coat from the floor where it lay clogging the bottom stair. "I don't need to be shouted at. I'll go catch last orders."

"Don't go, Mike. I'm sorry I shouted," said Becks, suddenly panicked. She really didn't want to be left alone in the peak of her misery. She grabbed Mike's arm. "Can't we just talk? You know I'm always like this at the start of my two weeks," said Becks. She desperately needed someone to be kind to her. She wanted Mike to tell her she was being stupid getting in a state about Susan and that all would be OK. That she would get pregnant again one day and that even though she had grown a little bulgy around the hips and bum, she was still sexy and had her own unique set of curves.

"Not now, Becks. You've totally killed a good mood. If you're going to be like this for the next two weeks, then I don't want to be here."

Mike opened the front door and disappeared out into the cold sting of the night.

All alone, Becks dragged her feet into the sitting room and sat down heavily on the sofa. She picked up Mike's dirty plate and licked it clean. God, she loved curry. Next to it was the empty chicken tikka masala container. She wiped her fingertip around the edge of the tin foil, amassing dollops of crusty orange sauce, and licked her finger clean, and then she drained the remnants of backwash from Mike's beer can. Unsated, but with nothing left to consume, she buried her head in a cushion and screamed.

It was all Susan's fault. Susan had put her in this spin. How dare Susan announce her pregnancy on the same day Becks was embarking on her dreaded two-week wait? How insensitive. It was going to be so much harder now to endure the days and days of waiting.

Now, thanks to Smuggy Susan, Becks wasn't going to be able to see any of her friends. How could she? They all had their new baby worlds in common, what did Becks have to add to the friendship? At least before, it was her and Susan who made up the 'un-pregnant unit', so it felt like a personal choice. Now it felt like physical inadequacy. Which was about right.

I am physically inadequate, thought Becks, *compared to my friends. At least they all have their full quota of fallopian tubes.* If it had not been for the ectopic pregnancy, so would she. Becks had begged the doctor not to make the surgical removal, but it was ,apparently, a matter of life and death. There was no other choice. She had been assured that having only one fallopian tube would not prevent her getting pregnant, but, er, hello? Why no baby? *No wonder I'm mad,* thought Becks, *the doctor doled out misinformation, leaving me potentially infertile, and now Susan has gone and ditched me.*

There was also the matter of Mike's low sperm count, not low enough to render him sterile, obviously, but he was not in the realms of virile. And Hector, well, Becks was sure it was just his age, but he was so demanding. He wanted every second of Becks' waking moments to himself. She could not remember when she had last had any quality time just to browse on Instagram or create the photo collage of Hector's life to date. Getting through each day was enough of a chore and now, she had two weeks to wait and see if her dream of getting pregnant was ever going to come to fruition.

Peering inside Mike's empty beer can, Becks wondered if she was at her rock bottom.

She lifted out the iPad from where it was lodged down the side of the sofa and typed TWW into Google. It was not the first time she had typed in the acronym for the 'Two-Week Wait'. She navigated through to the 'Trying to Conceive' forum. There were always people worse off than her on these fertility forums – maybe reading other people's stories might make her feel better. The heading of the top posting caught her eye:

"ANYONE ELSE STARTING THEIR TWO-WEEK WAIT?? SHALL WE WAIT IT OUT TOGETHER?"

"Yes," said Becks, "I don't see why not? I've not got anyone else to talk to." She clicked on the heading and began typing:

Becks@desperatemumof1

Hi, I'm starting my two-week wait, don't want to wait it out alone...

Monday 1st February
Day 1 of TWW

Fern tapped her foot impatiently, glancing down at her watch, spinning the heavy Rolex face towards her. Fifteen minutes late. She looked around the empty, tastefully decorated consultation room. Where was that receptionist? She had disappeared off and was nowhere to be seen. She went back to scribbling furiously in her Smythson notebook, jotting down production notes about her forthcoming show, her mind working overtime on ideas. It was infuriating having to leave work early to catch the only available appointment, and now the doctor was running late. She really didn't have time for this.

"Mrs Abbott?"

Without bothering to look up, Fern jammed her Fendi bag under her arm and slotted her notes into the front pocket of her work tote.

"The doctor is ready for you."

"Thank you?" Fern said with a touch of hostility – nothing annoyed her more than being kept waiting. She herself lived by the 'better to be an hour early than a minute late' rule.

She brushed past the receptionist into Dr Forester's office.

"Ahh, Mrs Abbott. Apologies for the slight delay."

Dr Forester was a tall man, with thick grey hair sweeping back off his sun-speckled forehead. He stepped forward from behind his desk, briskly shook her hand and pulled out a chair, inviting her to sit.

Dr Forester was charming enough, despite his poor time-keeping. Her mood mellowed. She would forgive him keeping her waiting – this time.

Fern switched on her million-watt smile, hoping that her vibrant red lipstick hadn't transferred onto her front teeth. One could say it was a look that was too bold for an eleven o'clock fertility appointment, but she knew it suited her gleaming dark skin and fiery West Indian temperament. No one dared question or challenge her when she had her MAC 'Ruby Woo' warpaint on. And frankly she didn't care what time of day it was, or what occasion. She wore her Woo with pride.

Dr Forester looked at her, momentarily distracted by her smile. "Mrs Abbott. As you know, we have run a fair few tests on you these past weeks." Dr Forester shuffled through the pile of result papers stacked in front of him, then peered at the screen.

Fern nodded in annoyance. Of course she knew. She had paid him substantially to do so.

"The very good news is…" He paused and pulled his chair forward to peer closer at the monitor.

Fern sighed in impatience, tired of the waiting. For the appointment, for the results, for her baby.

"Yes?" Fern said, brightly, in an effort to move him along with his diagnosis.

"…the good news is… there is nothing gynaecologically wrong with you. Well, that we can find."

Silence.

"That's it?" Fern asked, finally.

"Yep! That's it." Dr Forester smiled over and sat back.

"What do you mean?" Fern asked, head cocked.

"Well," Dr Forester said slowly, "according to these extensive tests you requested, there is no reason whatsoever why you and your husband should not be able to conceive."

This was not the news that Fern was expecting.

"Well, do more tests," she said. "There is obviously something wrong – in here..." Fern waved her hand over her flat stomach in agitation.

Dr Forester looked at her blankly.

He was clearly a fool.

Fern tried to explain. "I have been trying to get pregnant now for a full six months. Intercourse scheduled and written in pen in the diary. Temperature taken, ovulation stick peed on, sexy lingerie bought and worn. We stick to the schedule, almost to the hour. My husband is at home, so he is available night and day. It's all been running like clockwork..."

Including her period, admittedly. Arriving month after month, a text-book twenty eight days apart. Not ideal.

"Trust me, my husband has been keeping a closer eye on this one than I have! We are doing everything by the book. There must be another explanation?"

Fern gave a deep breath and smiled tightly after her temperamental outburst. She awaited the doctor's solution. He must have one. But, Dr Forester was looking alarmed.

He cleared his throat. "I'm sorry – if we can't find anything wrong, there is not much we can fix. We call this in fertility circles, 'Not trying for long enough,' if you will forgive the technical term." Dr Forester chuckled.

Fern stared at him in disbelief. "Not trying long enough? Half a year! Not trying for long enough? It has been plenty of time. Why does no one get it? I have a show that I have to get into production before the summer break, so..." Fern took a deep breath and glared.

Dr Forester sat back, crossed his fingers together, raised an eyebrow and waited for her to finish her rant.

"I NEED to get pregnant, pronto!"

Dr Forester shrugged his shoulders, clearly unimpressed and not interested in her tight programme-scheduling problems. He patted his papers into a neat formation and shoved them into the brown buff folder before him, signalling the end of the consultation.

Fern sat there in shock. There must be another test that they could do. This couldn't be it. She needed an action plan. Fern lived by action plans. They could be written into her diary, like her monthly cycle or work commitments, and stuck to.

IVF was obviously the solution. She could take her drugs, do her exercises, have her implant. She would tackle it like a military exercise.

"Er, I thank you for your time, Dr Forester, but I want you to know, I shall be getting a second opinion." Fern was not able to contain her fury as she gathered up her coat and snatched her bag up from the floor.

Mr Forester looked back, bewildered. This was a new one for him – he had never encountered someone so unhappy with a good news diagnosis. He was used to delivering awful illnesses: blocked tubes, polycystic ovaries, fibroids, severe endometriosis. News to make desperate women cry; worlds shattered, turned upside down.

Yes, Dr Forester mused – he had been quite excited to tell one of his patients today that there was nothing physically wrong, that there was light at the end of the tunnel.

He was not anticipating fury.

Fern strode down Harley Street in a dark mood and hailed a cab.

"10 Mansion Drive, Kennington Park, please."

She sat back and closed her eyes.

"Jon, I'm home." Fern threw her keys in the bowl in the hallway. Jon was working upstairs in his home office. She had convinced him that he didn't need to come with her to the appointment, but he had created such a fuss about it, they had settled on him working from home so that they could deal with the news together, whatever that news might be.

Fern took a deep breath and put her hand on the post before making her way slowly up the stairs. It wasn't that Jon was needy, exactly, or a fusser – it was just he was so EARNEST about everything. He was going to approach this problem with the same enthusiasm he did everything else, and it was going to irritate the hell out of her, she could feel it. She didn't have time for enthusiasm.

"Hey!"

Fern tried to quell her irritation as he bounded towards her. Jon was a large athletic man, more hound than human, with his large brown eyes and thatch of thick floppy hair.

"I am going for a second opinion," Fern stated firmly, holding him at arm's length after his all-engulfing hug.

"Why?" Jon asked, stepping back. "What did Dr Forester say? Is it bad news? I knew it was going to be bad news. Oh God. What are we going to do?"

Fern waited patiently for Jon to finish his catastrophising.

"Jon, it's fine. He said we haven't given it enough time. There is nothing physically wrong with me. Or you, for that matter."

"Oh my goodness. Best news." He gave her another hug. "Sooo?"

"So… as I said, a second opinion."

"Oh-K," said Jon. He knew better than to force an issue with Fern when she was in a prickly mood. "I'll start on a celebration supper. Sea bass alright? I have three different types of kale and spring greens to go with it, keep your iron levels up. And sea bass is good fish – low mercury levels. Not like that tuna sashimi you love to eat at Nobu!"

Jon was already halfway down the stairs, calling up his menu to her. Fern sighed again and closed her eyes. She could see it starting already. He was going to make her his project.

Jon had been the one keen to start their family. Fern was less disposed to the idea of children. Month after month, Jon would casually enquire about her period. It had started grating after a while, and Fern was annoyed that his constant questioning was making her feel anxious about it herself. Fern hated feeling anxious. Jon had the monopoly on that in their relationship. If they both started losing the plot, it would be disastrous.

Fern thought back to their last serious argument on the subject of starting a family. "My mum already had five children by the age of thirty," Jon had said. "You are going to be thirty-seven next month. What are we waiting for?"

"I don't know what *we* are waiting for, Jon, but you know what *I'm* waiting for. I have fought so hard, professionally, to get where I am. I have seen other women dropping out of the industry to have children, leaving the door open for the men to grab their well-earned promotions. Well, I haven't let that happen, have I? And now I am in 'their' boardroom making a real difference. I can make substantial and lasting change for the women struggling behind me. I can be their voice – but only if I am there to be heard."

"But what about our family? I want one. I want a baby. It's amazing what you are doing for the advancement of women in your industry. Truly, it is. But I am your husband. And I would also like to be heard." Jon had walked out of the room, grabbing his keys from the hallway table and slamming the front door shut.

He was right. It wasn't fair on him and that was why Fern had booked her now seemingly futile appointment the very next morning.

Fern followed Jon down the stairs and slumped onto the kitchen chair. Ever since the argument she had felt bad for Jon, feeling the weight of his disappointment when she broke the news to him each month at the arrival of her period.

She watched as he cheerfully prepped his vegetables.

Fine, Fern decided. She would accept the doctor's diagnosis of 'nothing wrong' and apply the same determination to getting pregnant that she applied to everything else. She was going to focus on this two-week wait, and she would get her result.

Her pregnancy would not inconvenience her, and she could be back at work within three weeks once the baby came. Jon had already said that he would be happy to take care of it when it arrived. All settled. Also, she was on day 14 of her cycle. It was time to get busy, and no time like the present.

Fern spun her laptop around and typed rapidly into Google.

The first hit was a forum with the title:

TWO-WEEK WAIT

"ANYONE ELSE STARTING THEIR TWO-WEEK WAIT?? SHALL WE WAIT IT OUT TOGETHER?"

Yes, thought Fern, rapidly signing up for the chat. *I don't want to wait it out again on my own.* This time she was going to get involved. She was going to pass the time with some other 'two-week waiters'.

Who knows? It could be fun. At the very least she might get some creative inspiration for her next show. Fern perked up at the idea. She could use it for professional and personal reasons. Two birds with one stone. Very efficient. She was going to start taking back control.

She started typing.

Fern@toobusytoTWW

Hi, I'm Fern…

Monday 1st February
Day 1 of TWW

"This bloody well better work," said Mandi, downing the last drop of blood-red pomegranate juice and retching into her hand. "Disgusting." She threw the fruit juice carton to the floor and stamped on it with all the might she could muster in her fabric slipper, disposing of the flattened cardboard in the recycle bin. "Stupid old wives' tale."

"Why are you drinking it?" asked Jay, her young nephew, delighted at any distraction from his biology.

"It's meant to help me become a good mother."

"But you're not a mother."

"I might be if I keep drinking this poison."

"But don't you become a—"

"Alright, Jay, get on with your homework. I promised Mammi you'd have it done by the time they get back from Roh's match."

Mandi glanced at the clock, willing the time to ground to a halt as the familiar feeling of dread took hold.

Had a month gone by that quickly? Was it really dinner again with Agila…?

"How does she do it?"

"Who?" said Jay.

"Oh, sorry, did I say something?"

"You said, how does she do it?"

"Did I? I have no idea why I said it."

"I know who you're talking about." Jay's dark eyes narrowed, and he stared unnervingly deep into Mandi's soul.

"I wasn't talking about anyone... come on... photosynthesis."

"It's Nani, isn't it?"

"How did you know?"

"I just know."

"Shhh, well, don't tell her, will you?"

"Might not."

"No, will not... please."

"And I know why you're sad all the time."

"I'm not sad."

"It's because Uncle Gav works all hours and you are left alone."

"You think, huh?" said Mandi; a sharp panic seized her stomach wall.

"That's what I think, because I heard Nani say it to Mammi. They said that you need to spend more time together."

"You shouldn't listen to other people's conversations, Jay.»

"I wasn't listening."

"Sounds like you were to me."

"My ears were just in the same place that they were talking."

"Nani says you need to work harder."

"What's that even mean?" said Mandi, her fingers were quivering with... what was it? Rage? Humiliation? She didn't know what it was, but for some reason her heart had set off on a canter.

Jay shrugged. "I don't know what it means, it's just what Nani said... Are you alright?"

"Back in a sec," said Mandi, giving Jay's hair a brief rub and edging herself out of the kitchen for a quick getaway.

Mandi ran up the stairs into the bathroom, locked the door and clasped on to the edge of the sink. She stared at herself in the bathroom mirror, her face a mass of red blotches, and breathed in deep. "In through the nose, out through the mouth; one, two, three, four." As the increasingly customary blotches faded, returning her complexion to its natural deep olive, she felt immediately calmer. Tabu's advice had worked. One more for luck: "In through the nose, out through the mouth."

"Are you alright, Auntie?" Jay called up the stairs.

"I'm fine, I'll be down in a minute."

"Your phone's ringing." Jay's feet were thudding up the stairs, the rings getting louder with each step. "It's Uncle Gav, shall I answer it for you?"

"It's OK, I can call him la—"

"Hello, Uncle," said Jay. "I'm fine, thank you. She's in the bathroom. Do you want to speak to her?"

Mandi opened the bathroom door, throwing Jay a cool smile. "I'm here. Now go back to studying, Jay."

Jay handed the phone to Mandi but stayed rooted to the spot.

"Hi, Gav," said Mandi, taking herself into the spare bedroom and closing the door.

"When will you be back? Mammi wants to know what time we'll be heading over?"

"I don't know. I'm babysitting. Depends on when your sister gets back from football with Rohan."

"OK, so go directly to Mammi's house and I will meet you there," said Gav.

Mandi lay back heavily on the spare bed and stared up at the ceiling. "Do we have to go?"

"You know we do."

"But I'm not feeling great tonight. I've... I've got a stomachache."

"Yah, Mands, you need to lay off the pineapple rings."

"Pomegranate, actually."

"Pomegranate, then, whatever it is, it's not going to get you what you want—"

"What we want—"

"Yes, what we want, so just quit all the superstitious crap."

"It worked for Ravi."

"Stop this, Mandi, I'm not going into this at the office. Just meet me at Mammi's."

"OK, but I'm telling you I don't want to go."

"It's not a choice, Mandi, it's a duty. We eat at 7.15pm. Don't be late."

Mandi parked up on Kingscliff Crescent several doors down from number 53, her mother-in-law's two-up two-down, semi-detached. She always did this. Gav couldn't understand why she didn't just park right outside the house; there were always spaces, but the short walk to the front door was essential. It gave Mandi the chance to gather herself, position her mouth into a fixed smile set to proffer the false jollity that Gav expected of his beloved bibi when in the company of his, equally beloved, mother.

'Bibi...' Pah. How proud she'd been the first time she heard herself referred to in this way. Such hope, expectation... such promise lay before Gav and her, his young bride, barely out of her teens, as they became intimately familiar on that marital bed. How awkward and pained the world had become in the eighteen months since. What regrets must Gav have?

"How can you be a bibi and not make me babies?" That was what he had dared to ask of his wife. Only once, mind you. Mandi, embarking on a series of severe panic attacks, had ensured those same insulting words never fell from his lips again. But wow, hearing him say them; it was like someone had injected burning treacle through his beloved bibi's veins.

He was right, though. However modern Mandi considered herself to be – a city girl, dressing how she pleased, staying out late with her friends… There was no getting away from the reality that the role of the wife is to bring new life into the world. A biological duty, one that, as every unproductive month passed, she was failing to fulfil.

The monthly dinner with Agila, her mother-in-law, that she so dreaded, was not centred around hospitality, or love or even the need for company on her mother-in-law's behalf. It was simply a form of checking up. As Mandi walked up the garden path, through the immaculately pruned, ornamental front garden, she decided on fifteen seconds before the dreaded question. Last time it had been longer than this, but this time, she could sense a greater urgency. Gav had been strict about the 7.15pm start time. Agila was obviously keen to assert yet more control.

"You're here, at last," said Gav, opening the door.

"Where's Agila?" said Mandi, forgetting to look at the clock.

"In the front room," said Gav. "Entertaining."

"Entertaining who? You never said anything about guests."

"Sorry, forgot."

"You know I get nervous when you spring things on me," said Mandi, feeling the heat rising in her neck.

"It's only some of the committee members from the temple. Don't worry."

At that moment, Agila came bustling into the hall and, as expected, took Mandi into her fleshy arms. "Any exciting news to share?" she whispered in Mandi's ear, mid-embrace. "I love good news."

And, there it was, the fifteen-second question.

"Not as far as I know," said Mandi.

"You are not to say a word about your problem to my guests. Do you hear me? If anyone asks, you are simply waiting to start a family until Gav gets his promotion. Got it?"

"Yes, Saas," said Mandi. "Although they might say a prayer on our—"

"No, Mandi, not a word. Last thing we want is for our family problems to be whispered far and wide. No-one must know."

It was a great relief to Mandi that she could come home separately from Gav, sneaking out and driving herself home, early. Two hours, three courses and at least four thousand questions relating to her and Gav's fertility, or lack of it, was enough to bear. It was no surprise. Eighteen months married with no sign of procreation, and tongues do waggle. Mandi remained loyal to Agila's line, and consequently, Gav got an armful of questions he ended up having to deflect, all relating to his non-existent upcoming promotion.

Mandi threw herself down on the sofa in her living room, deciding to give herself a night off her daily dose of hormone-balancing royal jelly. Only effective on an empty stomach, anyway, and seeing as she was still experiencing the sugar rush from too many of Agila's super-sweet gulab jamun, it made sense to steer clear of anything too rich.

The TV remote control was just out of Mandi's reach and she couldn't be bothered to move an inch to get it, so she browsed Instagram on her phone, her mood deflating as she saw endless photos of Bina out with her uni friends, drinking cocktails and looking like her best friend from home was the last person on her mind. If Sara was here now, and Bina, she wouldn't have to pretend that there was an upcoming promotion for Gav. They would know everything already. They most probably wouldn't care because, unlike Mandi, starting a family aged twenty-one was the furthest desire from their minds. But they'd at least make fun of her, tease her and make her feel like she was worthy of being more than a vessel for embedding Gav's semen.

The next two weeks of waiting, wondering and, no doubt, the accompanying panic attacks, stretched endlessly and emptily ahead. For not the first time that evening, Mandi felt totally alone but at the same time suffocated. Her inability to conceive was the talk of Gav's family. They were all at it. Gav was most probably having a head-to-head about it with Agila at that precise moment. Everyone was talking about her, but no one was talking *to* her or listening.

Mindlessly, Mandi flicked through her apps, landing on the one place where she could find comfort, of a sort. The online infertility community. Agila had told her not to share her fertility problems with the local community, but she never said anything about online. The Two-Week Wait forum was active as ever. Mandi browsed the top posts and her heart gave a small leap.

Jane@closetoTWWentyyearsandcounting
"ANYONE ELSE STARTING THEIR TWO-WEEK WAIT?? SHALL WE WAIT IT OUT TOGETHER?"

Mandi@LusciousLocks

Hi Jane, I'm starting my TWW today and dreading it. I could really do with support getting through xxx

Monday 1st February

Day 1 of TWW

Star swept her long blonde hair back off her face as she transitioned from Ahdo Mukha Svanasana (downward-facing dog pose) into a backward bend. She closed her eyes and breathed with conscious intent into her lower ribs, opening her heart chakra to the universe. Running her right hand over her toned belly in a gesture of self-love, she stretched up to the sky and closed her eyes, summoning the energy from the universe down through her reaching fingers to rest in her receptive womb.

"Namaste," she murmured, pressing her hands together at her chest and bowing her head in fervent prayer. Star squeezed her eyes tight against the tears threatening to escape onto her cheek and down onto her yoga mat. She didn't want the rest of the yoga class to see.

Please. Let today be the day, she thought.

"All OK, Star?" Tasha asked, running to catch up with Star as she strode from the yoga studio towards her bicycle.

"Sure!" Star said brightly, fumbling with the chain lock. She flashed a brief smile at Tasha and swung her slim leg over the weathered leather saddle, balancing on long toes as she spun her long hair into a bun at the top of her head. Hair tousled and effortlessly chic, Star put her foot on the pedal, ready to set off. She was surprised when Tasha placed a cold hand over hers on the handle bar to stop her.

"Well, it's just I felt your energy was a little 'off' today. I hope you don't mind me saying. I'm very sensitive like that," Tasha said, half closing her kohl-rimmed eyes in compassion. Still gripping Star's hand, Tasha was now squeezing her fingers alarmingly.

"Fancy grabbing a matcha latte, babes? Then you can tell me all about it, if you like. Get it all off your chest," Tasha said, breathily.

Star stared at Tasha's hand holding hers hostage on the handle bar, and felt a stab of irritation. No, she did not 'like'. Star had absolutely no interest in talking to Tash, with her big eerie eyes, her 'sensitivity' and her crazy hair.

"Soz, Tash, got things on. Hope you understand, babe. Catch you next week."

Star delicately prised her fingers from under Tasha's firm grip and waved goodbye, her bracelets jangling in the nippy February air as she embarked on her cycle ride home.

Twenty yards down the road, Star stopped peddling. *Come on, Star,* she said to herself, *what harm could it do?* Maybe it would feel good to chat to Tasha over a hot drink. She could finally put out into the universe the one subject she was finding impossible to talk about, get her whirring thoughts out in the open.

"Hey!" Star called out, wheeling her ancient Pashley round and cycling back to an expectant Tasha.

"Actually, babes, I've changed my mind. I've got time for a quick one."

"OK Tash, you have to swear you won't tell anyone," Star started, blowing cool air across her ginger tea.

Tasha looked at Star, her huge eyes glowing with anticipation. "I promise, pinky promise. I won't tell anyone, ever. You can trust me."

Hmm. Star doubted that, but for the purposes of this 'opening up' experiment, she would have to believe her for now. She didn't have anyone else.

"What's your opinion on sprogs? You know, babies," Star said, delicately breaking open a carrot cake muffin and passing half over to Tasha.

"BABIES?" Tasha squealed. "OH, STAR! Are you pregnant? I didn't even know you had a partner, you secretive minx! You always talk about self-love and self-partnering in your posts, no mention of anyone who could give you sweet bambinos!"

Star could see Tasha's mind spinning with excitement at this potential piece of gossip. Tasha took a huge bite of the cake, crumbs falling all over the table.

"No. No, Tash, I'm not. I…"

Star paused.

Tasha was busy licking her finger and picking up the crumbs scattered all over the vinyl tablecloth to pop in her mouth.

"I have…" Star tried to start again, then swallowed hard and hesitated. She was regretting this now.

"Yes?" Tasha had stopping licking her finger and was now staring at Star in excitement and curiosity, her big eyes even larger than normal.

Star stared back into those round eyes, making calculations. This was all very risky. What had she been thinking, trying to open up to someone? Star had spent so many years relying on herself only, keeping all her secrets close to her chest. Tasha was sort of a friend, sure, but they hadn't known each other that long. Star was famously nomadic by nature; she had no true mates, really. Friends came and went, and changed as often as her location.

Star was now having serious second thoughts. She could envision Tasha running to the press the minute Star finished her last mouthful of tea.

"I mean to say, I have..." Star was desperately searching for a problem, any problem that didn't involve confessing – that.

Aha!

"...I have a very co-dependant, dysfunctional relationship with my parents. My mum is very critical of me, my body, everything I do, say or wear. I will forever be eight years old in their eyes. If I ever had a baby, I just wonder whether that would change. Whether they would finally take me seriously. That's all," Star said regaining her composure, the half-truth tumbling from her mouth before she could think about it too much.

Star had bottled it. She couldn't tell Tasha about her fertility issues, about her diseased womb. Not when Star's whole brand was based on perfection, both physical and spiritual. Tasha would blab her deepest secret to everyone; she just knew it. It could ruin her career.

Star laughed inwardly that the potentially explosive *I have a toxic relationship with my parents* statement felt less terrifying than telling the truth.

The 'dysfunctional family' angle still made a newsworthy headline – Star knew this from experience. She could cope with the fallout from that story, as it was half true – hell, it might even make her follower numbers go up! The things she read about herself online often made her mind boggle, yet her following grew and grew. But it was not what was actually bothering her. Talking about her family seemed less personal and intrusive than the real issue that kept her awake all night, chest tight with the worry and anxiety of it all. Much easier than discussing her infertility, and her agonising two-week waits.

"Wow. I also live at home and hate my parents too. They are always interfering," Tash said sympathetically. "But I am only nineteen."

"I'm twenty-nine! I should be old enough to have a civilised relationship with the old boomer's by now, without every conversation ending up with me sulking," Star replied truthfully. She did feel a bit embarrassed about her situation, thinking about it. It was bad enough living at home at that age, without having teenage-style tantrums on top.

"But don't you have millions of pounds to go with your millions of followers? Why are you still living at home! Move out! You totally need a perfect home for your perfect life," Tash said, earnestly.

Star laughed sadly. "They just don't get me, Tash. Or what I do for a living. My mum suggested this morning that I get a proper job as a receptionist at a beauty salon," Star said, ignoring Tash's comment about how much money Star had. Everyone assumed Star was minted, but it couldn't be further from the truth. Not after all the expensive alternative fertility treatments she shelled out for. Weekly acupuncture, Chinese herbs, hair testing, supplements, cupping. She had tried it all, and the cost kept adding up.

Tasha's mouth had dropped open. Star could see carrot cake stuck in her back molars.

"Doesn't she know you're famous? Like, properly famous? Working in a beauty salon is great, but why would you apply for a job there when you are so successful already?" Tasha asked, agog.

"They just don't understand what I do. Different generation," Star said, shrugging.

"It must be awful. I don't really have that problem because I work in the family nail bar business, so I never get that hassle." Tasha looked down at her perfectly manicured nails as if to confirm her excellent life choice.

"Sounds great. My dad's an accountant, but I can barely add up numbers, so that was never an option for me," Star said.

"How did you get to be an Instagram influencer anyway? Tell me your secret. You're like a phoenix rising from the ashes of misery, to guide your millions of followers into the light," Tasha said dreamily. "I love all your posts. Did you know you were going to be such a hit? Like, did you have a plan when this all started?"

"No plan." Star laughed. "Just my pretty face, hot bod, and huuuge ego…"

Tasha laughed too, as if Star had made a joke.

But Star wasn't joking, far from it. It had been exactly the way it had happened.

"I learnt the best way to get loads of likes and comments, and the rest is history," Star explained. "Just do yoga in a bikini! Turns out, people like to look at a semi-naked girl in a pretzel pose on a beautiful beach, preferably in front of a stunning sunrise or a mellow sunset. Who knew?"

Star twirled her empty cup. She was annoyed at herself for making it sound so formulaic. But it was true.

Star had been at the right place, at the right time. It had all started after she had hit rock bottom after her devastating diagnosis two years ago. She had started posting more and more spiritual and yoga-related content, and before she knew it, she had become an overnight internet sensation with millions of followers. At the time she had also been desperate for money, so the gifted exotic holidays, paid adverts for organic skincare and juice cleanses had finally started to provide her the income she needed in order to pursue her dream of becoming a mother.

"You make it sound easy!" Tasha said.

"It's not that easy, really. Loads of editing and content generation to do. Never a day off. I work hard, actually," Star said defensively.

Star did think she deserved her success, and she did work extremely hard, in her own way. She knew deep down that she was a living cliché, but it was how she managed to cope. If her life looked perfect online, then perhaps a little of that magic would rub off onto her offline existence. Her deeply lonely, empty life.

Also, she couldn't lie to herself – she had become addicted to the praise.

"Your body is so perfect…"

"Life goals right there…"

"OMG I can't even… you're so spiritual. I stan…"

Comment after comment, endlessly telling her how wonderful and inspirational she was.

If only her followers knew the truth. That she was a lonely girl from Surrey, rapidly approaching her thirties, no way of holding down a relationship, most probably barren and now living with her parents. The self-love mantras she was so famous for, the ones that gave genuine hope and light to so many… well. They didn't even touch the sides with her.

Star air-kissed Tash her goodbyes, and left her sitting at the cafe table, probably texting all her friends the latest Star gossip. Star cycled home slowly, drizzle stinging her face the whole way. She tried hard not to think of Romero, her latest Latin lover. He had looked pretty virile the last time she had seen him, lying tangled in her pink sheets that morning. Oh well. It was all in the lap of the gods now. As always, she was doing it alone, whatever.

Back in her childhood bedroom, with the familiar pink curtains and fluffy bedspread, Star crossed her legs and started to type.

TWO-WEEK WAIT
"ANYONE ELSE STARTING THEIR TWO-WEEK WAIT?? SHALL WE WAIT IT OUT TOGETHER?"

Star@Gaiababe
Namaste! Glad to meet you, ladies...

PART TWO

Tuesday 2nd February

Day 2 of TWW

Jane@closetoTWWentyyearsandcounting

Hi everyone, happy Tuesday!

Good to hear from you.

It's going to be a long wait, so I am thinking it would be good to get to know each other. I have put in a few questions below, so answer if you like. I often find it helps as an ice-breaker.

What's your name?
Partner's name?
How long have you been TTC?
Do you already have children?
Any infertility issues?
Anything else about yourself, feel free to share...

So, my name is Jane and my partner is called Keith. We have been trying to conceive for not far off twenty years. Yes, I'm pretty ancient now, but I live in hope. We have no children. Have had countless fertility tests over the years, but no one has ever managed to diagnose the reason. The last examination showed poor egg quality, but that was two years ago when I was forty, so not surprising.

This is most probably going to be my last TWW. If I get a BFN, this time, we're getting a twelve-week-old puppy. I love dogs, but I am not sure I am ready to throw in the towel on TTC. Let's see how things go. Not expecting any great shakes. Keith and I did two rounds of IVF a few years ago, but have had to give up on this, too expensive and too stressful. Thank you, NHS postcode lottery! Everyone I know has kids – I feel I have missed the boat on their worlds of baby and motherhood. This is sooo hard, but I am a quietly determined person and once I set my mind on something I don't want to let it go, especially when the letting go would mean never having a family. Anyone else got any stories to share? Really find it helps if you do!!!!

Mandi@LusciousLocks

Thank you, thank you, thank you for starting up this chat. Do NOT want to wait this out alone. Super nervous with anticipation (and maybe a tiny bit of excitement).

Hi. My name is Mandi. I am twenty-one years old and my husband, Gav (thirty-five) and I have been trying to conceive since marrying eighteen months ago but only now beginning to worry as being made to feel like I am not a true woman by unmentionable family members (Gav's mum).

I am new to fertility forums and so apologies if I am not speaking the correct jargon. I suffer from polycystic ovaries so knew that making babies would be a battle – but now beginning to get tense as lots of pressure coming in, which is making matters worse. We don't have any children yet and Gav's mum is broody for a whole bunch of grandkids (she already has two from Gav's sister, but they are seven and nine and she says she wants babies!!!). Most of my friends are still at uni and they think I'm mad for wanting to start a family so young, but me and Gav decided to try immediately before the polycystics get too bad.

Am drinking soooo much pomegranate juice I am nearly drowning in the stuff and shoving fertility-enhancing medjool dates into practically every meal I cook. Gav is getting pretty wound up with all my fan-dangled potions, as he calls them (he loves his food)... He nearly exploded when I started sucking garlic in bed the other day (I read best health results if taken before sleep). I'm getting that desperate. Really appreciate any support you can offer me. Xxx

Jane@closetoTWWentyyearsandcounting
Hi Mandi. Welcome to the TWW chat. I am sorry to hear you are under pressure. There is no excuse for that, and can I assure you (as someone twenty years your senior and fully female) that you are 100% woman AND an individual, regardless of what the wider world is telling you. Out of interest? Has Gav been tested himself for his sperm count? Contrary to popular belief, it's not always the woman!!!

Thought you might appreciate a jargon buster as there are quite a lot of acronyms when it comes to infertility chat:

AF	Auntie Flo (AKA your period)
BBT	basal body temperature
BFN and BFP	big fat negative/positive (result on pregnancy test)
HPT	home pregnancy test
MIL	mother-in-law (sounds like this one might be relevant to you!!)
OH	other half
OPK	ovulation predictor kit

PCOS	polycystic ovary syndrome
PG	pregnant
POAS	pee on a stick
TTC	trying to conceive
TWW	two-week wait

Mandi@LusciousLocks

Fantastic. Thank you for that, Jane. You asked if Gav has been tested? Funnily enough, just last week. He eventually agreed but only because I spun some kind of baloney about it being necessary if one day, down the line, we need to go down the IVF route. He said it was a waste of time because it was almost certainly not him 'at fault', but let's wait and see, shall we? Results in a few days. That would be an interesting new angle, if it was him!

Becks@desperatemumof1

Hi there. Thank you for starting up this thread, Jane. I have just been for a 10k run to kick off my dreaded TWW. Feel calm and ready to go (bites nails). Here's hoping.

In response to your questions:

My name is Becks. I am married to Mike. We have been TTC for around twenty months. We are mega fortunate to already have one son, Hector, who our lives totally revolve around (I am a SAH mum), but we really want him to have a little brother or sister soon so that they can be close in age.

I had an ectopic pregnancy and so only have one fallopian tube, which is most probably the reason why I am not getting immediately pregnant like I did with Hector. Also, Mike has a low sperm count (although don't tell him I told you haha) but I am sure it is more because of the ectopic pregnancy. I am a very impatient person and so find having to wait really hard especially when all my friends have got (or are about to get) their little number twos already and so are bonding big time second time round. Bit left out, but hopefully not for long – fingers and toes tightly crossed...

I am really into fitness and so thinking through a healthy diet and a lot of exercise I will be able to conceive naturally. Mike is more patient than me and so happy to bide his time. I find this hard, but I also respect his decision. He was an only child so doesn't appreciate how much Hector will want to have a sibling, down the line.

What is good is that Mike and I have grown so close during this difficult waiting time. I am not sure if it is parenthood that has mellowed us or that we are both working through this challenging time together – teamwork! So that is us right now, a little family of three desperate to expand.

Star@Gaiababe

Namaste! Glad to meet you, ladies... I'm Star and before you ask, there is no partner/husband/lover in this whole baby making mix... I'm going it alone. Scared. Moi? Not at all. In fact, positively relishing the chance of a beautiful mother-child journey. Don't get me wrong, I have full respect for anyone planning on sharing babyhood with a father, so go girls, but not for me.

My story. I have been TTC for a couple of months with a finely toned selection of Latino lovers and feel confident that the stars are aligning this month as there was definitely a spiritual connection between my latest hot Latin lover, Romero, and me.

You said you wanted advice, Mandi – highly recommend full moon lovemaking for recharging those sacrals. Ha ha, having a bit of a forward day today, must be the PCG (post-coital glow). Fertility backstory to date: no enfants yet, but once I get my chakras in tune with my rose quartz and moonstone rituals, I intend to have quite a flock. No fixed abode to speak of, unless you call 'under the stars' a postal address. Have no intention of settling down... every intention of remaining a free-world traveller. Here's to two weeks of peace and love, ladies. Ciao for now.

P.S. Hope you are all hugging your orange calcite stones... recharge that sexual energy, ladeez.

Mandi@LusciousLocks

Hi Star. Any particular tips for full moon lovemaking?

Star@Gaiababe

As it says on the tin, Mands. Find a spot that swathes you in peace and tranquility. My go-to is the Vale of Kashmir – the landscape has fertility written all over it – but it can be a forest or meadow. Wherever. Meditate under the stars, limber up with a few bee breaths, hold Gav close and when the full moon is at max revs, allow your minds, bodies and spirits to unify. I kid you not, the result is nirvana...

Becks@desperatemumof1

Pleased to meet you, Star, I've never heard of the full moon as being a successful remedy for fertility.

Star@Gaiababe

Babes, the moon is a life force, full moon yells oestrogen. Trust me. Lunar guru at your beck and call, no pun intended BECK(s)...

Mandi@LusciousLocks

Love the idea but not sure Gav will go for it. He is quite conventional.

Star@Gaiababe
A beneath the duvet, socks on, kind of guy?

Mandi@LusciousLocks
Ha ha, not far off, he wears socks with sandals in winter!

Jane@closetoTWWentyyearsandcounting
Not sure there are many peaceful, tranquil spots for swathing here in the Midlands!

Fern@toobusytoTWW
Hi ladies. Am new to this forum, flicking through and found this thread. I'm Fern, married to Jon. Been TTC for six months, getting pissed off having to wait (girl hates waiting). Been to doctor who told me there is nothing wrong, which to me reads as, 'can't be bothered to do thorough checks'.

I am not sure I qualify to be on this chat, as I am most probably not as devoted to the idea of having kids as you all seem to be (forgot to say, no kids to date), but as I am the only woman in my department at work, it is most probably healthy to find a few women to share this wait with. Jon is waaaaay more into the idea of starting a family than I am. I love him for his dedication but need an outlet for my irritation, as he has fallen into the habit of catering to my every need. Trust me, ladies, that is not a brag. I, like you, Star, value my freedom and fiercely protect it.

Fern@toobusytoTWW
Shit, clicked send when I wasn't done. Well, I most probably was done, just ranting. Doctors always wind me up. Anyway, that is my story. Post-coital blazing cow seeks bunch of post-coital glowing females to share in agony of long sodding wait.

Why do I have a feeling you are going to tell me to start mediating, Star?

Star@Gaiababe

It did cross my mind, Fern, haha. High five to freedom, babes.

Fern@toobusytoTWW

Hang on – you're not the Star of mega Instagram fame with a million followers Star, are you??

Star@Gaiababe

Well, that's me busted! I was going to keep my identity hush-hush! Want to keep my private life private, if you get what I mean…

Fern@toobusytoTWW

Sure thing. Might need to DM you – you could be great for a segment we are doing on rising stars (haha!).

Jane@closetoTWWentyyearsandcounting

OK, OK, you two, enough of the networking… sounds like you live in a man's world at work, Fern. Welcome to a good dose of female connection. Totally agree, doctors can be frustrating. Keith and I have bashed our heads against many a medical wall over the years, all to no avail. TTC is quite a minefield, which is why it helps to have people to talk to. When I first started on this infertility journey there was literally no one around. Those were lonely times. So, thank you for being there, ladies.

Mandi@LusciousLocks

OMG, cannot imagine a world without people twenty-four seven to talk to. It would totally freak me out. Social media is my lifeline. Sometimes I go whole days and realise I have been chatting all day but not opened my mouth!!! Anyone got any plans for how to spend the next two weeks?

Fern@toobusytoTWW

Mid-production at the moment (I work in TV) and so it's going to be full-on work for me – except for this weekend when Jon has booked some swanky hotel with spa for me to supposedly relax and let the hormones flow. I will most probably bite his head off in the sauna (#female mantid).

Mandi@LusciousLocks

Lucky you. Gav is going to be away all weekend playing golf. Bad timing, but he loves his golf and it gives me a break from having to shop and cook for a change, plus it means I can gorge on high fertility foods. Anyone got any recommendations for fertility-enhancing foods?

Fern@toobusytoTWW

Just eat what you want, Mandi. This is not a time to be overly hard on yourself.

Becks@desperatemumof1

Yeah, just don't gorge a whole bottle of gin, Mandi! I can't remember the last time Mike and I went anywhere by ourselves. Sounds like a luxury, Fern. Most weekends we hang out at the duck pond. Hector loves ducks, bless.

Mandi@LusciousLocks

Thanks, Jane. Will heed your advice on being kind to myself. MIL came around the other days with four mackerels wrapped in newspaper, complete with head, eyes and backbone, having read an article on eating oily fish bones for pregnancy. Will need to find a backbone myself to endure her interference.

Star@Gaiababe

Positive thinking, Mands, babe. Remember mind, body, spirit is one. You need to will that egg to work its magic.

Jane@closetoTWWentyyearsandcounting

That's day 2 down now, ladies. Seems like it is the five of us on this journey together. Now that we are all so hormonally in tune, anyone got any objections to me making this a closed chat? Keep it small and personal? Also avoids anyone popping up telling us that they already have six kids but have been trying one month for their seventh.

Becks@desperatemumof1

Fine by me.

Mandi@LusciousLocks

Agreed. Intimacy suits me.

Tuesday, 2nd February
Day 2 of TWW

"Fancy a sausage, Stacey? I'm doing a batch with mash and gravy." Janet Ruddin hovered awkwardly in Star's doorway, never sure nowadays whether hovering was best or to stride in with purpose.

"Are they Linda McCartney's textured soya protein with rapeseed oil?" said Star, lying on her bed barely raising her eyes from the iPad balanced on her tummy.

"No, they're Walls from Tesco. Is that a yes?"

"Mum, you know I don't eat meat." Star threw the iPad onto the bed and jumped up with frustration. "It makes my skin break and my stomach bloat, and I hate a bloated stomach."

"You always ate sausages before you went on your travels," said Janet calmly. She anchored both feet firmly on the carpet and stood as tall as her lower back pain allowed.

"And now I don't, because, believe it or not, Mum, travel changes people."

"I'm not sure Majorca did much for your dad or me, except the food poisoning your dad got from that calamari. It was definitely double defrosted. I never told you about that, did I? Sick as a dog."

"Not that kind of travel, Mum, the kind of travelling where you find your inner self, get into the zone, make peace with the universe—"

"Oh, speaking of finding yourself, did Romero find you? He came over earlier, straight from work, still had wet paint on his jeans."

"I hope you told him I wasn't here." Star's heart started racing; last thing she wanted – correction, last thing she *needed* right now – was Romero in her face, reeking of Dulux. Star thought she had been very clear with him that morning. A repeat visit to her bedroom would not be welcome.

"Well, did you?" Star demanded.

"Why would I do that?" Janet asked, confused.

"Because we broke up."

"With all due respect, Stace, I didn't even know you were together."

"It depends how you clarify 'together'. We weren't courting, if that's what you mean."

"So, basically, you were sleeping with each other?" Janet ventured a few steps into Star's room, sensing a tiny opening for bonding.

"Look, Mum," said Star, steering her back out. "I might be living here now, but it doesn't mean I need to share all the details of my life. I'm not a teenager anymore."

Star wished with all her heart that she could share all the details of her life with her mum. There had been so many lonely nights over the past couple of years, moments when she had wanted to call home to talk about the hell she was going through. A hell that had started the moment she had decided she wanted a baby.

Star had been struck with such a strong vision during one Spring Equinox Cacao Ceremony a couple of years ago, it had affected her profoundly. She couldn't shake it, the powerful image of her walking down the beach with a papoose strapped to her chest. A baby! That was it. That was the missing piece in her empty life. A baby could help her rekindle a stronger relationship with her parents; maybe she could even go home to have it. Her pride was the only thing stopping her from contacting them, nothing else. Star knew her mum was desperate for a grandchild; she had brought it up often enough in the past. Star would be welcomed back with open arms, if she had a babe in hers.

Star couldn't contain her excitement about her plan.

"I'm going to have a baby," she told Indira, friend du jour.

"You don't have a husband, or a boyfriend," Indira had pointed out. "What's it going to be, an immaculate conception?"

"I'm going to do it my way, don't you worry. I don't need anything as boring as a boyfriend, Indira. I just need some friendly sperm. Men just dampen my free spirit."

Indira looked unconvinced, and Star smiled with the certainty of someone who had discovered a great solution.

Star started tracking her cycles with the moon. She meditated on crystals and chose tall athletic men from the international yoga circuit to seduce, not worrying about whether they were ready to be fathers or not. It didn't matter to her. They weren't going to be involved anyway.

Every month Star had been bitterly disappointed to find her period turning up without fail. Finally, she had to confront the bitter truth: all the chanting, water fasts and vegetable detoxes were not going to produce the baby she wanted with all her heart.

Star booked in to see a conventional doctor during a short stopover in Australia on the way to Bali. She had been scanned, then a laparoscopy booked.

"It's definitely endometriosis," the doctor confirmed.

"What?" Star asked.

"A chronic, incurable and often progressive condition, but manageable through a protocol of painkillers, various chemical interventions such as inducing artificial menopause, and drugs such as tranexamic acid to help with excessive bleeding. Your fertility is probably compromised. I recommend laser treatment to remove most of the adhesions. When you have healed from the surgery, start trying for a baby sooner rather than later, or it might never happen."

Star walked the beach for hours that night and cried her eyes out. Her beautiful yoga-fit womb and left ovary were riddled with disease.

"Or it might never happen…"

The doctor's words kept ringing in her ears.

At the time, Star was totally alone. She wasn't speaking to her parents. Her traveller lifestyle and flighty personality meant a steady romance was not on the cards. But sitting in the doctor's office that afternoon, barely understanding a word he said, one thing had become clear.

Star was going to do everything in her power to have a baby, and she was going to do it her way. Sod the poisons and the contraceptive pills she had been necking since she was fourteen. She had only taken them to help with the extreme pain of her monthly curse. No wonder her body was rebelling. She was going to meditate, take herbs and acupuncture. Star was going to look to the East rather than to the West for her cures. The more partners she had, the more chance of success. She was going to have her 'mini' Star if it was the last thing she did.

So here Star found herself, two years and countless lovers later, back in the family home, arguing with her mum as always. She placed her hand over her belly, instinctively crossing her fingers to give Romero's sperm a good-luck boost, and glanced over at her mum standing forlornly at the door. She gave a deep sigh.

"You still here, Mum? Chat's over."

"I just want to be sure you're happy, that's all," said Janet, her voice catching an unexpected wave of emotion.

"Happiness is a choice, not a result, Mum," said Star. "And I surf that on the crest of happiness."

"What does that even mean?" said Janet, looking at her funny, strange, beautiful and clearly very lost daughter. "It's not that I'm saying, you need a man to fulfil you, it's just, well, you're twenty-nine, Stacey, perhaps the time has come to anchor yourself a little." Janet held her breath. It was a bit of a gamble. She knew how much Star hated people questioning her life choices.

"Look, Mum. I know what I'm doing, OK? I have thousands, no, millions of people hanging on my every word. I am life guru to the masses and all you do is question me. Do you know how demoralising that is?"

"I don't mean to belittle you, Stace—"

"It's Star."

"I don't mean to belittle you, Star, it's just that, well, every so often I catch you with such a sad look on your face that I… I worry about you. Are you really fine? I know I've not always made it clear, but I hope you know that you can talk to me?"

"Yes, I know," Star lied, trying to remove the tension from her voice and failing. She turned away from her mum standing in the hallway and plonked back heavily on her bed, picking up her phone, eyes fixed firmly on the screen.

"I am fine. It's just you know, no rain, no flowers."

"If you say so. But I'm here, OK. And so's your dad, although maybe less now that he's taken apart his entire motorbike engine."

"Thanks, Mum."

"So, was that yes to a sausage?"

"Go on then. And a load of gravy."

Tuesday 2nd February
Day 2 of TWW

Jane watched from bed, as Keith brushed his teeth walking around the room as he always did. How he managed never to drop a dollop of toothpaste, she didn't know. Jane had to stand over the sink, otherwise the toothpaste dribbled everywhere.

"Tired?" asked Keith, wiping his mouth with a towel.

"No more than normal." Jane opened her book and snuggled down on the pillow. She was fifty pages into the winner of the Man Booker prize, but god, it was dull as ditchwater. The temptation to stop reading it was overpowering, but Jane was not a quitter. She would muddle through, perhaps skip a few pages, avoid all the long-winded descriptions on rooftops and varying shades of green forest, and get through to the end.

"Had any response?" asked Keith.

"Yeah, four women, all beginning their two-week wait like me."

"Like us," said Keith, climbing into bed beside Jane and carelessly throwing a leg over her tummy.

"Are you going to join in the chat too? Man's perspective?" said Jane.

"I can if you want. Ooh, got a bit of a pain in my ovary."

"It's going to be a bit like that," said Jane. "Everyone seems to be a newbie. One of them is only twenty-one."

"Ouch."

"Tell me about it. I feel like her grandma."

"Why on earth would you worry about not being pregnant at twenty-one?"

"We were only twenty-two, if you remember, and it really mattered to us."

"I suppose, it just sounds so young now."

"When you get the urge, you get the urge, Keithy boy." Jane pushed Keith's leg off and turned onto her side. "And before you ask, no, I don't have the urge. Oh, yes, and we've got this earth mother, called Star. She's really into mantras and breathing. Makes love outside in I think she said Kathmandu."

"That is my kind of girl."

"Bad luck, she only goes for Latinos."

"They haven't got a patch on this Middle England torso," said Keith, flexing the muscles on his pale arms.

"No, they have not. Give me a strawberry blond, verging on the skinny man any time," said Jane, yawning. "Except tonight. I'm going to sleep. Busy day tomorrow getting to know all my new infertility friends."

"Just let me know if I can have any kind of a role in your life for the next two weeks."

"Hmm, there might be a few bins to empty," said Jane, giving Keith a long, tightly closed-lipped kiss and turning over.

"My work here is done," said Keith.

"Yes, my darling, it is," said Jane. "For now."

Tuesday 2nd February

Day 2 of TWW

"I think it is really good that you're connecting with other women. For support," said Jon, placing a cup of milky, sweet tea next to Fern, who was still firmly ensconced beneath the duvet.

"It's not going to lead anywhere," she said, yawning and nestling deeper into the pillow. "You can't get pregnant through solidarity."

"Just having other women going through the same as you has got to be good for support?"

"Yeah, maybe… is that milk in my tea?"

"Isn't that what you wanted?"

"I was going to go milk-free for a bit, but that's OK."

"I can make another one." Jon went to grab the mug.

"No, it's fine."

"So, any advice or tips gleaned?"

"Maybe one or two things, someone mentioned oily fish and there's some tree-hugger who talks about sex under the stars."

"Any particular kind of oily fish?"

"Mackerel, maybe? But sex under the stars?"

"I'll pick some up today. You never know."

"So, mackerel instead of sex under the stars? Jesus, Jon, should I be worried?"

"Would you be up for sex under the stars, Fern?"

"No. Not right now."

"There we go. I'll roast some mackerel with sweet potatoes and ginger marinated pak choy for supper tonight. What time will you be home?"

"Meetings all day, probably 9ish."

"Can't be good for us eating so late, but I'm sure it's healthier than grabbing a takeaway to eat at your desk. You can never trust the amount of salt they put into food nowadays. I've completely cut back on the salt I add to our meals. Have you noticed?"

Fern dragged herself into a sitting position and picked up her phone lying beside her on the bedside table. "What's that? Salt? Er, no. Not really." She started flicking through the messages. "Big meetings this morning with all the finance. I'll have to have a runner pick up breakfast for me."

"I can make you an omelette."

"No, I'll be fine. What time are we leaving for the hotel on Friday?"

"It's an hour's drive, so 6ish, if you can be back by then?" Jon was putting on his socks, perched at the end of the bed.

"When have I ever managed to leave work before 8pm?" said Fern, looking up from her phone and clocking that the socks were not a matching pair. It was a regular occurrence that normally endeared her to her utterly un-vain husband, but for some reason today, she was riled.

"Exactly, it's a rare event," said Jon. "They can't say no."

"I'll get bad looks."

"Do you care?"

"No. But I like to lead by example." Fern clambered out of bed, throwing her phone onto her pillow. "So, what are your plans for today?"

"I've got a phone interview at two."

"Oh, is that today? For the two-monther in Malta?"

"Yes, but I'm not sure I want it."

"Why not? It would do you good to get some sun."

"It's just not a great time to be away, what with… you know." Jon looked across at Fern, almost apologetically. He was fully dressed now, bottom of jeans tucked carelessly into his socks, creased shirt. "I just don't want to miss any window at the moment," he continued.

"There'll be weekends back home," said Fern. "For all the mad hanky panky."

"…and I need to take care of you, make sure you're eating OK and not working too hard—"

"Believe it or not, Jon, I managed to live thirty-four whole years before we met without suffering from malnutrition or sleep madness." Fern disappeared into the bathroom and turned on the shower.

"I know, but it's different now," said Jon, poking his head around the door.

"Only in your mind."

"That's where most differences take place."

"You can get your mum around to look after me – you know how much she would love that."

"Stop that, Fern. It's only because she cares about you."

"Er, she cares about *you*, oh yes, and my womb."

"That's by the by. Anyway, I don't actually think I want the job, it's not an ad for a product I even endorse."

"What is it?"

"Some heavy-duty diesel car. I'd most probably get asphyxiated from fumes just standing behind the camera."

Fern cocked an eyebrow at Jon. "Steady on the fast living there, lover."

"What? I care about my lungs, OK."

"Look, David Attenborough, you might have the morning to swan about, but I've got a big meeting starting in no time. Can you pass me the shampoo and bugger off?"

"Careful you don't slip on the soap," said Jon, handing Fern the organic, chemical-free, natural, hibiscus-scented shampoo. "What? Is it my fault I care?"

Tuesday 2nd February

Day 2 of TWW

BECKS – Offline

Becks woke up at 2.07am with a jump.

"Coming!" she yelled spontaneously, causing Mike to grunt and stir.

"Mummy," called Hector, crying in his bedroom.

"Ughh…" grunted Mike.

"Don't worry, I'll go," said Becks, staggering out of bed, making no attempts to tread quietly across the wooden floorboards.

"Ssshh." Mike rolled onto Becks' side of the bed, barely conscious.

"You ssshh," said Becks, crossly, and then to Hector, "Mummy's coming."

Turning on the hall light outside Hector's room, Becks could tell before glimpsing him that Hector had thrown up. She had a supersensitive nose for strong smells and if there was one thing that made her gag more than anything, it was someone else's vom. Even her own son's.

"MIKE," she called, not expecting any response from her husband, who had stumbled into bed two hours before, waking Becks, moaning at her for turning off all the lights, and consequently filling the room with the sour exhalations of Claxton Real Ale. Yes, she knew the smell.

Hector was sitting up in his bed, covered from the side of his head down to his toes in last night's chicken nugget tea.

"Wait there," Becks said, going into the bathroom, grabbing a towel and switching on the shower.

"Come here, I'll carry you into the bathroom." Becks took a deep breath and held on to it as she lifted Hector onto the cold bathroom tiles and stripped him down.

"Well, this is going to bugger up my day."

Becks plonked Hector in the shower and, keeping his pyjamas at arm's length from her nose, threw them in the laundry bin.

"COOOLLLDDDD," screamed Hector, causing Becks to jump.

"Just wait, OK? It takes a while to heat up." Becks tried to subdue the irritation coursing through her, but it seemed to have become a default reaction to most things nowadays.

"Cold, cold, cold," mumbled Hector.

"I'm washing off the sick, OK? Just be patient."

Thirty minutes later, Hector was back in bed; fifteen minutes after that, he threw up again. This time successfully into a saucepan that Becks had left beside him on the floor. As she sat on the edge of the bath, watching Hector spew out every dribble of bile from his hopefully now empty stomach into the toilet bowl, she felt tears prickling her eyeballs.

What, no, Becks, surely not here? Not now, let it go. But she couldn't. No matter where Becks was at whatever time of day or, so it appeared, night, she lugged around the same nagging feeling, as much a part of her now as the stretch marks and an unsightly sun spot on her cheekbone. *There's only one thing*

I want in my life, one thing. She glared at the bathroom wall, through which Mike was still sleeping, dead to the world. "Something he," she said, stroking Hector's back soothingly, "my sweet little throwing-up son, cannot fulfil."

Rubbing her own tummy, weighed down by a sense of dread and dismay, Becks blinked back the tears and took a deep breath. She was certain that if only she could get pregnant, like her friends, all would be good with the world. No one would judge her, Mike would become reinvigorated by their marriage, which, yes, Becks had to face facts, did feel quite loveless at the moment, and Hector would have a little buddy for life.

"I'm finished, Mummy," said Hector, looking at Becks, stringy saliva hanging from his lips.

Inwardly gagging, Becks took a handful of loo roll and wiped his mouth. "Are you sure? We don't want any more sicky, do we?" Steering Hector back into his now stripped-down bed and placing him directly onto the mattress with a blanket over him, Becks permitted her mind to swerve sharply left and crash into images of Susan. *I bet she never gets up for Frankie – Josh does it all. I am sure of that,* she thought. *Let me go to Frankie, my darling, you rest here, leave the sweet-scented sick to me...*

It was past four when Becks eventually crawled back in besides Mike, shivering and dog-tired. She stole as much of the duvet as was available to her, shoved Mike as close to the edge of the bed as she dared, and snuggled down, desperate to sleep but remaining restless, half expecting Hector to call out at any moment.

Lying there, she ran through the list of women on the forum: her so-called TWW chums. A mixed bag. At least she was the only one so far to have a child; that gave her a firm footing. She could offer helpful advice, no, she wouldn't be smug – she would be there to answer any questions. It gave her a role; she could be useful – honest, but useful. Best to tell it like it is; people always respect honesty, especially at difficult times.

"Wahhhhsdgy," burbled Mike suddenly, following up with a long, rumbling burp.

"Oh, foul," said Becks, bringing her hand up to her nose and squeezing her nostrils shut. Using the soles of her feet, she pushed Mike even further away, until his legs were swinging over the floor.

Actually, fuck being honest, thought Becks. *Who wants honesty? And, for that matter, since when does anyone speak the truth online?*

Tuesday 2nd February

Day 2 of TWW

It was past midnight when Gav eventually rolled in from his Mammi's house, forehead glistening with sweat, bottom set of buttons undone on his shirt to reveal an overfed belly.

"Yah, you're still up," he said.

"Of course," said Mandi. "You don't like it when I go to bed before you." She was stretched out on the sofa, still in the same clothes she had worn all that day. Not particularly comfortable clothes at that: skinny jeans suffocating her legs and a black top with an annoyingly loose strap that kept falling down her arm, but she hadn't got around to changing into something more suitable for lounging.

"Are you going to look at me or do I need to report your phone for committing adultery with my wife?"

"Oh no, are you pissed?" said Mandi, looking up from her Instagram and assessing the state of her husband.

"No, just pleasantly mellow." Gav was gently swaying in the middle of the room, out of rhythm with Ed Sheeran on the AirDrop, but clearly in rhythm with whatever soundtrack was in his head.

"You ought to sit down."

"In a bit."

"How was Mammi after I left?"

"So-so," said Gav.

"So…?"

"So-so-ciable… ha ha, see what I did there?"

"Did her guests all stay as late as you?"

"No, I was the last to leave. Mammi kept feeding me more food, telling me I look half starved."

"I hope you told her I feed you like a pig."

"I might have done, I can't remember. Anyway, what kind of son refuses his mammi's cooking?"

Gav weaved a route around the mahogany coffee table, past Mandi on the sofa and plonked down heavily on the red and gold armchair identical in all but size to the sofa. He threw his legs carelessly over the tasselled arm and clutched his belly.

"Ugh," he said. "Man feels good. Man full."

"I'm pleased for you," said Mandi. "So, does that mean I still have to be up at six to get you breakfast?"

"Yeah, I have a 7.30 meeting."

"Oh, Gav, you know I need all the sleep I can get."

"Oh, on the subject of sleep, Mammi told me to tell you… ummm… what was it?" He stuck his finger on the side of his head and agitated his temple. "Something about lying on your tummy not your back… I think I drifted off halfway through her interesting insight. You should call her and ask."

"Yeah, I think I can figure out how to sleep, but thank you for imparting the message in such a clear way."

"You're welcome."

"Can't you just pick up breakfast somewhere?" said Mandi, stretching. "You like that egg, mushroom and bean cup they do at Pret."

"No, lazybones, you can make me breakfast – we need to save money, remember?"

"What are we saving for, remind me?"

"Yah, come on, Mandi, new golf clubs!" Gav sat up, trying to straighten himself on the chair but failing. "How many times do I have to tell you?"

"I wonder *why* I keep forgetting?"

"Look, I told you that you could have something too. Why not treat yourself to a manicure, or, I don't know…"

"What with these?" Mandi waggled her fingers in front of Gav.

"Well, stop biting them then."

"I can't – you know I'm stressed."

"Then stop being stressed. You need to find something to do with yourself rather than sitting around all day worrying."

"I don't sit around worrying." Mandi jumped up from the sofa and went to lock the front door. "I have plenty to do to keep me busy."

"Stuck in front of a screen all day doesn't mean you're busy, Mands." Gav scratched his protruding belly and yawned loudly. "You should find a hobby. Speak to Mammi – she has loads of stuff she does every day."

"I'm quite capable of amusing myself." Mandi picked up Gav's discarded shoes and lined them up in front of the door.

"By being bored."

"No, I have loads to do. Look around, the house doesn't mysteriously tidy itself."

"It looks like shit in here, Mand. All those magazines, empty plates and that must be at least five of your coats in a pile."

"So, I didn't tidy today because I was out, if you recall, looking after your nephew, but normally it's immaculate."

"If you say so, my darling." Heaving himself up off his chair, Gav staggered over to Mandi. "Come on, my busy little wife, let's go to bed." Throwing his arms around Mandi's shoulders, Gav transferred all his weight onto Mandi, allowing her to drag him up the stairs.

"Why don't *we* ever go away for romantic weekends?" said Mandi once she had recovered her breath on the landing.

"It sounds like you are implying someone does." Gav was leaning against the bedroom door, attempting to coordinate his fine motor skills enough to unbutton his shirt.

"Oh, just someone I spoke to today. Her husband is taking her to some swanky hotel."

"Who?"

"You don't know her," said Mandi, gathering up the dishevelled duvet and huffing it straight.

"Is this one of your 'virtual' friends?"

"Yes, actually, it is."

"And you believe her? She could be saying anything. How do you know she even has a husband?"

"I know she does. Otherwise what would she be doing on my two-week wait forum?"

"Spying."

"That would be really weird. There's nothing to see."

"Except for a lot of miserable women talking about their shit husbands." Gav threw his tie onto the bed.

"That's not true."

"Course it is. Forums, for-'ummm', moaning."

"I find them comforting."

"I think you should stop using them, Mand," said Gav, taking Mandi's hand. "We don't know that they're safe. All that data you're putting out about us to strangers."

"You sound like your mam."

"She has a point. You might be happy airing your dirty underwear for all the world to see, but I don't want you showing anyone mine."

"It's not like that." Mandi recovered her hand from Gav's firm grasp and rubbed her wrists. "Everyone's friendly. We're all in it together."

"In what, Mands?"

"In our fertility journeys."

"You're not on any journey, you're just taking your time to get pregnant. That's not a journey. It's biology. Who even are these people?"

"It doesn't matter, God, I should never have said anything. I'm only trying to share my life with you, like married couples do. Am I doing that wrong too?"

"Then share it only with *me*, don't share it with all the world. Do you know how embarrassing it is having everyone know my business?"

"This isn't about you, Gav, it's about me."

"And what so, you're a 'me' now, not an 'us'?"

"Just forget it, alright?" Mandi scrambled out of her jeans and fell into bed. She would give her teeth a doubly good brush in the morning. "And anyway, it's a closed group now, just five of us, so no public airing of your underwear."

"I still want you to quit."

"Why? It's me who can't get pregnant, not you, apparently."

"So, focus on getting yourself better then." Gav climbed in beside Mandi, angrily thumping his legs on the mattress. "You know how private I am."

"As I said, Gav, this isn't about you. No one even needs to know your name. I can change it."

"Oh, what? You've already put it out there?"

"I can't remember."

"You're really pissing me off, Mandi," said Gav, shaking his pillow and lying his head down firmly. "Never talk to me about this forum again. I don't want to know."

Wednesday 3rd February
Day 3 of TWW

Jane@closetoTWWentyyearsandcounting
Morning all. How are we today?

Fern@toobusytoTWW
Bearing up. Got a big meeting with five middle-aged male execs to prepare for. I wonder if they will be interested in hearing about my fertility journey?

Jane@closetoTWWentyyearsandcounting
It might bring the meeting to a rapid close.

Fern@toobusytoTWW
There's always a silver lining. What are your plans?

Jane@closetoTWWentyyearsandcounting
Out for lunch with my sister and mum. It's my mum's eighty-fifth birthday! Not quite sure I'm in the mood for it, but one learns to grin and bear it.

Fern@toobusytoTWW
Swap your day for my meeting with execs!

Jane@closetoTWWentyyearsandcounting
So kind, but I'll muddle through!!

Becks@desperatemumof1
Aaargh, Hector's down with a bug so no nursery and no getting to the gym for me. I warn you, ladies, there is always something in the germ department, when you have a toddler.

Jane@closetoTWWentyyearsandcounting
I'm prepared to take that risk.

Becks@desperatemumof1
I can assure you it is not that fun. I haven't been to the gym for two days now and I am feeling sooo bloated. Wall-to-wall CBeebies here I come… yaaawwn.

Becks@desperatemumof1
Oh wow, Jane. Sorry if I upset you. Remember, I am suffering the same as you, that is why I'm here. Apologies if I already have a child, it doesn't make it any easier, I can assure you.

Fern@toobusytoTWW
It must make it a bit easier, Becks. Don't rub our noses in it.

Becks@desperatemumof1
OMG. Perhaps it would be better if I left this chat. Hector is a big part of my life. Does that mean I can't mention him at all?

Jane@closetoTWWentyyearsandcounting
It's fine, Becks. Of course, he is a part of your life and that is

fine. I just meant tread delicately – maybe I am overly sensitive. Years of self-preservation!

Star@Gaiababe

Ladies, ladies. Just clocking in, now, namaste and peace be amongst us all. Have we done our morning heart chakra alignment? No, I didn't think so. Altogether now, deep breath in, reciting the words 'I love' ten times. I love, I love, I love, I love, I love, I love, I love, I love, I love, I love, and exhale. Feeling the love?

Fern@toobusytoTWW

Nope, only the hairs on the back of my neck stiffen. I think it's called cynicism.

Star@Gaiababe

The love mantra works every time. Sometimes we just forget to love ourselves, which makes it so much harder to share the love.

Fern@toobusytoTWW

Are you always this positive at 8am?

Star@Gaiababe

A smile is the best make-up a girl can wear!

Fern@toobusytoTWW

I prefer red lippie.

Star@Gaiababe

Whatever works for you, babe. You were born to sparkle.

Jane@closetoTWWentyyearsandcounting

Might have calmed me down too. Sorry to be irritable with you, Becks. We are all in this together, as you say.

Becks@desperatemumof1

It's OK, Jane. I was most probably being insensitive. Another reason why the gym would have been good… work off some of my stress. Meant to be out for coffee with my friends today, but TBH, can't face them all discussing their newborns. Everyone in my world seems to be pregnant. Am sure they are looking pityingly at me. So, guess I'm sensitive myself.

Fern@toobusytoTWW

Hope you're not looking at us pityingly.

Becks@desperatemumof1

Sorry, that came out wrong. Can't seem to say anything right today. Need some me time and some sleep. At least Hector is happy to sit in front of the telly for hours.

Jane@closetoTWWentyyearsandcounting

My SIL is ridiculously strict about screen time for her kids. One hour a day maximum.

Becks@desperatemumof1

I'm strict too. It's Mike who is the softie. He loves all the kids' shows himself.

Star@Gaiababe

Could that be the reason for his low sperm count? Just a thought? Inactivity?

Becks@desperatemumof1
NO! He's super busy the rest of the time when he's at home, helping out, doing the shopping…

Star@Gaiababe
Hmm, maybe it IS good to have a man around.

Fern@toobusytoTWW
Stick to what you've got, Star, if I were you – there's a lot to be said for being a single mum (should it work out). Removes any pressure.

Becks@desperatemumof1
Mike doesn't pressurise me.

Fern@toobusytoTWW
I didn't say he did, but when you've got to make all the decisions as a twosome, it gets a bit tiring. Maybe it's just me, but I sometimes feel I am carrying all the weight of Jon's expectations along with mine, and that is a heavy load.

Star@Gaiababe
Sounds like you've got yourself a stayer there, though.

Fern@toobusytoTWW
Yeah, Jon will stick around come hell or high water. I just don't want to disappoint him, you know.

Jane@closetoTWWentyyearsandcounting
Remember you're in this together and so whatever disappointments he has, you have too, Fern.

Fern@toobusytoTWW

True, except, luckily for me, I can lose myself in my work. Speaking of, meeting in ten, gotta roll.

***

Mandi@LusciousLocks

Anyone around? Had row with DH last night and feeling really bad.

Becks@desperatemumof1

What's up, Luscious Locks?

Mandi@LusciousLocks

Hi Becks. DH cross about me sharing my fertility news online. Not sure what to do.

Becks@desperatemumof1

Er… ignore him. This is your journey, not his.

Mandi@LusciousLocks

He doesn't like the word 'journey' either. Says it's not a journey.

Becks@desperatemumof1

Hmm, he sounds pissed off. It's up to you. From my experience, DH's are always happier if we do our talking about stuff like this with friends rather than with them.

Mandi@LusciousLocks

That's what I think too. DH has far better things to think about.

Becks@desperatemumof1
I'm not sure 'far better' is the right way of putting it, ha ha.

Star@Gaiababe
Hey gals… you don't have to tell him, Mands, although, from my understanding, it is good to involve your partner in your concerns as much as possible, so that they can understand what you feel.

Becks@desperatemumof1
Spoken like a true 'free spirit'.

Star@Gaiababe
I know, hardly practising what I preach – but keeping communication channels open is a proven way of maintaining healthy relationships.

Mandi@LusciousLocks
Even if he doesn't like it, I'm not going to stop. I need this chat group. I don't have anyone else to talk to.

Star@Gaiababe
Cool coyotes, Mands. Stick with what you believe. There are always doubters out there. I have based my career on getting people to believe in themselves.

Mandi@LusciousLocks
Have you had any success? You sound like you are good at it to me.

Star@Gaiababe

I like to be the best I can be and have others do the same, so it depends what you call success.

Mandi@LusciousLocks

My DH is very conservative. He believes in people keeping their private affairs to themselves. I agree with that too, but I also think that a problem shared is a problem halved and I know I could not do this alone.

Star@Gaiababe

It does help to surround yourself by people who understand. Protection from negative, upsetting comments.

Jane@closetoTWWentyyearsandcounting

Hi all. On the subject of upsetting comments, my mum just told me at lunch that if I stopped being so stubborn, I would have a family by now.

Becks@desperatemumof1

How much wine had she had?

Jane@closetoTWWentyyearsandcounting

That was the problem. She is normally very subtle. I would be lying if I said it didn't hurt.

Fern@toobusytoTWW

Haha The Stubborn Ovary, I like that… someone call Netflix. Oh. I'm in TV. That would be me.

Jane@closetoTWWentyyearsandcounting

I had to bite my tongue, which I have become quite good at over the years.

Star@Gaiababe

It's a shame that we should have to curb what we want to say just to avoid other peeps insensitivity. Sounds like you did well, Jane.

Jane@closetoTWWentyyearsandcounting

Not sure I did well, just what was essential to keeping the peace on her birthday. The problem is, I do feel bad that I haven't been able to give her grandchildren. At least she has loads from my sister!

Becks@desperatemumof1

I wouldn't feel too bad – she's had kids of her own. And other grandkids. Take the pressure off.

Fern@toobusytoTWW

Be grateful she didn't tell you to 'just relax' – that's what my MIL says to me ALL THE TIME, and it drives me up the wall. What does it even mean, 'just relax'?

Becks@desperatemumof1

Yeah, that's totally patronising too. If a hot bath and a yoga session were the solution, I'd have a bus-load of kids by now.

Jane@closetoTWWentyyearsandcounting

And there is something about the word 'relax' that instantly makes you feel tense, especially when you feel so rubbish at the best of times.

Star@Gaiababe

Although, gotta be said – decreased stress equals increased libido'. Hygge is my lifesaver, living in the present and enjoying the present. Lighting a candle, drinking a mug of rooibos, chanting affirmations, and ten minutes of ashtanga yoga. That's how I start my day.

Fern@toobusytoTWW

Wish I had the time.

Star@Gaiababe

Time has a wonderful way of showing us what matters.

Fern@toobusytoTWW

Deadlines do it for me.

Thursday 4th February

Day 4 of TWW

Mandi@LusciousLocks

I know it's nothing, but I had a dream last night that I was pregnant. Anyone else had one of those?

Becks@desperatemumof1

I remember having one when I was pregnant with DS, so that could be something, Mandi.

Mandi@LusciousLocks

Oh, wow. Now you've got my hopes up.

Jane@closetoTWWentyyearsandcounting

Sorry to be the voice of reason, but early days, girls.

Mandi@LusciousLocks

You're right, Jane. I'm just digging around for any hope, that's all.

Jane@closetoTWWentyyearsandcounting
I know, I am sure we're all doing it. It's quite common at this early stage in the TWW to get psychologically geared up.

Fern@toobusytoTWW
Who needs a theme park rollercoaster when there's a TWW to contend with?

Becks@desperatemumof1
I will most probably get my head bitten off for saying this, but having been pregnant once before, I'm on hyper alert for the same sort of feelings… and I am pretty certain, nothing yet.

Mandi@LusciousLocks
What's the earliest we can test?

Jane@closetoTWWentyyearsandcounting
I never test before fourteen days. No point.

Becks@desperatemumof1
I did hear about someone once getting a BFP at six days.

Jane@closetoTWWentyyearsandcounting
Hmm, not sure about that one, Becks. I think for our sanity, we should keep an eye on the long-term wait, rather than get hyped up too early on.

Becks@desperatemumof1
Told you I was impatient. I do not have the disposition to wait. I like to write a list and then tick things off.

Mandi@LusciousLocks
Yeah, wish I could be as patient as you, Jane.

Jane@closetoTWWentyyearsandcounting

You will need several more years of disappointment before that happens, Mandi… (let's hope not).

Becks@desperatemumof1

I find it hard because people think that as I already have one child, there is nothing wrong with my fertility, so they come right out and ask. And often they ask Hector direct, which really winds me up. "Bet you want a little brother or sister, don't you?" Grrr… Hector just shrugs. I am sure he picks up vibes from me.

Jane@closetoTWWentyyearsandcounting

That must be hard. All of my close friends have stopped asking us now, or maybe we have just shut ourselves off from all but a handful of the most sensitive. It is the first question strangers tend to ask, though, especially if Keith and I are out and about together. "Any kids?" they ask. And they make it sound like such a casual question when inside both Keith and I are screaming.

What you need to do is have some stock answers that you just give to people so that they back off and you can leave your emotions out of it. When people say, "Any kids?" nowadays. I just answer with, "Always on the cards."

If I were you, Becks, I would say something like, "Happy little trio." Keep it simple. And right now, remember, you and your DH are the only things that matter to Hector. Oh, and Hector himself, of course.

Fern@toobusytoTWW

Hi all… hang in there, Mandi. Maybe Gav is stressed like you. Hearing you, Jane, on the 'casual questioning'. At least in my world, people tend to be married to the job, so babyland is less of an issue. One of my ex-colleagues did come in the other day to show us her newborn and I actually felt quite sorry for her because we were too busy to take much notice.

Mandi@LusciousLocks

I am literally the only one in my world trying to get pregnant. All my friends are away at uni or looking for jobs. They think I'm mad wanting a baby. I just really worry that when they are all ready to settle down, I will still be trying.

Jane@closetoTWWentyyearsandcounting

I know how you feel, Mandi. Keith and I started trying at twenty-two, but it doesn't mean it's going to happen to you.

Mandi@LusciousLocks

Deep down, I don't think Gav actually wants a baby right now. He is most probably secretly pleased. It is only because of his 'duty' that he is even considering it.

Becks@desperatemumof1

What duty is that, Mandi?

Mandi@LusciousLocks

Our families come from Delhi: kids = wealth, especially boys! Family pressure mounts when you are married to have a family ASAP.

Jane@closetoTWWentyyearsandcounting

What about you, Mandi? Do you actually want a family or are you just doing it because of the pressure?

Mandi@LusciousLocks

I've been wanting children since I was about five. That's all I cared about. I was never into the idea of going to uni or being a career woman… Maybe I've wanted them too much!!!!!!

Becks@desperatemumof1

That's tough, although they say if you want something bad enough it happens, right?

Jane@closetoTWWentyyearsandcounting

That's one for our Gaia guru – where is she when we need her?

***

Star@Gaiababe

Hello, beautiful women. Just come back from two hours of self-love. How am I feeling? Lovely. Walking in the forest. Forest bathing. I swear, trees are the best remedy for anxiety.

Jane@closetoTWWentyyearsandcounting

Forest bathing?? Actually sounds quite nice. I love the fact that you connect with nature so well, Star. Lesson to us all.

***

Becks@desperatemumof1

OK, guys, confession, just eaten half a chocolate cake. My friend dropped it off at my house yesterday afternoon, when I didn't show up for coffee. I told her I would share it with DH and DS but ate the whole lot myself. #fatnotproud

Fern@toobusytoTWW

Let it go, girl. Comfort eating is what gets me through. DH is all into preparing healthy meals, but I gorge when he's not looking, haha. Burger in a bun anyone? Makes me feel better and to be honest, right now, I need all the good feeling I can get.

Fern@toobusytoTWW

And don't say anything, Star…

Star@Gaiababe

My lips are zipped.

Fern@toobusytoTWW

So not much comfort food going to get past them then.

Becks@desperatemumof1

I wish I could feel as relaxed about it as you do, Fern. I'm really conscious of my weight and right now, I feel horrible – inadequate and horrible.

Star@Gaiababe

Would it help if I said, 'feel good about your body, whatever the size'?

Becks@desperatemumof1

Nope. I'm going to have to double my time at the gym this morning. That's going to hurt.

Mandi@LusciousLocks

At least you get to the gym, I've become such a couch potato recently.

Thursday 4th February, evening

Day 4 of TWW

"Romero, please don't call me. Yeah? It's over, babe. I wish you well, but you need to set me free."

Star hung up and placed her phone against her chest as she lay down on her childhood bed. She closed her eyes, allowing a tear to roll onto her pillow. Squeezing the bridge of her nose, she stemmed the sob brewing deep in her chest. If she made so much as a hint of a noise, her mother would come running. Star could not cope with having an anxious Janet in her face right now.

"Breathe in for four, hold for four, out for four," she whispered.

It was no good. Her monkey mind was chattering – meditation wasn't going to cut it this time.

She leapt up gracefully and went over to her desk to where her pink fluffy-topped pens poked cheerfully out of her familiar old pen holder. Her fingers ran over the crystals and precious pile of smelly rubbers that she had collected so carefully as a child.

Star snapped open her laptop, picked up her phone and took a selfie. She checked it critically and adjusted the light exposure. She hesitated, then added a filter and cropped the shot. Her childish cherry wallpaper, unchanged since the '90s, was not the background her million-plus Instagram followers would want to see.

"This is me #RAW #REAL," she wrote.

Star checked the close-up image of her face one last time. Her eyelashes were suitably glossy, eyes brimming with glittering tears.

She held her breath against the familiar wave of anxiety that bubbled up every time she was about to post. This was not a typical upload for her. Star was much more comfortable sending beachside photos of herself in front of sunsets in exotic places. Her finger hovered, then pressed decisively. The whoosh sent a surge of adrenaline, followed by instant regret.

"What… why did I just sent that?"

Less than twenty seconds later, her phone vibrated. Here we go. The likes were starting to come in thick and fast. Who were these people? One hundred, two hundred, one thousand followers taking time out of their day to let her know their feelings about her post.

Star scrolled down.

Threeoftree	Babes, ooo no! What's happened? I hope you are OK? Sending light.
Stuckinarut	Stunning but so sad! Why?
Helpahiphi	Gorgeous, always and forever.
Snarky3274	Attentionseekingbitchhead.

She sighed and flipped her phone face down on her desk. It didn't seem to matter what she posted. The trolls and haters wormed their way into her feed pretty quickly these days. Once one person posted something mean, it was like a wave.

Plenty more negativity would surface before someone stepped in with a positive comment and changed the mood again.

"Stacey?"

Oh no.

Star groaned and wiped her eyes. She had forgotten her mum followed all her posts.

Star opened the door and yelled down, "Mum! It's fine! I'm fine! Just… just had a bit of a bust-up with Romero, that's all."

Star peered down the stairs. Her mum was standing at the bottom, clutching her phone, prepped to come up.

"Stacey!"

"You don't need to come, Mum." Star flashed her an overly cheery grin. "See? I'm fine. I like to shake things up on my grid. It gets a bit boring just posting all those happy-go-lucky shots. And I didn't have the energy to find the right mantra tonight. Don't worry about me. Go back to making the tea. What are we having? Not sausages!"

"Stace, can I—"

Oh God, Janet was oozing concern.

Star walked back into her room and closed the door, listening to her mum's approaching footsteps and then the knock on her bedroom door.

"What, Mum? I told you – I'm fine!"

Janet pushed the door open, walked in and sat on her bed, uninvited. Star felt too emotionally exhausted to complain.

"OK. Stacey – I am going to say this again, for the last time, and I want you to listen." Janet sounded really stern.

Star was taken aback at her mum's bold tone. She wasn't used to being challenged.

"OK, OK, chill the chill. I'm listening." Star sat down on the little white leather stool at her dressing table. She picked her fingernails and toyed with her long hair. One firm word from her mum and she instantly regressed to her eleven-year old self.

"You're twenty-nine years old and you're living here, in your old bedroom."

Star rolled her eyes.

"This isn't a criticism," Janet continued. "Dad and I are of course delighted that you came home. But we're confused. Why are you here? Now? Are you on the run? Escaping? Is he… is Romero abusing you?"

"What, Mum? No!"

Star couldn't help herself from smirking. Romero? The idea of the mild-mannered, ukulele-playing (fit and toned) earth child Romero being cruel to anyone or anything was laughable. Although maybe it was a fair question – sometimes evil can be found in the most surprising places.

"Mum – he's a vegan! He rescues battery farm chickens. He… just… NO. No, he is not abusing me. And please… call me Star."

"What is it then?"

"It's just that I don't want a boyfriend and he can't accept it. That's it, OK? End of."

Star sighed. "Look, Mum, I know you got married at twenty, and you and Dad are very happy, but it's just not the life for me. I don't want to be tied down. I don't want a man telling me what to do. Romero is lovely, and I'm sure he wouldn't want to tell me how to live my life. But – even the IDEA of it gives me goosebumps. I like being able to pick up my backpack and head off wherever I want to go, with whoever I want. Or don't want. I like being single. It makes me happy."

Janet sat quietly. "It's selfish of you, Stacey."

"How?" Star asked defensively. "I'm not hurting anyone. I'm just living my best life."

Janet looked at her, eyes blazing. "What about us? What about grandchildren? How can you deny us that pleasure? All my friends keep bringing in little snaps of gurgling babies. And what do I have to show them? Your latest yoga pose on Instagram."

Star snorted. "Here we go again. I'm never good enough, am I?" she said.

Janet slumped. "You are. You're more than good enough! And that's the point. You are more loved than you know, Star. I just don't think you're as happy as you make out."

Janet stood up to leave.

Star felt the familiar rumble of irritation.

This time it was with herself. Her mum was right. What *was* wrong with her? Why couldn't she settle down?

"What do *you* know, Mum? You don't know anything. Why do you say these things? It's not all about you and your friends. Of course I'm happy. I chose this life, remember?"

Come on, Star, stay zen, she reminded herself. If there was a little life starting, all this negative emotion could hurt it.

Janet took her phone out of her back pocket. "If you're so happy, why post this?"

Star stared at her mum's phone and saw her tear-filled eyes gazing back.

"It's nothing, OK?"

"It doesn't look like nothing to me."

If only Janet knew what lay behind the tears. If only she knew how all Star wanted to do was give her mum the grandchild she longed for. If only Star could open up to Janet and let her in. Share her deepest longings. But it wouldn't work. Janet would never understand. The gulf between their two worlds was too wide.

"Really, Mum, I'm OK," said Star, going over to Janet and clasping her sleeve. "Please stop worrying about me. I'm not as lost as you think."

"You know, Stace... Star, the door's always open," said Janet, patting Star's hand.

"I know, Mum, and by the way, that's really cliché."

"Is it?"

"Next you're going to tell me that when a door closes a window opens."

"I was, actually," Janet said with a small smile. "Anyway, look, I'm pleased we've had this chat. I don't feel any the wiser, but at least I know you're not sobbing into your boots."

"Boots, Mum? Er no, Valentino Rockstud sandals, if you don't mind."

"Oh yes, sorry, I forget you favour flip-flops nowadays."

"Yeah, thanks, Mum..."

Janet left the room and closed the door.

"... for everything," said Star, quietly under her breath.

Picking up her phone she lay back on her bed and gently, mindlessly, stroked her tummy.

Thursday 4th February, evening

Day 4 ofTWW

JANE – Diary

Reasons to remember why I love myself:

> *Thoughtful*
> *Sensitive*
> *Perceptive*
> *In love*
> *Loved*
> *Secure*
> *Inventive*

If unable to be a mother, I will find alternatives:

Get a puppy. (Hmm – Keith's wish. Is it mine?)
Find a fulfilling job. (Coping with covering for mothers needing school hols/assembly, etc. Could I do that? Not strong enough… might get bitter… will get bitter.)
Set up/work at an orphanage… Where? Romania? Yemen? Yes. Possibility. Convince Keith… hmm. Adopt. Hmmm. Foster. Hmmm. No, want our own child.

Secret (secret) thoughts.

If fertilised, baby T = size of a grain of sand right now.

Did you make the journey, Baby T, through to my pesky uterus? Are you burrowing? Please tell me that you are. I can give you the happiest home. I know I will. I KNOW I will.

Positive thinking.

Small row with Keith (hate rowing). Stupid reason. Puppy. Frustrated. Puppy replacement to baby T. No I don't want to believe that. Does Keith want to give up? Am I alone in wanting to go on and on until I have baby T in my arms? Am I living in a fantasy world? Hate myself. Inadequate.

Sshh, STOP IT!!!

> *Thoughtful*
> *Sensitive*
> *Perceptive*
> *In love*
> *Loved*
> *Secure*
> *Inventive*

Thought for the day:
We spend half our fertile years trying desperately not to get pregnant and the other half willing it to happen.

Feel old on the forum. Everyone looking up to me for advice. Deep down pitying me? Think I am a lost cause? Maybe. But it is their hope that spurs me on. I have as much chance of getting pregnant as any of them. I DO. I can do this. Are you listening, Baby T? The best life – that's what I can offer.

All the other women have time to wait. Even Fern — thirty-seven. Ha. Only thirty-seven. Does Fern even want a baby? Can't tell. Career versus baby. Er, baby, yes please.

Princess Diana died at thirty-six and this sounded soooo old when I was twenty, and now, I'm years past. Forty-two. ONLY forty-two. Rachel Weisz pregnant… she's forty-eight. Sooo — years of fertility left in me. Probably.

Turned down making love with Keith tonight. He understood, but I feel bad. Scared of dislodging Baby T. I know. Scientifically unlikely. Neurotic me. Neurotic mother… No. Never. Keith is all I have so mustn't reject him ever…

He loves me = must be doing something right.

Plans for forum:
Suggest writing journal. Private place to be totally honest.
Suggest ways of occupying mind for the TWW.
Comfort Mandi… hold her handi!
Keep the peace… potential to get personal… everyone tense.
Find ways of coping if one of us gets BFP… don't want to think about this. Will I be strong enough to show happiness?
Learn positive thinking.

Keep crying. Why? Keith – giving up? Puppy? Sad. Why so sad, Jane?

List for tomorrow:
Go for swim – twenty lengths.
Go to art shop for canvas and paints. Start working on making art studio in spare room.
Meet Maisy – Caffe Nero. (Be sympathetic – divorce, eek. Sound and look interested in Seb (fifteen?) and Sam (nine?).) Come up with soundbite on TWW. Keep it brief. Don't get emotional. DON'T GET EMOTIONAL.

Buy Birthday card: Sue, Gramp L.

Write thank you text for theatre tix – Annie.

Madcap plan... Research orphanage opportunities in... somewhere... Not giving up. Just looking ahead. Baby T might like orphanage too. Lots of friends.

Puppy – don't dismiss. Keith's coping mechanism. Support him.

Keep thinking positive thoughts. Brave face, Jane... BRAVE...

Thoughtful
Sensitive
Perceptive
In love
Loved
Secure
Inventive
Lots to give life even if my purpose as mother is not fulfilled.

Thursday 4th February

Day 4 of TWW

"It's OK not to be OK, you know," Jon yelled.

"What?" Fern called back, wobbling on her bicycle as she attempted to turn around and hear what Jon was saying.

"Stop. Stop. For God's sake." Jon wheeled his bike to a stop and hung over the handlebars, panting. Fern pulled up and put her foot down.

"This was a terrible idea," Jon gasped.

"Nope, it was a brilliant idea. I was going crazy in London, imagining what was going on inside me. Fresh air is supposed to be good for conception, isn't it?

"The cycle route didn't look this hard on the map," Jon grumbled. They had taken their bikes to Clapham Junction early that morning and hopped on a train to Brockenhurst in the New Forest on a whim. It was cold and grey and very February.

"Oh, come on, fatty. It's not that bad. One last bit, and then we're at the pub. You can have a nice cold pint and cheesy ploughmans. Race you!"

"Grrr," mumbled Jon. "Why do you always have to be so damn competitive?"

"What were you shouting earlier?" Fern asked, setting down a large glass of bitter in front of Jon. She sipped her green limeade and winced. "This is not as tasty as yours," she said.

"Well, you can't take the chance. Stay off the booze, Ferny... just in case." Jon wiped the white froth off his top lip.

Fern rolled her eyes at him. "You're liking this, aren't you... Daddy in charge."

She took another gulp of fizzy lime. "So? What did you say?"

"I said, it's OK not to be OK," Jon said.

"Who said I'm not OK?" Fern replied, sensing a surge of irritation.

"Don't get cross. It's just... you always feel the need to be STRONG... all the time, and sometimes... I just think it might be healthier for you if you let go... just a bit."

Fern twiddled with the black straw in her drink. "I'm fine, Jon. Well, I thought I was. This Two-Week Wait forum has got me thinking a bit more about stuff." She cocked her head at Jon, huddled in her jumper and leant forward over the pub table towards him.

"There's someone on there, Jane, who is forty-two and has been trying for twenty years. Twenty!" Fern exclaimed. "We've only been trying for six months and already it feels like an eternity. How the hell has she kept going?"

Fern sat back and looked into the pub fire roaring in the hearth. "I guess I feel impatient because of my deadlines," she said quietly. "I just want to get it over with."

Jon put his pint down. "'Get it over with', Fern? That's harsh."

"You know what I mean. It's just how to progress with work and balancing career and baby and... I am a black woman at the top of the ladder, Jon. The reason I've got to where I am, as I keep reminding you, is—"

"Hold on, is it because of your grit and determination?"

"Yes," said Fern, throwing a napkin at Jon. "And quit with the teasing, OK?"

"You forgot to mention natural talent and flair."

"Yeah, well, that goes without saying."

"And stunning good looks?"

"Your words, not mine." Fern flashed her white teeth against her signature red lipstick.

"The most stunning in all the world," Jon replied, lifting her hand and kissing it.

This was not the time to unravel baggage. Jon could sense that none of this was easy for Fern. She always carried a lot more than she let out.

"Do you think the fact you were sent away to boarding school so young makes you want a family more than me?" asked Fern out of the blue, causing Jon to sit back.

"Woah, where did that come from?"

"Just popped into my head," said Fern. "I grew up in a huge busy household and couldn't wait to leave home."

"No. I loved school. Best days of my life," Jon said affably.

"I'm just curious, that's all," Fern said, shrugging. "It's just quite unusual. From what I can gather on the forum, most of the other men are just happy to go along with what their wives want. Some don't even seem bothered about the whole trying to conceive thing, and take no interest!"

"I just want a family of my own, Fern. What's wrong with that? I can't wait to take the kids to the playground, to swimming lessons, teach them how to fish, ride a bike, kick a ball," Jon said dreamily.

Fern's look of – what was it? Horror? – caused Jon to snap out of his dream.

"Sorry, Fern, but is it a crime to want to be a father?"

Fern picked at the limp lettuce draped over the side of her cheese sandwich. "OK. You can dream. I'm just sweating over here under the weight of your expectations!" Fern said. "One step at a time and all that."

Jon took a huge bite of his doorstop bloomer. A blob of mayonnaise dripped down the front of his faded rugby shirt. Fern noticed the collar was frayed. How long had he been wearing that? Come to think of it, she didn't think she had ever seen him not wear it.

"So, do you feel any different?" he asked, daring himself to broach the icy ground.

"No, Jon! You must have asked me this already a hundred times! It's too early to tell. Stop asking. I'll tell you if I do."

Fern did feel upset for some reason. Could it be that she wanted this more than she realised? Surely not.

"Won't you miss working, Jon?" Fern asked, trying to get off the subject of what was happening in her body. She had been wanting to ask Jon this for months, but it had never seemed the right time.

"You are joking, right? Miss careering around on planes, with tight deadlines, never knowing when the next job is coming in? No, thank you. I can't wait to be at home, making you and the kids supper. Keeping house like daddy bear."

"Oh my God, I don't even know what to say to that?"

Truth was, it did sound perfect. A world Fern could only imagine.

"Only question is – will you still find me sexy with baby sick on my shoulder?" Jon said.

Fern tutted. "Pah, Jon."

But wait, *would* she find him sexy? What's more, would he find *her* sexy? Her toned body would totally change if she got pregnant.

Fern was scared. Scared of being pregnant, scared of not being pregnant. What if she couldn't do it? She was not used to feeling so many emotions... so much confusion. For the first time in a long time, Fern felt totally out of control.

Thursday 4th February

Day 4 of TWW

"Come on, Hector, hurry up!"

Becks grabbed his arm and tried to poke it through the arm of his little yellow raincoat.

Hector immediately made his arm as stiff as a metal pole. Whatever Becks did, she could not bend his arm at the elbow to get his raincoat on.

Hector had his defiant look on.

"Fine, fine. You'll just have to get wet. Let's go."

Becks threw the raincoat on the floor and picked up the large beach bag she used as her handbag these days. No more dainty clutches for her, or smart leather totes she used when she worked in HR. Now she carried huge, freebie canvas monstrosities, to lug all the millions of things her child in theory needed. She turned to scoop Hector up around the waist. He immediately screeched and straightened his body like a surfboard, causing Becks to lose balance and drop him on the floor.

"Stand up, Hector," Becks wailed. "We're really late! Don't you want to see your friends?"

Hector stood up and crossed his arms, little mouth pouting. *Where do kids learn to make that face?* Becks wondered.

"Hector…" Becks was wheedling now, bending down with her face right next to his.

"Chocolate," Hector said stubbornly.

"No."

"CHOCOLATE!"

"FINE!"

Becks rummaged around in her bag and dropped the bag of Buttons in Hector's hand. "Happy now? Let's go!"

Hector trotted after her, whining for her to open the packet.

She strapped him into the car seat, tore open the Buttons and chucked them at him. They immediately spilled all over the car seat and on the floor.

Hector started to wail.

"Look, just eat them from the seat, they'll be fine," Becks said through gritted teeth.

Hector stopped crying enough to realise he could reach most of the Buttons from where he sat.

Becks heaved a sigh of relief. Looking for them would keep him occupied for the next few minutes.

"So sorry, sorry," Becks gasped as she reached the gathering in the park. She knew she was purple in the face and sweating through her too-tight floral cotton shirt. Her thighs were sticking together under her knee-length dark denim skirt.

Mike was already there, with a beer in one hand and a sausage roll in the other. Becks' heart sank. He had come straight from work.

"Ah, look! It's Becks! So nice of you to turn up. My wonderful wife, everyone. Perfectly on time as normal… not…"

Becks blushed.

"Sorry, I… had a little problem. With Hector."

Becks laughed apologetically in the direction of the group of mums surrounding Mike. Their shirts didn't seem to be gaping, and none of them had sweat patches under their armpits. She crossed her arms self-consciously.

"Always a problem with Hector, hey?" Mike said. "The monster…"

Becks glared. "No, no… not always. Just today."

"Doesn't feel like 'just today'. It's every day. Isn't it, sweetheart?" Mike's eyes bore into Becks', provoking her, willing her to react, like he didn't give a damn about airing their marital difficulties far and wide.

How dare he? This was her NCT group. Her support network… not his.

She gave him a warning look and shooed Hector off to join the other three-year-olds running in zig zags around a bright blue plastic Dora the Explorer ball.

"Anyhooooo," Becks said brightly, turning to her friends. "How are we all?"

"Exhausted. You have no idea, Becks. You think you have your hands full with Hector. Wait until you have two!" Molly gasped theatrically.

Becks found Molly a bit smirky, and tried to avoid her at coffee mornings. She couldn't avoid her now.

"See, Becks? We are better off just sticking with one," Mike said slyly, addressing the group.

Becks closed her eyes and counted to three. She was going to kill him. It was fine that he was insufferable and awful at home, where no one could see, but here, in front of all these judge-y women?

"Yes, Molly, I'm sure you're right," Becks answered through gritted teeth. "That's why we're waiting."

"Waiting? What for? Don't leave it too long or you'll have the horror of a large age gap between them. It's very difficult when that happens," Amanda with the swishy hair murmured. She patted the fine golden wisps poking out of the top of the baby Bjorn papoose she was wearing around her size eight frame. "My little Lydia plays with Georgia all the time. It's so sweet to watch." Amanda smiled down at her infant.

"How does your three-year-old play with a three-month-old baby, Amanda?" Becks snapped irritably.

"Well…" Amanda looked put out. She thought for a few moments. "She brings me nappies, and muslins, you know. Just generally very, very helpful."

"Yes, Amanda, that's sweet. But Becks has a point. You should have planned for an even smaller gap!" Molly the Smirky piped up. "I'm thrilled we only have eighteen months between ours. It means our children are going to be BEST OF FRIENDS as they grow up. Practically twins!"

Becks looked at Amanda and Molly speechless. How could these awful women who were supposed to be her friends be so insensitive?

To be fair to them, Becks hadn't told them that she was struggling for the second one. So they had no idea that every word they said was like a barb in her heart. Like her old uni chums, Angela and pregnant Susan, the traitor. They had no idea either. Becks felt so alone.

Becks instinctively put her hand on her belly and turned her head to search out Hector. He was lying over the blue ball possessively, and the other three-year-olds were attempting to kick it out from under him. There was a lot of shrieking.

"Think positive thoughts, think positive thoughts," Becks said under her breath.

"What?" Amanda asked, swishing her freshly washed glossy head towards her.

"Oh, don't mind her. She's always muttering to herself. Mad as a box of frogs, aren't you, Becks?"

Ahh, here was Mike again, chirping up with his two pennies' worth.

"Oh, dear. I sense a domestic brewing," said Molly, making a mock-awkward face and laughing in a silly way.

"No, you don't," Becks said breezily. "It's just Mike's sense of humour. He's very witty. Always cracking jokes. When you've been married for as long as us, you gain a unique understanding of each other's humour."

Molly took a sharp intake of breath and frowned at Becks.

"Becks, that's not very sensitive, is it? You know Molly is going through a horrible divorce right now," Amanda said.

"Oh, of course. I forgot. Sorry, Molly."

Becks knew full well Molly was going through a divorce. Molly had spoken about nothing else for six months at their monthly NCT coffee mornings.

"Hector! HECTOR!" Mike was bellowing.

He turned to Becks. "For God's sake, Becks. Take control of your child. He's causing a riot over there."

"No, he isn't, Mike! It's called playing. That's what kids look like when they're interacting. Not that you would know!" Becks said sulkily. She took a quick peek at the bundle of three-year-olds on the playing-field floor.

Shit. Was that Stella's auburn pigtail in Hector's mouth? Becks hurried over and subtly extricated him from the melee.

"Time for tea, Hector, let's go. I'll give you some more Buttons," Becks hissed before he could kick off properly.

When she got back to the group, Mike was apologising loudly to the other mums. "It's all a bit much for Becks. Hector is very strong-willed. Takes after me." He laughed proudly. "She can't handle that much masculinity."

Becks turned her back on Mike and stormed off to the car, dragging Hector and his prize Dora ball with her. She could feel the eyes of her so-called friends boring into her sweaty back. If only she had another baby like they all did. Everything would be so much easier. She could blame tiredness, hormones, whatever, on not being able to keep Hector in line. As it was, she felt totally alone. It was Mike, Hector and the world against her, and it wasn't fair.

"Please let this baby happen," she muttered aloud. "I don't think I can take this any longer!"

"Buttons!" Hector shrieked, kicking her in the shins.

Friday 5th February

Day 5 of TWW

Becks@desperatemumof1

Hi guys. So, I went to the gym yesterday, and now I have all sort of aches and pains. I can't work out if I just went double hard on the treadmill and have given myself a hernia... Or – dare I say it – it's my womb stretching! I've definitely got more of a pot belly today. Although that might be the tub of Ben and Jerry's I snuffled like a pig last night.

Mandi@LusciousLocks

Ooo! Can you tell so early? My tummy is still flat. Did you feel anything like this with Hector the first time round?

Becks@desperatemumof1

Umm – to be honest I can't remember, LOL. But I guess because I've been preg before, my body might have some sort of muscle memory and be stretching out? I can't do my top buttons up.

Fern@toobusytoTWW

Wait – what? Becks – you've been pregnant before?! Why haven't you told us…?

Becks@desperatemumof1

Yeah, thanks, Fern.

Star@Gaiababe

Morning all. What a glorious day. Fern… enough of the *wit*… Becks can't help it if she's been pregnant before. It doesn't make this TWW feel any less awful, am I right, Becks?

Becks@desperatemumof1

It's worse this time. I know you guys won't believe me. It's just… I KNOW what I've got to lose, what I have to gain. And with Mike, he's great. But bit of a weird situ yesterday.

Jane@closetoTWWentyyearsandcounting

OK. Normally that sort of 'lose/gain' comment would piss me off, but I'm going to cut you a break, Becks. You and Mike… what's going on?

Becks@desperatemumof1

Oh, nothing really. He's just… so alpha, you know? We went to an NCT barbecue, and… I don't know. I wish I hadn't invited him. Don't get me wrong, I like to take him along – he's always great with Hector. I couldn't ask for more support really #soblessed. It's me. I feel so insecure. He was surrounded by all these yummy mummies with their flowing blonde locks and pert tits. He looked like he was having the best time. God, don't any of them breastfeed? Especially as they all have two now. My boobs look like spaniel puppy ears. Hector's destroyed them.

Jane@closetoTWWentyyearsandcounting

LOL, I hear you. Mine are rapidly heading south, and I can't even blame nurturing a babe. Nowadays I go into M&S and ask for boulder holders. They always know exactly where to direct me. Funny you should mention puppies. Keith brought up the subject of puppy last night in bed. I was LIVID! Nearly sent him out to sleep with his precious gnomes. Psycho me!

Star@Gaiababe

From what I've gathered about your Keith, Jane, that sounds very un-Keith… isn't he normally pretty good?

Jane@closetoTWWentyyearsandcounting

Yep! He is! It really upset me. Chatting about how excited he was about this new puppy we're potentially getting and I mean potentially – NOT CERTAIN YET. I'm lying there, wishing with every bone in my body that my fertilised egg has reached my womb, and he's wibbling on about a puppy. I've been through this TWW process so many times, and he knows not to push my buttons. He found out soon enough – they were well and truly pushed!

Fern@toobusytoTWW

What did you feel when he said that?

Jane@closetoTWWentyyearsandcounting

Like he'd given up. To be honest, I'm preparing myself already for a BFN, so I feel a bit like that myself. I just don't want Keith to. He's always been so good at staying positive, loads of cuddles and tea and tissues when it doesn't work out. He's the strong one… the puppy thing threw me…

Mandi@LusciousLocks

Aww, that's sad, Jane. It must be really tough, going through this so many times.

Jane@closetoTWWentyyearsandcounting

It's hard. At least this time I have you lovely ladies to cheer me up. Someone tell me something positive and fab – we all need to stay upbeat!

Star@Gaiababe

Well, it's not marvie, but there must have been something in the air last night. For some reason I felt really sad, chakras not aligned, out of sorts. So I posted a picture of me crying on my grid! My mum saw it *HORROR* and came up to have a heart-to-heart. Did not like. She's so desperate to have a grandchild, it's really grating on my relaxed vibe. Having anger hormones raging around is not good for the safe space of my welcoming womb!

Fern@toobusytoTWW

HA! I love that you describe your womb as a 'safe space'. Mine is a viper's nest, clearly! I've been meaning to ask. WHY do you want a baby, Star? I follow you on Insta – saw your post last night. (How can you look so gorgeous when crying, bitch! JK…) I look like a hot snivelling mess. You didn't caption why you were crying – I was going to ask but then got busy and forgot.

Star@Gaiababe

Gosh, babes, I'm glad you didn't ask. All the questions about me becoming a mum have died down recently – it might have sparked them off again! Followers have goldfish-level attention spans, thankfully. OK, FINE. You have to promise me. What's said on TWW stays on TWW. Yes? Can't have all this personal stuff floating around online. Would ruin my brand image.

Mandi@LusciousLocks

Pinky promise.

Fern@toobusytoTWW

Too self-centred to gossip. What is it?

Becks@desperatemumof1

OO, TELL US.

Jane@closetoTWWentyyearsandcounting

Of course I wouldn't dream of it. Mum's the word. Or – non-mums the word, ha. Apart from Becks, of course. I think she mentioned she had a child and is therefore technically a mum.

Becks@desperatemumof1

!!!!!!!!!!!!!!!!!!

Star@Gaiababe

LOL, but TIME OUT! Enough already. Poor Becks. Stop. OK. The reason I want a mini-me is simple. I want to give my mum a grandchild. Of course I'm also desperate for a little travelling companion, and can't wait to experience the blinding pleasure of childbirth. I dream of primal roars and vaginal orgasms... really! I do!

Jane@closetoTWWentyyearsandcounting

LOL. We must mix in very different circles. I hear about ripped lady bits and bleeding nips. I like the sound of yours better. Anyway, carry on.

Star@Gaiababe

My mumma's a treasure. All she wants is a mini-me. I was a terror of a wild child. Such a disappointment to them. I think this would make me feel better, ya know? Give them someone else to love who might be a bit better behaved. Bit more THEM.

Jane@closetoTWWentyyearsandcounting

What does 'THEM' mean? And sorry, it's like twenty questions here. I get you don't want a partner... But I was thinking last night how lonely it must be for you. You know. When times get tough. These first few days are the hardest, I think, in TWW. You're excited but know there is no way you can tell if anything is happening. And soooooo long to wait before day 14. How are you doing it solo?

Star@Gaiababe

Haha. A lot to unpick there, babes. Them. OK. Here's the background. My parents are very conservative. Homely, suburban people. They think I'm some sort of sprite creature that lives in their house. My free spirit is confusing to them. When I was young, I was too busy wanting to do cartwheels, stare at flowers, run off into woods. My poor mumma used to have kittens waiting at home for me to return from my 'escapades' – her word. Maybe my baby would enjoy the baking and the knitting and the hours of reading my mum used to want to do with me.

Becks@desperatemumof1

Sooooo... it sounds like you are trying to have a baby for her??

Star@Gaiababe

Like I say. I'm not very good at expressing myself properly, babes. That's why mantras are my friends! Ready-made to express what I want to say. I just want to re-build my relationship with my folks. I think I can do that if I have a baby. And I also really, really want a baby. End of story.

Jane@closetoTWWentyyearsandcounting

BUT WHY ALONE?

Star@Gaiababe

Cos my parents' marriage is perfect. I could never compete with that level of relationship goals. EVER. It's not for me. I might as well have no one than bounce along with Mr crap pants.

Mandi@LusciousLocks

That's one of the saddest things I've ever heard. Gav isn't perfect, but he's mine. And if his mother wasn't always interfering, it could be good. Being in a partnership is great.

Jane@closetoTWWentyyearsandcounting

Are you an only child, Star?

Star@Gaiababe

Yep. Why?

Jane@closetoTWWentyyearsandcounting

Just thinking. If your parents have such a perfect marriage and love children so much, why did they only have you?

Becks@desperatemumof1

Nothing wrong with only one child.

Jane@closetoTWWentyyearsandcounting
Ssshh, you know what I mean.

Star@Gaiababe
I dunno why. Maybe cos I was such a handful?

Jane@closetoTWWentyyearsandcounting
Hmmmmm.

Becks@desperatemumof1
I'm back in the room... Hector needed a bum wipe, never ends. But BTW I agree with Mandi. Being married is a joy.

Fern@toobusytoTWW
No disrespect, Becks. Tell me to butt out if you like, but your marriage doesn't sound so joyful if you're worried Mike is lusting after pert tits.

Becks@desperatemumof1
Butt out... let me create an illusion.

Star@Gaiababe
And on that note, peace, love and sunshine, girls.

Saturday 6th February

Day 6 of TWW

Mandi@LusciousLocks

Good morning, everyone!

Becks@desperatemumof1

Morning, Mandi.

Mandi@LusciousLocks

Just wanted to check in on everyone. Last night got quite personal.

Fern@toobusytoTWW

Who's got time to worry about that?

Jane@closetoTWWentyyearsandcounting

We all should worry. This is supposed to be a nice space of support. For my part. Apologies, Becks. I was out of order yesterday. Just very jittery and on edge after my fall-out with Keith. All feels a bit desperate now.

Star@Gaiababe

Morning, my little celestial chickadees. I have news.

Mandi@LusciousLocks

WHAT – you haven't tested already?!

Star@Gaiababe

What, on DAY 6? I'm not crazy.

Mandi@LusciousLocks

What then?

Star@Gaiababe

Jane's questions started me thinking, you know. I asked my mum why I was an only child. She said that it was complicated, and she would tell me another time! I was dashing out to a moonlight yoga session so that suited me, but it sounds like Jane was on to something. Funny, I never thought to question it until now… self obsessed… moi??

Jane@closetoTWWentyyearsandcounting

Ahh… sounds encouraging. It's the sort of thing that will be bonding, a chat like that. Good luck. Let us know what she tells you!

Star@Gaiababe

Of course. No secrets here.

Becks@desperatemumof1

No, absolutely not.

Fern@toobusytoTWW

Sorr,y girls, I've been cheating on you.

Jane@closetoTWWentyyearsandcounting

What?

Fern@toobusytoTWW

Just checking out other forums, to see if there was any other information out there that might be helpful.

Jane@closetoTWWentyyearsandcounting

Well, let me proffer you some free advice: NO FORUM-HOPPING!!

Fern@toobusytoTWW

Why?

Jane@closetoTWWentyyearsandcounting

Why? I've been doing this a long time. I did the same as you at first. All it does is cause confusion and anxiety. Best to stick to our closed chat. We can get to know each other properly, and I have loads of tips and tricks on how to get through.

Mandi@LusciousLocks

Pleeeeease share…

Jane@closetoTWWentyyearsandcounting

OK – first rule: NO to forum-hopping. That way madness lies. People can say and do anything they feel, and completely rock your already-fragile world.

And the next important one – NO SYMPTOM-SPOTTING. From one day to the next you will feel pregnant, not pregnant, high and very low. It's a proper rollercoaster. I learnt years ago to ignore my body as much as I could. Only time I allow myself to get excited is just before I POAS (pee on a stick, Mandi!).

Third titbit – I found keeping a diary really helped me. Helped me stay grounded. Writing things offline was much less anxiety-inducing than anything I wrote online.

Becks@desperatemumof1

Are you saying we cause you anxiety? LOL.

Jane@closetoTWWentyyearsandcounting

Haha, no. BUT! Only stay on positive forums. Things can get negative pretty quickly.

Star@Gaiababe

I can second that!! Honestly, babes. Only stay online where you know the peeps are friends. Loads of trolls and psychos out there, waiting to sap you of your good energy – trust me, I meet them on a near-daily basis.

Fern@toobusytoTWW

To be honest, I was getting a little irritated with all the advice. Eat this, don't do that, feel this, etc. It was like stepping into an online version of Jon's head!

Mandi@LusciousLocks

LOLOL.

Mandi@LusciousLocks

But – what were they saying, these other forums. Like what advice?

Fern@toobusytoTWW

Oh God knows, really weird tips on when and what to eat and no deodorant and no fluoride and no heavy metals, no pollution – I live in central London. How am I supposed to avoid that? Also I value my teeth and I work. Hard. Can't be wafting around meeting rooms with stinky pits.

Mandi@LusciousLocks
I've heard all those things can really help people though.

Jane@closetoTWWentyyearsandcounting
AAAAND here is what I was talking about! So, take it from me. I have tried everything. EVERYTHING. Nothing has worked. Nada. So far. But my friend, she went on a clean diet, only ate organic, used crystal deodorants under her armpits whilst TTC. Did she get pregnant? Er, no. She had to have six rounds of IVF with all the chemicals. She now has a bouncing boy, and she gives him loads of Wotsits and Haribo. My other friend ate value sausages, drank red wine (only one glass, before the alcohol police jump in), really stressy night shift job and got pregnant after her third go. All our bodies are different, our symptoms different. There is no one size fits all.

Star@Gaiababe
That's a bit depressing, Jane. I am convinced doing my yoga and eating plant-based is going to help me. Are you of the belief that I'm doing all this for nothing?

Jane@closetoTWWentyyearsandcounting
Well, it's not for nothing, is it, Star? You love doing those things, don't you? And exercise and good food are always better than the alternative. Look. The most sensible thing I heard on this long and torturous journey has been this. Take care of yourself as you would your baby! Whatever that means to you. For me, that means eating a wide and varied diet, squeezing in as many veg as possible, resting if I feel tired (naps are seriously underrated in the adult world, trust me) and cutting myself some slack if I fall

off the wagon once in a while. And never ever blaming myself for what I did the month before if I don't get PG.

Mandi@LusciousLocks

I read somewhere that pomegranate juice can really help…

Jane@closetoTWWentyyearsandcounting

If you love the taste of pomegranate juice – go for it!

Mandi@LusciousLocks

I've been reading a lot. It gets quite confusing. To be honest, I'm not sure what to believe anymore. It frightens me. I think that everything I'm doing is harming my chances and I'm setting myself up for a BFN…

Jane@closetoTWWentyyearsandcounting

Yes, I hear you. Remember I have done twenty years of this, and every month there is a new fad, new advice. I just had to keep my head down and go on my intuition a bit. I know that eating all the pies and drinking booze and not keeping active isn't going to help my chances. So I try and do the opposite of that. Seems to help me mentally, anyway.

Mandi@LusciousLocks

Yes, I have been really tearful today. Anyone else?

Becks@desperatemumof1

I'm like Tiny Tears over here. Someone has turned on the tap and I can't turn it off!

Jane@closetoTWWentyyearsandcounting

I confess I've been a bit weepy too. What has really helped me in the past is journaling. I keep a gratitude journal and I write in it without fail every single day. Three things that make me feel grateful. That has nothing do with being pregnant, or being a mum. I read those back to myself when I'm feeling low. It really works! For me at least.

Mandi@LusciousLocks

OK, I'm running down to Smiths and grabbing a journal now. Do you use a special one?

Jane@closetoTWWentyyearsandcounting

Nope – you can use whatever you have to hand, seriously. Don't spend money or make it complicated. Unless you want to, of course. I bought a really nice daily diary that I love writing in – keep it by my bed and use it every day.

Fern@toobusytoTWW

God, sounds like something else I have to add to my to-do list!

Jane@closetoTWWentyyearsandcounting

Takes five minutes before I go to sleep. Not a huge burden. I also jot down social media accounts that are really useful, and also the ones to AVOID AVOID AVOID! It's a good reminder of which accounts to steer clear of. I find the whole journaling thing super therapeutic.

Star@Gaiababe

Sounds awesome. I do something similar with my daily meditation, but I haven't been writing it down. Gonna give it a crack.

Becks@desperatemumof1

Sounds good. I just don't know what I would write in it, that's all.

Fern@toobusytoTWW

Errrrr... you've got to be kidding, right? Maybe for starters... writing about how you are UNBELIEVABLY LUCKY to have a child already??????? And a fantastic husband that you love?

Becks@desperatemumof1

Oh, great. Here it starts again. Of course I'm grateful for Hector. It's just nothing else is springing to mind right now...

Jane@closetoTWWentyyearsandcounting

Hang in there, Becks. You might feel like that now, but once you start writing you could be surprised. Let me know how you get on.

Saturday 6th February
Day 6 of TWW

"Oops!" Fern said, shutting down her computer.

"What have you done now? You're such a stirrer," Jon said, hooking Fern's discarded coffee mug off the kitchen table. He took it over to the dishwasher. Fern felt irritated as she heard him re-stacking the plates surreptitiously but decided to let it go. She would have commented, but she felt too exhausted. Exhausted. Hmm, now was that a sign? Fern knew what Jane would have to say about symptom-spotting so early on.

"I think I might have riled a few of the ladies off on the TWW forum!"

"You? Really? Surely not?"

"I told them I had been surfing other forums. Jane, the one that's been TTC for twenty years told me off... no-go, apparently."

"TTC?" Jon asked.

"Trying to conceive, you *know* that, Jon," Fern said. Her patience was definitely wearing thin this evening.

"Just so many unfathomable abbreviations. Why don't people just spell it out? It's only a few extra letters..."

"People don't have time to write everything out. Anyway, why bother, if everyone knows what it means? Everyone living in modern times, I mean." Fern poked Jon in his increasingly fleshy ribs.

"So why did she tell you off? Can't see what's wrong with getting info from wherever you can?"

"Well, to be fair, she did win me over in the end. She said that skipping around on different forums gets confusing. Makes sense – I was already getting annoyed with all the mad advice."

"So no more forum-hopping?"

"No more forum-hopping. There this young girl, Mandi, who hangs off every word Jane says. I think Jane had to shut down the idea of looking around for the sake of the girl's sanity! She's like a sponge, sucking up every bit of information like her life depends on it—"

"Drinking yak milk in the moonlight with Star?" Jon laughed. "God, Star has really caught your imagination."

"What... jealous?" Jon kissed Fern on the top of her head. "She just sounds interesting, that's all."

"She is, actually. I think there might be hidden depths to Star. Going to do a bit more probing, I think."

"Oh, good, a Ferny mission. New reality TV series? It will keep your mind off things at least. So... on the topic of nothing related... any symptoms?" Jon dared.

"That's the other thing she said – NO SYMPTOM-SPOTTING. It's too early to tell! You know that, and I know that. Come on. Let's get an early night. I'm whacked." Fern slotted her laptop into her work bag in preparation for the morning.

"Hmm, exhausted you say...?" Jon studiously stroked his chin. "Very interesting."

"Jon... I said stop!"

Saturday 6th February

Day 6 of TWW

JANE – Offline

"Managing this forum is like herding cats!" said Jane, digging deep into her beloved vegetable patch.

"What now?" Keith said, handing her a trowel. "Here, try this, I think the fork might be too big."

Jane accepted the trowel and began to lever the first of the new potatoes.

"Well, our career woman, Fern. She has decided to forum-hop," Jane said.

Keith whistled inwards. "She HASN'T... what a sinner."

"I'm serious, Keith, it's not good for morale. You know that's the worst thing you can do, especially around day 6. You have no idea how you feel, you try and symptom-spot, and every person has random advice to throw at you. It's hard enough trying to keep sane without the voices of a thousand nutters clamouring in your head!"

Jane sat back on her heels, wiping her hand across her forehead, leaving a long streak of soil. "I told them to start a gratitude diary. My new adopted daughter Mandi leapt on the idea."

"You're so wise. Thank God the other girls have got you."

"Are you being cynical?" Jane glanced at Keith.

"No, I totally mean it," Keith said, affectionately wiping the soil from Jane's face with his thumb.

"Well, I'm not sure I'm much support. I feel so tearful all the time, swinging between giving up the chat and needing to stay on. I dunno why it all feels so much more intense this time. Maybe it's because I know I am coming to the end of the loooong road. Every TWW forum I start, I hear from different people all suffering from the same problem. It's depressing and also uplifting. So confusing."

"Let's go eat the fruits of your labour," Keith said, removing a tiny potato from Jane's tight clasp.

They both burst out laughing.

"Well, phew… at least I'm capable of producing something!"

Saturday 6th February

Day 6 of TWW

"I might come off the TWW forum," Becks said to Mike over tea.

She speared her fish finger and shoved it mindlessly into her mouth.

"Good. I don't trust those things anyway. Namby-pamby. Spreading your business all over the internet. Can't be good. Will be giving you all sorts of fancy-pants ideas," Mike said, not lifting his eyes from *The Sun*.

"Have you finished there?" Becks asked. She picked up Hector's Thomas the Tank Engine plate and scraped the remaining chips and peas onto her own.

"Are you sure you want that?" Mike murmured behind his newspaper.

"What?" Becks asked as she lifted Hector out of his chair. He ran off and turned on CBeebies at full volume.

"Those," Mike said, pointing at the chips now on Becks' plate.

"Why?"

"You've already had yours. Do you want his as well?" Mike said.

Becks picked up her plate and roughly scraped the food into the bin. "I was just clearing up, "she said, familiar tears pricking her eyes.

"Good. Just checking. Bet Amanda doesn't nick leftovers from her kids' plates," Mike said, giving half a wink and turning the page of the paper. "HECTOR! TURN THAT DAMN THING DOWN! Not with a figure like that."

"You seemed to be getting on well with her the other day," Becks said brightly, back still turned as she wiped the mountain of crumbs off the surface and onto the floor.

"Yes. I always found her to be a bit stuck up before, but she's actually alright. You should go out with that lot. You never see them anymore. Well that's what she said, anyway," Mike said absently.

"Well, that's not true. I meet them once a month for coffee. At least!" Becks said defensively. "It's just a bit hard. With them all either pregnant or having two kids. I find it… upsetting," she continued.

"Why? Why can't you just be happy with Hector?" Mike boomed.

"I am! For God's sake. SHUSH!" Becks said in a panic, glancing over at Hector, who had a finger up his nose and his hand down his trousers. Hector looked at her to see if he was in trouble, and then swung his head back to look at the TV, his eyes glazed in concentration.

"Don't you want this, hmm, Mike?" Becks hissed.

"What, another baby? Sure. If another one comes along, that's great. But there's no sign, so I don't think we should get all twisty knickers about it."

Becks sat down and placed another beer in front of Mike. He picked it up and drank from it without looking at her.

"I think about my knickers all the time. If I get a period… if I see that blood in my pants this month… I don't know how I'll cope, Mike."

"Becks, stop. I don't want to think about that sort of thing. I've just had my tea, Jesus!" Mike said in disgust, taking another swig.

Becks looked at her husband. Why was he always such an arsehole? She heard Jane talking about Keith, Fern complaining about Jon. But only because he was over-attentive. So that was her issue, not his. Even Mandi seemed to love Gav, although she hadn't spoken much about him, to be fair. Becks knew more about Mandi's mother-in-law than about Gav. But still. Facts still stood. She felt completely abandoned by Mike.

What was she doing, trying to have another baby with him, when she wasn't even sure if their marriage would survive? Could she be a single mother with two children? Star seemed to relish the idea of single parenting. Becks didn't know if she could cope. Not that Mike pulled his weight in any way.

"What?" Mike grunted, nudging his empty bottle towards her.

"I didn't say anything," Becks said quietly.

"Well then, stop staring at me. It's putting me off my paper."

Becks snatched the bottle off the table and threw it furiously in the recycling bin. It made a very satisfying noise as it smashed. She looked around at the men in her life. Neither Hector nor Mike had so much as lifted their heads. She might as well not exist. Becks sighed. She prepared herself for the next battle. One which would rage whilst Mike sat oblivious downstairs with his beer and his sport.

"Come on, Hector. Bath time."

Saturday 6th February

Day 6 of TWW

"So," Mandi said, sipping from her beaker of Sprite.

"So? Spill the tea!" Her friends were gathered around the red plastic table, all eyes on Mandi.

"You said something exciting had happened," added Kyra.

"Not really exciting. Not in any of your worlds at least."

"Is it something really debauched?" said Meera with a grin.

"NO!" said Mandi. "I leave the debauched to you in your uni world."

"You don't know the first of it," Meera continued, giving a saucy wink. "So, what is it, Mands?"

"Nothing properly exciting, only that... I am on this brilliant forum, and there's this woman on there that's been trying to get pregnant for about one hundred years. She says forget all the rubbish you read about what to eat and drink and vitamins to take and all that. I'm so relieved. I was getting completely confused."

"Wahey!" said Naira.

"Stop!" said Mandi, giving her friend a nudge. "It's exciting to me, OK?"

"We're just happy you are able to get out to meet us. It's been a billion years since we all got together. Now you're not interested in going out, we never see you," said Naira.

"And we miss youuuuuu," said Meera. Meera was her oldest friend from her first years at school. Inseparable.

"Only question is," said Naira. "The woman who told you this – you say she's been trying to get pregnant forever?"

"Yeah."

"And you're taking advice from her?"

"Yeah, yeah. I get it, but she is wise. She knows her stuff inside out."

"Sorry you're still not pregnant, Mands," Kyra said.

"Thank you. Although I might be. I find out in eight days."

"So precise."

"I'm in this hell called the two-week wait. It's a weird limbo land where you might be pregnant, but you don't know. I'll only know when I take a test or if my period comes."

"Well, take a test then, girl," Meera said.

"I want to. The woman who set up the forum said there's no point testing until day 14," said Mandi glumly.

"Where are you now?" Naira asked.

"Day 6," said Mandi.

"Sheesh. So many rules," Naira said, shaking her head. Mandi watched her long gold earring become entangled in her glossy black hair.

"Here, let me," Mandi said, leaning forward and freeing the hoops. "I know, right? It's a torture."

"What does Gav say? Is he being supportive?" Meera asked.

"You've got to be kidding me," Mandi snorted. "You know what he's like. 'Just make sure it doesn't interfere with my golfing weekend, Mand.' But I bet you can guess who is interested. Or at least, who is trying to be…"

"Oh God, really?" said Meera.

"Yep. Bane of my life; the constant phone calls and offerings of dead fish and best sleeping positions, are killing me. She's always trying to impart old wives' tale advice. It's definitely making me feel like it's all my fault she doesn't have a precious new grandkid to show off."

"Is it? Your fault?" Meera asked curiously.

Mandi stared at her. "I... I don't know? Waiting to hear back from Gav's test. He succumbed in the end."

Meera snorted into her drink. "Eeeoiaw, I'm just picturing him in all alone in little room with a cup and a wipe-clean iPad..."

"EEWWWW," Mandi protested. "That's my beloved husband you're talking about!"

Mandi's friends rolled around laughing at the idea.

"Shhhhh," Mandi said, "you'll get us kicked out!"

"Of McDonald's? Like to see them try." Kylie jutted out her chin out and let rip with a withering stare at her fellow diners.

"OK, OK. All I know is I have polycystic ovaries. Have you seen the caterpillar crawling across my top lip? That's a sure giveaway, huh?"

"Haven't noticed the caterpillar, cos I was too distracted by the carpet on your arms," Naira said, pulling one of Mandi's arm hairs.

"Oi!" Mandi said, laughing, lightly giving her a slap.

"Come over. I've nearly got my beautician certificate. Just another few months or so. I'll practise my threading on you for free." Naira pulled her friend up by her hand, Mandi protesting and bending her head to suck up the last of her precious drink.

"No time like the present. Come on! Let Naira do it. We will give you moral support," Meera said.

"I guess. I have nothing to lose. I've been told I need to keep busy," Mandi sighed, allowing herself to be pulled and jostled out of her seat. "Just don't rip my skin off," she said.

As she walked out of the brightly lit restaurant into the dingy grey light, Mandi smiled inwardly. Thank God for her friends. They had no idea what she was going through and beyond sex, body hair and DJs, they really didn't care a damn, but at least they kept her sane.

Saturday 6th February
Day 6 of TWW

"Mum. Why didn't you and Dad have more children?" Star asked, slicing the lettuce to add to the huge salad her mother was preparing.

"Not now, Stacey. Another time," said Janet too quickly, flicking Star with a linen tea towel.

"Why don't I take you out for an oat milk matcha latte and you can tell me everything? You know how you love doing girlie outings with me?"

"Yes, yes, Star, whatever you want," Janet replied, handing Star a bunch of parsley. "Can you chop this up, please? Pam and Steve will be here in a minute."

Star rolled the fragrant herbs into a cigar shape and deftly sliced through. One good thing about her travels was that she had a variety of skills under her belt. Being able to read people's reactions was one of them. That was necessary. When travelling alone you always need to be one step ahead. Janet was hiding something. She was sure of that. When it came to jobs, however, working in a kitchen was her favourite.

"Would you like me to make a carve a swan in a carrot? It's a trick I learned in Chiang Mai? Not complicated?"

"No, thank you, darling, the parsley cigars will suffice."

"Also, have you got any spare notebooks or unused journals lying around that I could have, please?"

"I have an old one I never started. Was going to use it to make gardening notes, but worked out it was much easier just to go out and actually garden. In the cupboard under the TV. You're welcome to have it."

"Thank you," Star said, scraping the parsley into the salad bowl.

"What do you want it for, anyway?" Janet called, watching her daughter disappear into the TV room.

Star put her head round the door, holding the leather journal aloft. "Er, to write in! Found it! Thanks so much!"

"You're welcome. Now, are you going to run a brush through your hair, and maybe put on some more appropriate clothes?"

Star looked down at her favourite crop top and silky floor-length skirt. "What do you mean? This *is* my most 'appropriate' outfit!"

Once a child, always a child.

"Oh," said Janet. "OK, don't worry. You look… great. That's them coming now. Get the door, would you… please?"

Star rolled her eyes and glided off to open the door to her parents' old family friends, surreptitiously pulling her crop top down towards her navel.

Sunday 7th February

Day 7 of TWW

Mandi@LusciousLocks

HALFWAY THERE!!!!!

Morning! It's me again, first on today!

Guys, we have done a full week already. Did that go fast for anyone else? It's getting harder, though. I keep wandering round the house, not knowing where to put myself.

Jane@closetoTWWentyyearsandcounting

Morning, Mandi. KEEP BUSY! Get out of the house.

Mandi@LusciousLocks

Got any tips, Jane, for what to do? I bought my journal yesterday, I love it. Already feel calmer, just getting my thoughts down. And I tipped that bloody pomegranate juice down the sink. It was turning my stomach! And making me bankrupt. Gone back to apple juice... joy!!!

Becks@desperatemumof1

Hi all. So I tried that journaling thing. Made me cry. I don't think I'm any good at things like this.

Fern@toobusytoTWW

Why, Becks? I am sorry to hear that. I know I give you a hard time, but you know I don't really mean it.

Star@Gaiababe

Becks, babes. You need to find your inner self and be content with it. Say after me. "I am in charge of how I feel and today I choose happy."

Fern@toobusytoTWW

God, Star, where do you get all these mad mantras? You're like the Dalai Lama.

Becks@desperatemumof1

That's the probs, Star. I don't know how I should feel. I don't know who I am anymore. I used to be this competent person. People used to come to me for advice, I was great at my job in HR. I used to wear sexy little black skirts and court shoes. Mike used to notice me. Now I feel shoddy. Frumpy. BITTER. I feel bitter. It eats me up and I take it out on my family.

Fern@toobusytoTWW

I actually relate to this, Becks. But not about how I look or what I do. More I feel angst that all this baby stuff is distracting me from my work. Everyone keeps asking me what's wrong. But I can't say, can I? Sorry, I'm being an inefficient distracted cow cos I'm TTC at the moment and you've caught me in my TWW!!! Also, I have a double whammy – Jon can't think of anything else either. Keeps asking me about it. So even when it's not consuming my thoughts, he still brings it up!

Mandi@LusciousLocks

Sheesh, ladies, this all sounds heavy! At least you know who you are. Or were. I haven't even got to that stage! Literally no clue. No sense of self at all. I just bumble along, being told what to do, turning up and doing it. It used to be blissful. But now I feel like I'm missing out, and I'm not complicated enough! Jane, what do you think? Should I be worried?

Jane@closetoTWWentyyearsandcounting

Haha, Mandi. How should I know? I think you sound fine as you are. If you aren't stressed about yourself, long may that continue! I also don't worry. I am who I am.

Star@Gaiababe

I'm with Fern and Becks...

Fern@toobusytoTWW

Whaaaat????? Come on, Star – you of all of us know who you are, surely. Look at your lifestyle! Your commitment to having a baby on your own! Your frankly ridiculously perfect body! What the hell is there to be doubtful about?

Star@Gaiababe

Ahh, yes. I forgot you follow me. You see the curated parts of my life, and I admit. It does all look very peachy. Cos I've framed it that way. Not everything is always perfect, even if it looks it...

Becks@desperatemumof1

Intrigued.

Fern@toobusytoTWW
Me too… Sooooooo… Star?

Star@Gaiababe
Soz, gotta dash. Ciao, peeps.

Jane@closetoTWWentyyearsandcounting
You're not getting away that easily… Star.

Mandi@LusciousLocks
Jane – you mentioned before about me being busy – any
suggestions? I'm going out of my mind…

Jane@closetoTWWentyyearsandcounting
OK. I found this list at the back of my journal. I've done some
or most of these things over the years. They might help, they
might not. I might as well share here:

Day 1 – Buy a notebook… start a bullet journal.

Day 2 – Buy some wool and start a knitting project, or treat
yourself to a thriller to read, or a horror movie to watch, or
a club, political debate, games night at the pub… ideally, any
experience that takes you to the furthest extremes with your
emotions… takes your mind off the biggie.

Day 3 – Get outside: gardening, bike ride, train ride, walk,
borrow a dog if you don't have one…

Day 4 – Get a haircut and colour.

Day 5 – Go out for lunch... picnic, cafe, just make sure it is with someone who knows how to make you feel good about yourself.

Day 6 – Create something with pen, pencil or paint. Even if it's labelling your flour containers with a doodle. Sounds mad, but you do get into it.

Day 7 – Declutter your house... a personal fave. And take all the stuff you don't want to the charity shop. Good for the karma.

Day 8 – Give your house a really good clean (with eco-products – agree, Star?). I make my own... Happy to share recipes if anyone is interested.

Day 9 – Book tickets to go somewhere... anywhere. I am going to book New York (Keith doesn't know this yet, SURPRISE!). Puppy pending, of course, grrrr.

Day 10 – Give your partner a massage. I know – not top of the list, but making that connection with him will really help when it comes to crunch day. Remember... you're in this together!

Day 11 – Write down all your anxieties and put them in a jar.

Day 12 – Write down all the things you are grateful for and put them in a jar. Look at them when life is feeling grim. I tend to go back through my diary and use that as a starting point.

Day 13 – Get out of the house today. Go for a walk, a swim, ice skate, gallery, movie, spending spree... anything to keep your mind off stuff.

Day 14 – Today will either be a good day or a bad day. Make sure you have plans in place for either outcome. My plans normally centre around food as I love cooking, but whatever floats your steamer, ladies... Make sure you plan ahead and stick to whatever you decide, especially if you get a BFN... that way you don't mope all day :(

Mandi@LusciousLocks
Wow! Thanks for that. Just going to go and declutter now! I have a whole cupboard of doom that needs serious attention...

Jane@closetoTWWentyyearsandcounting
Yeah! Get stuck in... all very satisfying...

Fern@toobusytoTWW
Or can I suggest, as an alternative – going to work every day? Just a thought. Sorry to be modern!

Becks@desperatemumof1
Thanks, Jane. Sorry I didn't get on with the journal. Too many difficult emotions.

Jane@closetoTWWentyyearsandcounting
I get it, Becks. Digging deep is hard... and scary, especially when you're not used to it. Sounds a bit cringy, but you should try to think of all the comments or observations people have made about you in the past... friendly, funny, feisty... anything that comes to mind. You need to get some vocab together for tapping into your inner self.

Becks@desperatemumof1
Thanks again, Jane. Will give it another go.

Jane@closetoTWWentyyearsandcounting
You can do it, Becks.

Sunday 7th February, evening

Day 7 of TWW

BECKS – Diary

Hello Diary

Been told having a journal is like having a good friend to confide in. Need a good friend right now. Feel alone, lonely, like a failure. Like I am being left behind. Everyone living the dream and me, living a nightmare. No one understands what it is like. Everyone tells me to be happy with what I have. Happy because I have a child. But I'm not happy. I'm miserable and I don't know why. Why is Hector not enough for me? At least I have one child, but whenever I look at him, all I think is of what is missing, of what he needs, of what I need. I feel sorry for him all the time, like he is lacking something. How can he care? How can he miss what he doesn't know? It's me who cares. I am projecting my thoughts on to him.

Stuff to do today...
    Go to chemist, pick up Hector's prescription.
    Reply to Mikhala re: Hector's invite to Rolly's party.

Mike can't tolerate me right now. I know it. I don't think he even wants to be in a room with me. He thinks I'm miserable and moany. I am. I am miserable and moaning all the time... and irritable and grumpy. I don't want to be like this. I want to enjoy my son, to enjoy my marriage, to have fun... everyone else is having fun. WHY CAN'T I HAVE FUN? Is this angst going to plague me all my life?

Maybe I was never happy...

Maybe I am using my fallopian tubes as an excuse to be miserable? Am I blaming my gloomy disposition on something physical so that I don't have to face up to what I really am?

How can some people get pregnant so easily? It's just NOT FAIR. I'm sorry, journal, but I want to SHOUT. I hate my fucking body. I hate my home. I hate my friends and I HATE MY LIFE.

Playground with Hector = torture.

Too many happy families... siblings. Can't bear it. How can they have what they want and not me? I never want to go to the park again. EVER. Need to find park avoidance techniques.

Day 8 of TWW tomorrow. Tick, bloody tock.

I am in charge of how I feel, and today I choose happy.

Thanks, Star, but fuck it. I will only be happy when I have a baby growing in my womb. If I have a baby, I will have my husband back. And then... I can stop being such a miserable old cow.

Comments people make about me (Jane's idea):
Funny
Quite funny
Caring?
Glamorous – used to be. Still am?
Fit – ish

Clever
Independent
Strong
Good at my job – who cares?
Fat (hate my thighs)
Impatient
Miserable
Dissatisfied – in all ways
Inadequate
FAILURE
B*tch
Happy… Liar…

I am in charge of how I feel and today I choose happy.

Happy?
    Can't remember what I was… before Hector, before Mike. I think I was happy. Was I? Did I actually like my job? I used to moan a lot about having to go to work – all I wanted was a child, but I had to wait for Mike to come around to the idea. Always bloody Mike.
    MIKE… mike… MiKe…
    Was I happy before I met Mike? I wanted to find a husband, I know that. Mike was good-looking. Is that why I married him? Did I actually love him? Properly love him, or love the idea of him?
    Am I meant to go this deep in my journal?
    Where are all these thoughts coming from?
    I'm exploding thoughts… spewing thoughts… spew, spew, spew.
    Why did I get married? Because Mike said he loved me. Or did he? Has he ever said he loves me or did I tell him he loved me and tell him that he had to marry me? Am I a dominating, dissatisfied bitch? DO YOU LOVE ME, MIKE?

Question for the day... Does Mike love me?

Did I trap Mike so that Laura couldn't have him? Jealous of Laura? Did Mike prefer Laura to me? Has Laura got LOADS of babies. Check tomorrow. Don't check. NEVER CHECK, BECKS. You DON'T want to know.

I am in charge of how I feel and today I choose happy.

Plan for today. Go to chemist.

Reply to Mikhala re: Hector's invite to Rolly's party.

Remind Mike why he is with me. Stop having a go at him. Play our own version of happy families. Get babysitter. Go out for dinner alone with Mike. Tell everyone that Mike and I are going out for dinner — happy marriage! Remind him that he loves me and hasn't made a mistake being with me.

I am in charge of how I feel and today I choose happy.

Monday 8th February
Day 8 of TWW

BECKS – Diary

5am. I'm awake. House quiet. Mike's about to yell at me for putting on bedside light??? Waiting, waiting. Phew. All good... All VERY good. Am feeling excited! WHAT is going on? Weird feeling lower abdomen like something is about to happen... butterflies? What for? Something else? Don't want to symptom-spot (don't tell Jane) but something amiss. I feel it. Strange taste in my mouth as well. Want to wake Mike and tell him – don't. He will just tell me to shut up. Ha, that's support. Good to know we're in this together. Will tell Hector. Won't mention brother or sister, just tell him that I think I might have something growing in my tummy. He'll ask me if it's breakfast... ha ha...

Tell NO ONE, Becks.
   SAY NOTHING.
   You can do it.
   KEEP IT TO YOURSELF...

Monday 8th February, crack of dawn

Day 8 of TWW

Becks@desperatemumof1

Anyone else awake?
Hello?

Sunday 7th February
Day 7 of TWW

"Soooo," said Gav, coming into the apartment early evening and quietly shutting the front door. "Do you want to hear the good news or the bad news?"

"You know I always want the good news first," said Mandi, patting down the neat pile of bank statements created as part of her day's decluttering.

"Well," said Gav. He removed a box stacked full of DVDs from his favourite armchair and sat down. "The good news is, you are off the hook with Mammi."

"What?" said Mandi.

"It is highly likely that for the next eight months at least, Mammi will not be requesting your company."

"Why not?" said Mandi. "That does not sound like your mum."

"Which leads me on to the bad news…" said Gav slowly, all the while keeping his eyes pinned on his wife.

"Yes? Hurry up." Mandi was feeling uncomfortable, squirming under the intensity of Gav's stare.

"The bad news, well, that would be, that my brother is creating a new line of Chadhar offspring."

"What?"

"It appears, contrary to what you might be thinking, that us Chadhar men do not shoot blanks."

"What are you talking about, Gav?" said Mandi, an uneasy feeling creeping in.

"Rajul is expecting a baby."

"Rajul? But he's not even married or—"

"So, do you want to hear the bad news?"

"That wasn't it?"

"Oh no, there's more."

"Yah, Gav, get on with it. Why are you playing with me like this?" Mandi unfolded herself from her cross-legged position on the floor and sprawled onto the sofa.

"It seems Rajul has been messing about with a friend of yours."

"Who?" Mandi shouted, stomach lurching.

"Try and picture the least likely of your friends to want to settle down," said Gav, seemingly relishing Mandi's dismay.

"I don't know. They all consider it a bad idea."

"In that case, just pick one."

"I don't know, Naira?"

"Bingo."

"What? No. Get real Gav. Naira? Why are you saying this to me?"

"Naira is pregnant with little brother Rajul's baby."

"That's total and utter bullshit. I only saw Naira like two days ago and she never said a word."

"From my understanding, she only found out this morning, but Rajul is such a big mouth he was on the phone to Mammi like five minutes after hearing the news."

"It's total crap," said Mandi, feeling her cheeks turn red. "I know everything there is to know about Naira's life and she never mentioned anything about Rajul, except for… hold on. Except for that night she bumped into him at Oceanica! But she never said anything about talking to him, let alone sleeping with him, and Naira tells everyone everything. You've definitely got it wrong. You're just trying to get me all worked up."

Gav pulled his phone out of his inside jacket pocket and scrolled up the screen. "Hmm, let me see now..." he said. "Ah yes, here we go."

Gav handed the phone over to Mandi. There was a WhatsApp text from Rajul.

'Naira not happy.
Mammi thrilled.'

"See."

"I just know it can't be true," said Mandi. "Tell me it's not true because I'm just about asphyxiating over here." Mandi clutched her chest and wheezily inhaled.

"It's 100% true," said Gav. "Look." Gav snatched back his phone. "Got the photo to prove it." He shoved the screen under Mandi's nose.

"What the fuck is that?" Mandi turned the phone sideways. "Please don't tell me that's a pregnancy test?"

"I believe it is. Rajul forwarded it to me. He's so proud of himself."

"He makes me sick."

"Why? For being a man?"

"No, for messing up Naira's life."

"Oh, and what is she? A helpless victim?"

"No, but by telling your mum, he has totally trapped her." Mandi stood up and began pacing around the room, dodging the obstacle course of boxes she had created from her middle-of-winter spring clean. She was struggling to think straight.

There was no way that Naira could be pregnant because if she was… IF she was… she would have told Mandi, or at least said something the other day. Mandi cast her mind back to seeing Naira for any hint of comment, but really, there was nothing. They talked about Mandi's polycystic ovaries and Mandi wanting to get pregnant, which would have been the perfect opportunity to Naira to pipe up, but she didn't. She wasn't even behaving oddly. And then when she gave Mandi her wax treatment, what did they discuss then? Mandi thought hard. Nothing. Nothing unusual. How come Naira wasn't bursting with the news that she had slept with Rajul? Why keep that secret? Was that why she gave Mandi a free wax and fussed over her? Because she knew she was about to stick a knife in her back? She must have suspected she was pregnant as she did a pregnancy test the very next morning. But why say nothing? Mandi felt betrayed. What kind of friend keeps such a big thing hidden? And why?

"She most probably feels bad," said Gav, as if reading Mandi's mind. "That's why she didn't say tell you."

"That's not Naira," said Mandi. "Naira says exactly what is on her mind. I've never known her to keep a secret." Mandi grabbed her phone from the coffee table. "I'm going to call her."

"Good luck," said Gav. "Give my new sister-in-law-to-be congratulations from me."

"You're so immature, Gav," said Mandi. "You don't get the enormity of this, not from any angle."

"You're just upset, Mandi, that your friend can produce a grandson for my mammi after spending only one night with my brother, when you have been trying for nearly two years."

"You can't even begin to imagine how upset I am, on *every* level," said Mandi through clenched teeth. "Oh, and by the way, it might not be a grandson. Have you actually considered that? And then what will your beloved Mammi do?"

Mandi could feel the pulse in her neck hammering. *Stupid, stupid Rajul. Stupid Naira, and stupidest of all, Agila.*

"Oh don't worry," said Gav. "Mammi already knows it's a boy. According to Rajul, conception took place on the fifth day of the week, which is when Mammi says the male sperm are strongest."

"Oh my God, do you know how ridiculous you sound?" said Mandi.

"She's never been wrong before," said Gav.

"It's hocus-pocus, Gav. And anyway, if she is that good, why has she not helped us conceive?"

"It's not us, Mandi, it's you."

"Let's wait and see, shall we? Test results in soon."

Mandi lay down on the sofa and looked for Naira on her phone. She tapped the number and waited. After one ring, the answerphone kicked in.

Sunday 7th February

Day 7 of TWW

"Tell me honestly, Jon. Am I looking fat?" Fern strode into the bedroom, balancing a bowl of crisps on her laptop.

"Truthfully, Fern, I can't tell. Not when you have so many clothes on."

"I'm only in a T-shirt and underwear," said Fern, placing the laptop on the bed and handing the crisp bowl to Jon.

"As I said, too many clothes. Let me just take a look under your T-shirt." Jon grabbed Fern, but she nimbly wriggled out of his grasp.

"No, not now, I'm serious. Phineas in the script department told me I was looking 'healthy' – and you know what that means."

"Er, that you're looking healthy? Oh, hold on a minute, you mean healthy, like healthy?"

"I don't mean healthy at all, I'm just telling you what Phineas said."

"OK. T-shirt off, side profile, let me get a proper look." Jon sat up straight on the bed. "Are you feeling bloated?"

"I'm not taking my T-shirt off. I've got a budget to do by

tomorrow morning. I just want to know." Fern sat on the bed beside Jon and opened her computer.

"OK, soooo, let me see." Jon jumped onto his knees like an overexcited spaniel and eyed up his wife. "Looking at you when you're clearly overdressed and refusing to present yourself in the correct manner, my answer is no. You do *not* look fat. You look exactly the same as you looked last week. If you let me *feel* you, however..." Jon dared to run his hand over Fern's solid abdomen.

"...So, no indication of me looking pregnant?"

"Ohhh, so, that's what you're asking, is it?" said Jon, sitting back and eyeing Fern up. "You want to know if you look pregnant, so you introduce this fictitious weirdo called Phineas, and make out he is asking very personal questions in order to avoid asking them yourself. You know, Fern... you really are a total nutcase who needs to learn to open up about your true feelings."

"Phineas does exist."

"Aha. In your head?"

"No, in the script department, as I said. He collects *Star Wars* paraphernalia and dresses up manga-style for Comic Con."

"And asks you overly forward questions?"

"OK, OK. Fine. I just didn't want to ask outright because..."

"Because you're paranoid about looking like you care?"

"No."

"What then?"

"I just don't. I mean, I can't, it's just that—"

"Look, Fern," said Jon, removing the computer from Fern's lap. "Love of my life. This has been brewing for a while and it's OK, I get it. I understand. You don't need to do this."

"But I do."

"You don't. You forget, I know you almost as well as you know yourself and regardless of what you think, you are the most capable person."

"What if I'm not? What if the reason I can't get pregnant is because I'm somehow damaged? Not fit to be a mother. It's all instinctive you know."

"Fern, what happened, happened years ago."

"She was still my mother."

"No, Sadie was your mother."

"Sadie is my aunt… big difference!"

"But she loved you like a mother. Look…" Jon cupped Fern's small, determined face in his large, gentle hands. "It's totally normal to worry at times when things don't happen as you want, and to blame yourself and dig around for all sorts of stuff to pin things on. We all do it."

"*You* don't."

"Er, yes, I do. I often worry that I have planned everything in my life so perfectly, nothing will go to plan."

"But that's positive worrying. That's normal. My worries aren't normal. All I get is negativity, anxiety. What if I screw up the one thing I am genetically born to do? What if… what if I end up being HER?"

"Stop it, Fern."

"I'm serious. What if I eventually get pregnant and then abandon—"

"Stop it."

"The doctor said there was nothing wrong with me physically, so it all has to be psychological, right? What if I don't have the capacity to love. Properly love. Love like a mother?"

Tears welled like ponds in Fern's deep, brown eyes. "What if the reason I can't get pregnant is because I lack maternal hormones?"

"Come here," said Jon, taking Fern in his arms and allowing her to sob into his shoulder. "It's fine to feel like this. It's good, actually."

"Everyone thinks I'm strong and robust and… I'm not. I'm crying inside, Jon. All the time, crying."

"I know. And that's why you need to stop being so hard on yourself. Demanding so much. You need to let it out."

"You sound like Auntie Sadie…" Fern said, laughing and crying at the same time, while releasing her head and squeezing her nose with her fingers. "She used to say, 'Ya path not clear 'til ya shed a tear.'"

Jon laughed. "She doesn't sound that West Indian?"

"Nah, only when she was trying to teach one of us a lesson. I guess she equated wisdom with her Jamaican roots."

"Well, you certainly inherited her wisdom."

"Now I *know* you're lying," said Fern, sitting back and lightly thumping Jon. "But I did get her fiery temper."

"Ooh, I'm scared."

"You should be." Fern smiled, then juddered, letting out another sob.

"Look," said Jon, sitting back and holding Fern firmly by the arms. He stared intently into her eyes. "You can do this, OK, and you *will* do it. If – no, *when* – we get our baby, you will be the sweetest, boldest, scariest, overly efficient and outspoken mother to that baby. And I know this, because I know the determination—"

"And grit."

"That as well… that you carry inside you. Believe it or not, you have *so* much to give."

"At work I do—"

"In life as well."

"I just feel so… so out of control. It's like… all my life I've had a goal, a direction, and now I just don't know what lies around the corner, and it scares me. It scares me to want something, and it scares me more to fuck up the one thing I want."

"It scares everyone."

"But – I don't like to be scared." Fern distractedly stroked the keys on her laptop.

"Really, Fern? That's strange because I love it."

"You know what I mean? I just know I'll get hurt."

"For once in your life, Fern, give in to the pressure, OK? Wear your heart on your sleeve. You don't need to be the cool kid—"

"Cool kid? Yeah, right."

"The badass boss."

"Yeah, yeah, alright, I know what you're saying."

"Just accept that sometimes life throws a curveball and you don't need to try and catch it. Everyone fumbles."

"I just don't want anyone ever to look down on me and think I can't do something, that I'm less capable than they are, that I'm…" Fern lowered her voice to a rare whisper, "…that I'm not good enough."

"Only arseholes think like that, Fern, and you know what we say about arseholes? Fuck 'em."

"In your dreams."

"Hey, I didn't invent the saying!"

"Er, I think you did." Fern slowly closed the laptop and relaxed her head against the bedhead. "You know, I really can't be bothered to do the budget tonight. Emotion is *wearing*."

"How about we go to Hill's and pick up a big fat juicy steak?"

"Er, hello? What happened to Mr low salt mackerel man?"

"And we'll share a rum and Coke?"

"What? You're crazy tonight."

"Aww, come on, Fern, stop playing hard to get," said Jon, grabbing Fern's fist and holding it up to his mouth as a microphone. "*Try a little tenderness.*"

"Oh yeah, Otis in the house…"

"*Try a little tenderness.*"

"I love it when you sing *stulla.*" Fern slowly lifted Jon's rugby shirt up off over his head. "It's as if Otis is right here, in the room." She kissed the fine hairs on Jon's chest, sensing the heat rising. "Oh, and don't think I don't know what you're doing here," she said, moving up to kiss Jon's neck.

"What am I doing?"

Kissing Jon's earlobe. "You think you're the Fern Whisperer. Don't you? You think that by seducing me, and whispering sweet nothings in my ear, that you have the power to make me forget thirty years of mental anguish so that I'm miraculously cured and completely normal."

"Darn," said Jon, removing Fern's T-shirt. "Busted."

"I'm a lot more complicated than that, Dr Abbott."

"In that case, a lot more seduction necessary."

"You haven't even made a groove in my badass armour," said Fern, pushing Jon back onto the bed. "I'm waaaay more complex than that."

"So, you're saying you want me to go deep. Is that what you're saying Fern? Because I can go deep. The question is, will *you* be able to handle it?"

Monday 8th February
Day 8 of TWW

Jane@closetoTWWentyyearsandcounting
Becks, you were up early this morning. Thought I was the early bird. All OK?

Becks@desperatemumof1
At last! Someone's awake. I've been up for hours.

Jane@closetoTWWentyyearsandcounting
Any reason?

Becks@desperatemumof1
Couldn't sleep. Woke up with a jump and was raring to go.

Jane@closetoTWWentyyearsandcounting
That's energetic. I'm still in bed. Can't quite bring myself to get up even though I really need a coffee.

Becks@desperatemumof1

I normally need a coffee as soon as I get up but today, weirdly, I don't fancy one.

Jane@closetoTWWentyyearsandcounting

I can't live without my morning coffee.

Becks@desperatemumof1

When I was pregnant with Hector, I gave it up completely. Made me feel sick. Feel sick at the thought of one today…

Jane@closetoTWWentyyearsandcounting

Are you trying to tell me something, Becks?

Becks@desperatemumof1

I wasn't going to say anything, but I do feel quite weird. I have this strange but familiar taste in my mouth and odd twinges.

Jane@closetoTWWentyyearsandcounting

We talked about this, Becks. NO SYMPTOM-SPOTTING.

Becks@desperatemumof1

I know, I know. Trying not to. I'm sure it's nothing – it's just I've had these same feelings before.

Jane@closetoTWWentyyearsandcounting

I don't like to preach to someone who has already been down the baby road, but it really is best not to read too much into what you are feeling. From experience, the mind is a very powerful tool at times like this and can play all sorts of games with the body.

Becks@desperatemumof1

I know. Maybe I'm just excited. Mike and I are going out for dinner tonight. It's been soooo long since we were out and alone. And trust me, that is not a brag – it is a necessity. Our marriage needs it.

Jane@closetoTWWentyyearsandcounting

I get it. Nice for you. Where will you go?

Becks@desperatemumof1

Don't know yet. Need to arrange something.

Jane@closetoTWWentyyearsandcounting

You're getting a babysitter for Hector?

Becks@desperatemumof1

Yes, although, need to arrange that too. Only decided on dinner last night.

Jane@closetoTWWentyyearsandcounting

It's good to make time to go on proper dates. It's quite easy during the looooong wait to lose sight of who you are as people. To remember we are not just time machines, counting down the minutes.

Fern@toobusytoTWW

Morning, morning, one and all. How are we today?

Jane@closetoTWWentyyearsandcounting

Hmmm, bearing up. Always hate day 8. It's when the TWW really starts to drag. Past the middle point, but still a way to go. Today does not feel like a decluttering day, regardless of what my nifty little list says. Feels more like a 'snuggle up on the sofa and read a good book' day. Thank God I'm not working this week. Anyone else got pouring rain?

Fern@toobusytoTWW
Reading a book sounds like bliss. Lucky you having a week off, Jane. What do you work as?

Jane@closetoTWWentyyearsandcounting
Bizarrely enough, I work in a school…

Fern@toobusytoTWW
All those kids????!!!!!!

Jane@closetoTWWentyyearsandcounting
Thankfully not. School office – accounts department. Only three days a week – which is enough. I never really see the kids. Just as well. I really couldn't cope with spending the whole day with other people's children – my own, that would be OK, but other people's – no thanks…

Becks@desperatemumof1
Welcome to my world. I am looking for ways of coming up with playground avoidance techniques. So far, only technique I have is – avoid playgrounds!

Fern@toobusytoTWW
Yeah, at least I don't have any interaction. Well, not much. I do come from an enormous family and there are loads of kids at every get-together. Luckily no one ever asks when Jon and I intend to have babies because they think I am married to my career.

Jane@closetoTWWentyyearsandcounting

Are you?

Fern@toobusytoTWW

It's the message I put out.

Jane@closetoTWWentyyearsandcounting

But are you?

Fern@toobusytoTWW

It's complicated, but Jon has told me I need to get in touch with my inner self, so let me think about how to answer that.

Jane@closetoTWWentyyearsandcounting

Sorry, you can tell me to stop probing. I just find it quite refreshing to speak to someone online who is not solely obsessed with getting pregnant.

Becks@desperatemumof1

It is all-consuming, isn't it? I tried writing in my diary last night, and the only comfort I gained was the confirmation that I am undoubtedly a grumpy, dissatisfied cow.

Jane@closetoTWWentyyearsandcounting

Ouch. Bit hard on yourself, Becks.

Becks@desperatemumof1

I know. It's just every word that came out was angry.

Fern@toobusytoTWW

We're all a bit angry. Life makes us angry. So much expectation, so much to live up to.

Becks@desperatemumof1

No, but I'm REALLY angry. My dad always told me I was a 'grass is always greener' kind of child, and I think it has followed me into adulthood. I always think everyone else's life is better than my own.

Fern@toobusytoTWW

My aunt's motto for life: "Look at what you've got, not what you haven't got."

Becks@desperatemumof1

Wise words. I seem overly fixated on what I haven't got. And I know that makes me selfish and self-centred and miserable. A new baby would be the cure-all for all my life miseries, I'm sure of it.

Fern@toobusytoTWW

That's quite a lot of pressure there, Becks. On the baby, and you. There's always going to be something, or someone, who has more…

Becks@desperatemumof1

I know. When will it end?

Fern@toobusytoTWW

Don't get me wrong, I get it. We all think the perfect life is just around the corner, just that little bit out of reach, but I am not sure we ever arrive. I used to look at the bosses at work and say, "All I want is to be them." Now, I am them… and it goes on. I want a baby!! It never ends.

Jane@closetoTWWentyyearsandcounting

You're super wise, Fern. Agree with all the above... and unfortunately, wanting a baby is an unavoidable want on all levels: physical, mental, societal, and worst of all it is out of our control! No promotion or pay rise, or good grades or step up the hierarchical ladder, is automatically going to get you your baby.

And as I might have said before (a thousand times), social media does not help. No one has that perfect life. It does not exist, but we are all led into believing there is some kind of nirvana that everyone is blissfully enjoying, except us.

Becks@desperatemumof1

You mean there's not?

Jane@closetoTWWentyyearsandcounting

Haha... sorry to burst your bubble.

Becks@desperatemumof1

I'm actually serious. Fear of not achieving nirvana worries me.

Star@Gaiababe

No nirvana = no job for me, beautiful ladeeeezz. I nurture nirvana for a living, and as I've said before – it's all smoke and mirrors.

Becks@desperatemumof1

Coming from the free, floaty spirit who makes love to hot Latino lovers under the stars.

Star@Gaiababe

As I say, all smoke and mirrors...

Becks@desperatemumof1
You mean that's not the truth?

Star@Gaiababe
I don't even know what the truth is anymore, babes. Trust me,
I certainly didn't learn honesty from my upstanding middle-
class parents. #lasttoknow

Fern@toobusytoTWW
Last to know? What's going on, Star? Everything OK?

Monday 8th February, mid-morning

Day 8 of TWW

"I've only got thirty minutes," said Janet, bustling into Creams, eyes darting about for a place to hang her coat, flustered; blotches on her chest. She was purposefully avoiding eye contact with Star, who had been in the coffee shop nearly twenty minutes by now, calmly sipping her way through a smoothie.

"Mum, you said you wouldn't book anything else up this morning," Star said, trying (but failing) not to sound sulky.

"I'm sorry, Gilly needed a fourth for nine o-clock tennis and I couldn't come up with an excuse fast enough."

"How about 'meeting my daughter for the first coffee we have had out together in at least two years'? That might have worked…"

"Sorry, darling. It's usually *me* trying to pin *you* down," said Janet, picking up the menu. "What's that you've got there?"

"It's the Green Goddess: celery, apple, mint and lime."

"Hmm, I think I'll have a cappuccino," Janet said. "Just a cappuccino for me," she repeated, as a waitress appeared at the table.

There was a short silence while Janet gathered herself, inhaled deeply, smoothed down the tablecloth and, eventually, settled her eyes on Star.

"So, darling, to what do I owe this pleasure?"

Star, who had been relishing the thought of this coffee date, found herself suddenly taken aback at being hit with such a direct question. "I, er, just want to chat," she said, shifting awkwardly in her seat. If you were going to nitpick, 'pry' would be the more appropriate word. Any kind of less-than-superficial conversation with Janet, about Janet's life, was, considered by Janet, to be prying.

Truth was, relations between Star and Janet had always been awkward. For as far back as Star could remember, being alone with her mum was squirmy. Those mother-daughter very vital conversations about bras and periods and body odour – everyday, natural adolescent subjects – were always undertaken in whispers, behind closed doors, "away from dad," as if it was a sin to grow breasts and bleed. As if Janet herself had never experienced anything so alien. The same with boyfriends and sex and any kind of personal health problem. Hush, hush. Nothing to see here. Move on.

For years, Star thought there was something wrong with her, as if what she was going through was different from everyone else, or if not different, then certainly not to be openly discussed. She was even, once upon a time (and still shudders to remember) something of a prude – secretive, locking herself in the cubicle to get changed for sports at school when the other girls were content with letting it all hang out in the communal areas. It was only recently, within roughly the last five years, that Star had come to realise that it wasn't *her* with the weird body or the privacy complex; it was her mum. Her mum – the prude. It was this insight, this fantastic relief, that caused Star to catapult from one extreme to the other. 'If you've got it, flaunt it... yeah, baby."

And flaunt it she did, at first. Every where and any how. She was one lacy vest and a pair of hot pants short of fully-fledged naturist, and that was on the streets of Surrey... much to Janet's despair. Elsewhere, out of sight of twitching net curtains, she didn't bother with the vest. At least, that was what she told her parents... to wind them up. Even then she had a bone to pick with their nonsensical hang-ups. And that was before she was prompted to look at the reason *why* Janet was the way she was. Why so coy? Why so repulsed by something so natural as the human body? And the latest question going around in Star's head, ever since Jane had brought it up on the forum...

"Mum, I'm sorry, I do have to ask this and I don't want to cause to any kind of embarrassment, as I know you hate questions along these sort of lines, but... is the reason I'm an only child because you and Dad never had sex?"

Whoops. That wasn't quite how Star intended for it to come out.

"I mean," she added hastily, clocking the horror spreading across Janet's face, "you love each other, and you love kids and you most probably wanted a whole army, but you only had me. So, what's the reason?"

"Shh, Stacey, not here!" Janet used a napkin to mop up a drop of spilt frothy milk created by a nervous jolt.

"I mean, I'm very happy being an only child, don't get me wrong," Star ploughed on. "It's just, well, are there other reasons why I am an only child?"

"Stacey." The blotches had expanded to the cheeks. "Stacey, Stacey—"

"It's Star."

"Star, it's complicated. Awkward. It's..." Janet rolled the

milky napkin into a tight ball. "Look, darling, why do you ask so many questions?"

"Because I have a right to know. Were there other reasons why you only had me... besides the sex?"

"There is... and never has been... anything wrong with your father's or my sex life," said Janet in an aggravated whisper.

"I'm so pleased to hear it, because mine is pretty good too, in case you want to know. Well, it was, before I split with Romero."

Janet sat bolt upright, lips pursed.

"It's OK, Mum. We can have these conversations now. I'm not a schoolgirl, and, by the way, sex is kind of necessary when... when you're trying for a baby."

The blotches dissipated from Janet's complexion and a white sheet moved in. "No!" Janet clutched her mug, causing more frothy spillage.

"Yes, actually, although note the use of the word 'trying.'"

"But... how can you be trying for a baby? I mean, who with?"

"I'm going it alone... ta-daaa! Modern family."

"But, a baby? Alone?"

"No, Mum, 'trying' for a baby. This is not me announcing the imminent arrival of a grandchild; this is me telling you that I am *trying* for a baby, a grandchild. For you, and Dad."

"But trying?"

"Yes, Mum. Turns out I am not a 'get-laid, baby-made' type of girl. Sadly." Star felt a lump forming in her throat and swallowed hard. "Doctor says I've got this condition. It's called endometriosis, and it's when tissue similar to the lining of the womb migrates to other—"

"I know what it is."

"It can attach itself to the—"

"I *know* what it is," Janet repeated. "I-I've heard it's very painful." She lifted her hand to her mouth, preparing for an involuntary sob.

"Yep. It's excruciating – and currently only manageable, not curable. It means that baby-making is going to be a challenge. If I'm lucky, I might have one child. One, Mum. Like you and Dad."

"No. Stace... Star. Not now." Janet stood up abruptly, pushing back her chair. "I'm really sorry, I have to go. They'll all be on the court, waiting for me."

"They say it can be hereditary, Mum."

"Here, take this." Janet thrust a £5 into Star's hand. "For the coffee."

"I just want to talk about it, Mum, with you. I just want to understand," said Star, jumping up. "Please, don't go."

"I have to, I don't like to let people down."

"Mum, you're letting me d—"

Janet left, retreating, with her scarf tightly wrapped around her neck. Nothing to see here. Move on.

Star sat back, and exhaled, long and slow. So, there it was. Another unanswered question. She looked across at the now empty chair and found herself engulfed in negative energy. Fanning herself with a menu, she picked up her phone and logged on to the forum.

Monday 8th February

Day 8 of TWW

TWW Forum (Continued)

Star@Gaiababe

Hi Fern, thanks for the concern. Not really OK. I've just admitted to my mum that I am trying for a baby, alone, oh yes… and that I have endometriosis.

Fern@toobusytoTWW

You have endometriosis? I had no idea! You always look so vibrant and healthy. If you and your perfect body can have it, what hope is there for the rest of us mortals? Anyway, well done for telling her you are trying for a baby. Must have come as a shock to your mum?

Jane@closetoTWWentyyearsandcounting

Sorry to hear you have the old endo, Star. Bummer indeed. I'm a bit surprised, though – you mean she didn't know? About the endo? That you were trying for a baby? That must have been a lot for her to take in, first thing in the morning!

Star@Gaiababe

We met for coffee… big mistake. My mum doesn't do coffee dates – too confrontational. I asked her outright why she and Dad didn't have more kids.

Becks@desperatemumof1

And?

Star@Gaiababe

And… nothing. She didn't answer. Only told me that she and my dad have a good sex life!

Becks@desperatemumof1

Happy for them… lol.

Star@Gaiababe

Thinking about it, I am certain that she suffers from endometriosis too, but she just won't own up. Frustrating.

Jane@closetoTWWentyyearsandcounting

Why? It's not anything to be embarrassed about.

Star@Gaiababe

But it's personal and my mum doesn't do personal. Not even to me, her own daughter. Not even when I give her an open invitation to bare all…

Fern@toobusytoTWW

Did you ask her direct, like, "Mum, do you have endometriosis?"

Star@Gaiababe

Haha, no, babe. I beat around the bush. You should see me when I'm with my mum, I'm nothing like the Star that presents on Instagram. She makes me all clam up, and clammy for that matter... not a good look! One day I will get to the truth. TBH, I could really do with her support right now. And I never thought I would say that. Perhaps not as independent as I let on. Heading home now to submerge in healing crystals. Need to reconnect.

Fern@toobusytoTWW
Hang in there, babe. You'll do it.

Jane@closetoTWWentyyearsandcounting
What is it with mothers? Mine speaks her mind when drunk, yours doesn't speak, and Mandi's MIL, it appears, never knows when to stop...

Fern@toobusytoTWW
Conclusion: mothers = totally overrated!

Jane@closetoTWWentyyearsandcounting
Speaking of, Mandi's quiet this morning. You up yet, Mands?

Becks@desperatemumof1
I'm sure she's still asleep – she's a youngie, remember...

Jane@closetoTWWentyyearsandcounting
Oh, to sleep past 6am.

Becks@desperatemumof1
6am... that's a lie in.

Fern@toobusytoTWW
That's it... ciao for now, girls, some of us gotta pretend we work for a living.

Monday 8th February, evening

Day 8 of TWW

Oh my God, oh my God, oh my God.
   I am officially in shock.
   The worst thing has happened. Worst, WORST…

Monday 8th February
Day 8 of TWW

It wasn't a great start to the day. Rain never puts one in the best of moods and it wasn't just raining; it was pouring – water drip-dripping onto the outside windowsill which meant the drainpipes must be clogged with leaves. *Make note*, thought Jane. *Clear out drainpipes. Another job for the weekend. Another boring job for the weekend.*

Jane yawned once and once again. If it wasn't for the lure of coffee she could have stayed in bed all day. A totally un-Jane thing for Jane to do, but today, she really could not be arsed to get up. Really and truly un-arsed? *Non-arsed? Under-arsed?* Whatever… she did not care.

It's all Keith's fault for leaving too early to bring me my kickstart coffee, she thought to herself. *Correction, it's all Denise's fault for calling Keith into an early-morning meeting, otherwise he would have been here to bring me my coffee.* Jane yawned for the third time in less than a minute and picked up the novel from her bedside table: *Reasons to Be Cheerful* by Nina Stibbe, a comedy read. Just what she needed, bar the painful fact that the mother in the book had effortlessly succeeded in giving birth five times. Five times! And the author twice. Jane knew that about the author because she had looked her up. Hurray for Wikipedia. She was always looking other women up; it was a kind of masochistic pastime.

Her interest did not lie in their career path, make-up routine, favourite restaurant, but simply in whether or not they had children. That was it. *How narrow my outlook has become*, she lamented on a regular basis. And, if yes, what age were they when they had their children? If they were over forty, she allowed herself a glimmer of hope – *you too can do this, Jane* – along with an immediate sense of affinity – *we're in the older mums' gang*. If under forty (which she was the first to admit, most women are – even in this day and age), she felt despair, gloom. *She doesn't know how lucky she is.*

She never told Keith about her little 'stalker' game. It was weird, after all, a tad obsessive, especially when she began imagining the happy family of strangers going about their rich, fulfilled daily lives.

The 'game' was worth enduring for those rare occasions, those small hits of dopamine, when she came across a childless woman in her forties who was smiling, happy and living the dream. *I, too, can be childless and happy.* Sadly, these women were few and far between, and were they really happy? *Smoke and mirrors...*

Jane skim read a few pages then tossed the book aside and clambered out of bed. Her dressing gown was strewn on the bedroom floor and she attempted to put it on, wrestling with the inside-out armholes. Traipsing into the bathroom and staring into the mirror, a pale face stared back, worry lines already forming around the eyes. She gave a wide smile, checking in on her front teeth, and broke into another great yawn. *Jesus, Jane, sort it out.*

The post had already arrived by the time Jane tottered downstairs: boring as usual, bar one letter addressed to Mr K Hardwick, written by human hand. It was such a rare sight seeing handwritten ink that Jane was tempted to open it, a temptation that quickly became an action.

Dear Keith

Little pup Jemima coming along a treat. Eating well and growing fast.

Please find enclosed the Pedigree Heritage form as discussed. Jemima (or Huffle, as my daughter calls her) is looking forward to moving in with you both and getting to know her new loving family. Just give me a shout when you are good to go.

Cheers for now,

Suz

Jemima? Suz? Puppy? Loving family? Jane held on to the letter for a long time, tightly scrunching up one corner, but she didn't notice. Her heart was on a gallop and she was having trouble catching her breath. *No, NO, NO. Not right. I never agreed to a puppy.* At least not agreed to it right now, before she knew for certain this TWW had been as unproductive as all the others.

Quite giddy, Jane made a plunge for the bannister and sat down heavily on the bottom step. She clasped hold of her forehead and, holding her head in her hands, rocked back and forth, a brand-new sensation swamping her, one she had never experienced before, intensely painful, sickeningly intoxicating: betrayal!

Seconds, minutes passed before Jane got up from the stair and walked blindly into the kitchen, fumbling around for the components to make her coffee. She felt too sick for toast, too sick to eat. All-consumed by bewilderment. Keith had given up? He had given up and gone behind Jane's back. *He told me he'd wait. Wait and see. One final wait and see and maybe one more, for luck and now…* He and 'Suz' were in cohorts. What line had he fed to Suz? *"Looking pretty certain it's a yes on the pup, but just give me two weeks before I give the final a-OK."* Did the topic of infertility come up? Was there much chinwagging together over Jane's withered, ineffectual womb? Did anyone think to mention any of this to Jane? Best not. Too sensitive. Sore point. Uncomfortable to talk about. Best keep it between us… Suz.

Jane was shaking uncontrollably. *How dare they? How dare they pussyfoot around me, like I'm some glass statue?* Jane picked up the letter from the hall floor and, after rummaging for her mobile in her dressing gown pocket, dialled the number on the top lefthand corner of the letter.

"Hi, it's Suz from Adore the Paw. I'm not here at the moment, so leave me a message with your name and number and I will call you straight back. Thanks and ta-ra for now."

Jane instantly hung up – what was her game plan if Suz had answered? Yell down the phone? *Help me, I want a baby.* Breathing deep harnessing her surging rage, Jane went to 'Favourites' on her phone and tapped the top number.

"Good morning, my love," said Keith, muffling his voice so as not to be heard in the office.

"You bastard!" cried Jane in a shaky voice, only just stifling the scream that was hammering at her throat.

"Are you OK? Jane? Jane?"

"You betrayed me. I can't talk to you right now," said Jane. "Just… just fuck off, alright."

Jane hung up the phone and threw it on the kitchen table as if it was a burning log. Sliding her back down the kitchen wall, she crouched onto the floor and pulled her knees up to her chest. From this position of despair, she broke into merciless sobs. In over twenty years of contented, marital bliss, she felt, for the first time today, right now, totally and utterly, alone.

Monday 8th February, evening
Day 8 of TWW

Mandi@LusciousLocks

Hi everyone. I'm here. Sorry. Few things to sort out here. Be back soon.

Star@Gaiababe

Sure thing, babes, hope all OK?

Mandi@LusciousLocks

Hmm, not sure at the moment. I will let you know.

Star@Gaiababe

Of course. Here if you need us.

Mandi@LusciousLocks

Thank you. I need to hear that.

Tuesday 9th February, morning

Day 9 of TWW

"What's with you this morning, Becks?" said Mike, pulling on his socks. "Are you hormonal or summat? Asking because you are *raging!*"

"No!" said Becks, stomping into the bathroom and slamming the door.

"Just as well," Mike yelled. "Cos I got Samantha screaming down my neck doubling my workload, and I can't cope with the two of you."

Becks *was* raging. About to explode… any… second… now… *The fucker!* Becks slammed her clenched fist on the edge of the bathroom sink and swung the bathroom door open back on its hinges.

"Yes, I *am* angry," she cried, bare legs wide, chest heaving and eyes narrowed. "You let me down." She pointed an accusing finger at Mike and jabbed it back and forth.

"Whaaat?" Mike replied with disdain. He was looking Becks up and down like she was a wild beast.

"I said," Becks pulled her misshapen Primark T-shirt lower over her off-colour granny pants and wished she had

190

thought to get dressed before this showdown. "You let me down." Her voice was quieter now, which, to anyone clued up on the moods of Becks (Mike, for example), was more alarming. He took a step back and squared up, ready to take whatever was coming his way. "What the hell are you talking about?"

"We had a date, last night. You and me and dinner, and you never showed up."

"A date? What do you mean, a date?"

"I mean I booked us a table at Spiro's and sat there like some lemon tart, all by myself for forty-seven minutes. Did you not get the four hundred texts I sent?"

"No!" Mike scrunched up his eyebrows. In fairness, Becks considered generously, he did look baffled. "If I'd got your text I would have been there."

"Don't lie."

"Er, dolmadakia with ground lamb? Feta me meli? Hello?"

"Don't say that."

"It's true."

"You're lying." Becks experienced a stab of panic.

"I'm not."

"Please tell me you are."

"Nope."

"Oh my God, then who did I send four hundred texts to inviting them out for a hot date and then berating them for not turning up?" She darted from the bedroom, raced down the stairs and grabbed her phone from the hall table.

"Ohhh, shit! Shit, shit, shit." Becks buried her head in her hand.

"What have you done, Becks?" asked Mike, hanging over the bannister.

Becks clutched a hold of her hammering heart. "I've only gone and sent out four hundred messages to Mikhala."

"Who's Mikhala?"

"Rolly's mum."

"Who's Rolly?"

"Oh my God. This is the worst thing. I barely know the woman. Playgroup mum. The only time we ever talked was when Hector had chicken pox—"

"Ouch, Becks. She is going to think you're some crazy nutter."

"'This is SO humiliating. I only entered her in as a contact yesterday to reply about Rolly's party."

"Didn't you think it was weird that I didn't write back?"

"You *did* write back. Well, she did. She wrote, hold on…" Becks scrolled back up the long trail of one-sided messages.

"I wrote, 'Hot date tonight. Spiro's 8pm. Be there, Spongey SquarePants,' and she wrote back, 'Haha, LOL.'"

"What? And you thought that was me? LOL?"

"Well, yeah, I thought it was you being sarcastic. And then when you didn't reply to my later texts, I thought it was because you were in the car driving to the restaurant. And then when you didn't reply to my even later texts, I thought either that your phone was on silent, because it normally is, or… that you were cross with me for sending you so many texts and that you would just show up. And then when you didn't show up, I just started manically writing you texts about what an arsehole you are and then I came home and went to bed. And then you eventually came in at some shithole late hour and I was too annoyed/ asleep to speak. It never crossed my mind that it wasn't you I was texting."

"You do realise you are officially an idiot," said Mike, a cautious grin appearing in the dark stubble of his face. "I seriously do sometimes wonder about your mental state."

"Just shut up. OK?" At the sight of Mike's mirth, Becks allowed a small smile to creep across her puckered lips.

"Everyone is going to be laughing at you, you do realise that?" Mike continued.

"And *you*. You're the arsehole who didn't show up! You're Spongey SquarePants." Becks let out a short burst of laughter. It felt weird laughing with Mike. She cut it short.

"What the fuck was that even supposed to mean?" Mike asked, curiously.

"I was trying to be romantic."

"You make it sound like I'm got some problem with my bladder."

"Shit. This is so embarrassing."

"I've got to go to work. Good luck dealing with the fallout."

"I'm going to be the laughing stock."

"Can I suggest you change Mikhala's name in your contacts… so you don't fuck up again."

"Yeah, thanks for the support."

"You're welcome." Mike ruffled Becks' hair and raced out of the door.

I bet he's thrilled to be out of the asylum, thought Becks, putting three sixes before Mikhala's name in her contacts.

Things had not started well. Becks was not looking forward to the day ahead. Day 9. She went onto the forum and scrolled back to Jane's list of ways to keep busy:

Day 9 – Book tickets to go somewhere… anywhere. I am going to book New York (Keith doesn't know this yet, SURPRISE!). Puppy pending, of course, grrrr.

Yeah right, thought Becks, *like that's going to work. Maybe I should just invite Mikhala.* Becks shook her head. *What sluice gates have I just opened?*

Discarding the enemy phone on the hall table, she pulled down her overly revealing T-shirt and went upstairs, wearily, to wake Hector.

Tuesday 9th February, morning
Day 9 of TWW

Fern@toobusytoTWW

How is everyone this fine morning? Good snuggling up day yesterday, Jane? Hot dinner date with Mike, Becks? Any further chats with your mum, Star? Mandi – you still with us?

Jane@closetoTWWentyyearsandcounting

Thanks for asking, Fern. If you want to know, I spent the entire day yesterday in tears.

Fern@toobusytoTWW

Jane!!!! What happenin'? (Respecting your honesty BTW.)

Jane@closetoTWWentyyearsandcounting

Fern... I gave up putting across a rosy picture of my life years ago. Tell it like it is – that's my motto. I'll tell you what is happening. Keith, my beloved husband, has booked in the new puppy, correction, Jemima – yes, she has a name – and is in touch with the dog owner, etc., etc., etc. about her 'moving

in to our loving home' all ready to go. Except for the small fact
– he hasn't told me!

Fern@toobusytoTWW

Ohhhhkay?????? And?

Jane@closetoTWWentyyearsandcounting

And… we agreed we were going to wait until these two weeks
were passed before making any plans. As in, if things don't
work out this time round, then we make a plan for what plan
to plan next. And maybe the plan = puppy, maybe the plan =
we keep trying. Whatever we do, I feel like he is no longer my
partner in this long journey and is splintering off, ditching the
dream.

Fern@toobusytoTWW

I see. Shit. What a bastard – LOL.

Jane@closetoTWWentyyearsandcounting

If that is you being sarcastic then I'm a) sticking two fingers
up at you and b) signing off because I'm too gutted to find
humour.

Fern@toobusytoTWW

Sorry, I take it back. It's just that Keith sounds a bit like Jon
– overly prepared, overly planning for tomorrow. And in
someone else's husband, it sounds endearing. In my own, it
drives me nuts – so, Jane, I get it.

Jane@closetoTWWentyyearsandcounting

So… I cried all day, because I'm just not sure I'm ready to
accept the end.

Fern@toobusytoTWW
Why does having a puppy need to be the end?

Jane@closetoTWWentyyearsandcounting
It doesn't, not technically, but it's more what it symbolises.

Becks@desperatemumof1
Just joining in now... Jane, I'm sorry, I'm with Fern here. I don't quite get why you're so upset? Keith sounds like he is just preparing a soft landing. You don't know how lucky you are.

Jane@closetoTWWentyyearsandcounting
I'm going to dismiss that last comment because I know that other people's luck is what you measure your life on, Becks, but, I suppose, the reason I feel this so strongly is because I don't want to give up. And I don't want Keith to give up, but I know he is so weary from the waiting and wondering. And he wants to move on. And I understand. But I don't want to and... am I even making sense?

Becks@desperatemumof1
About to make another controversial comment, but, Jane, you sound a bit hormonal (hiding head from virtual swipe).

Fern@toobusytoTWW
Oooh, might just step away for a milky tea.

Star@Gaiababe
Rise and shine, and inhale the beautiful dew drops on the glistening land... ladies, ladies, ladies... I'm feeling the heat. Shall we take a step back? Becks...?

Becks@desperatemumof1
Was my comment too harsh? It's what I hear from my DH the whole time, so I reckon I've become desensitised. Men just blaming everything on hormones.

Fern@toobusytoTWW
Yep, and that's because many men are only semi-evolved (sorry, Mike). Let's keep it off this forum where we are all fully enlightened women, please, Becks.

Becks@desperatemumof1
Hearing you, Fern – sorry, Jane. I'm actually slowly dying here today, so don't trust anything I say.

Star@Gaiababe
All OK with you, Becks? Dinner date?? Dare I ask?

Becks@desperatemumof1
I seriously think I'm going mad. My brain is all over the place. The dinner date didn't happen because (don't judge – very embarrassed), I sent the dinner date invite out to the wrong person.

Fern@toobusytoTWW
Oooh I'm liking this… sorry, I mean, oh dear! What do you mean, Becks?

Becks@desperatemumof1
Let's just say, I found myself inviting a complete stranger out to dinner.

Fern@toobusytoTWW
Male or female?

Becks@desperatemumof1

Female – very female. As in, one of the yummy mummy's from Hector's playgroup who I barely know and it's worse, because when Mike didn't show at the restaurant, I started writing all these really personal texts to this woman thinking it was Mike and… OMG, ladies, I'm so embarrassed.

Becks@desperatemumof1

Hello?
Hello?
Comments hugely appreciated?
Anyone there?

Becks@desperatemumof1

Hello?

Tuesday 9th February
Day 9 of TWW

Fern@toobusytoTWW
Hi Becks… are you there? We're on tenterhooks here.

Star@Gaiababe
Where's she gone?

Fern@toobusytoTWW
Don't leave us hanging… I need something enlightening and/ or hilarious to get me through this spreadsheet.

***

Becks@desperatemumof1
You're there, phew! I had a problem with my WiFi… thought you'd all ditched me to have a good laugh. Weirdly enough, I just had the woman, Mikhala, turn up on my doorstep. (!!!!) She was really concerned about me.

Fern@toobusytoTWW

Hmm, kind of her?

Becks@desperatemumof1

Humiliating, actually. She wanted to know if I was alright and said if I ever needed to talk, that I could call her. I pretended I was on the phone so that I didn't have time to chat. And anyway, not kind, Fern – I sense she was only prying.

Star@Gaiababe

Are you sure, babe? You know, women shine brightest together. Some of us can love with an open heart.

Fern@toobusytoTWW

Mantra morning, Star.

Star@Gaiababe

Sorry, it's my natural default.

Becks@desperatemumof1

I just can't really talk to anyone at the moment – except you guys. Everyone else thinks I'm a bore. And I am – I only have one topic of conversation. No one wants to hear about my fallopian tube and infertility, especially when they don't have the same problems I do.

Jane@closetoTWWentyyearsandcounting

You're right. Although I don't think it's necessarily because they don't want to hear – it's more because they don't know what to say. The strength of the 'want' us TWW-ers have for a baby is so visceral, words don't always work. "I'm sorry," sounds lame and, anyway, why is it someone else's fault? "I feel for you," sounds fake. "It must be hard for you," sounds like 'you're on your own' and if they dare say, "Just relax, it will happen…" Well, you know how I feel about that!!

Fern@toobusytoTWW
That's a good take, Jane. Humans like to fix things, find solutions, and when there is no fixing or obvious solution, we just flounder. It's like grief. It's something you have to suffer on your own. Support is good as is kindness, but at the end of the day, it doesn't alleviate the pain.

Becks@desperatemumof1
I think my problem is that I project my sadness onto other people, make out my problems are their fault.

Jane@closetoTWWentyyearsandcounting
That's perfectly normal, Becks, we all do it… Look at me, I nearly yelled at a complete stranger from the puppy kennel, not only because of the puppy but also because she mentioned she had a daughter. A daughter AND a puppy. My first thought was, *Bitch, how dare she?*

Fern@toobusytoTWW
You go, girl.

Becks@desperatemumof1
But did it make you feel any better?

Jane@closetoTWWentyyearsandcounting
We-ll, yes, but then no. Luckily, I did realise quite quickly that I was being irrational and so… took it out on Keith instead.

Fern@toobusytoTWW
At least he can understand where you're coming from.

Fern@toobusytoTWW

Sooooo, what I want to know, Becks… is at what point did you realise your texts were going to the wrong person?

Becks@desperatemumof1

This morning! Mike came in when I was asleep last night and so I kept my yells until today. It was actually quite funny, somewhere… deep down. We laughed about it, briefly. Maybe things *are* meant to happen for a reason. Maybe Mike and I needed something funny – but not very funny to happen – to take my mind off stuff. It's all got so heavy lately.

Mandi@LusciousLocks

Good morning, everybody. You are all sounding very wise and philosophical. Sorry, but I'm about to let the side down. #heatmagazine

Jane@closetoTWWentyyearsandcounting

There you are!! Hey Mandi!

Fern@toobusytoTWW

Welcome back, stranger.

Star@Gaiababe

Om shanti, Mands.

Mandi@LusciousLocks

Namaste, ladies. Oh, wow. A lot of s*** going down in my world. Would really, really value your wisdom and advice.

Becks@desperatemumof1

Does it involve messaging a complete stranger, because we've already covered that today?

Mandi@LusciousLocks

TBH, I really wish it did, the problem is there are not enough strangers in my world.

Fern@toobusytoTWW

Spill it, Mands.

Mandi@LusciousLocks

In a nutshell, my best friend has just announced that she is pregnant with Gav's brother. My mother-in-law is not angry, as you might expect, even though her son is still only nineteen. In fact, she is delighted. I am now confirmed as the incompetent waste of space, while Gav is parading around clutching his manhood, extolling the potency of the family sperm.

Becks@desperatemumof1

Ouch. Wasn't it you who mentioned semi-evolved men, Fern?

Fern@toobusytoTWW

That is a lot to take in there, Mandi. First off, so I'm guessing, Gav is no longer going to take any responsibility for his sperm in your attempts to get pregnant? Am I right?

Mandi@LusciousLocks

Correct. He is shooting perfect sperm on all cylinders. It's a family given. That said... ha ha... wait until we get the test results. Due in any day.

Jane@closetoTWWentyyearsandcounting

And your MIL is happy because??

Mandi@LusciousLocks

Because she wants a new baby – well, a new grandson.

Star@Gaiababe

I can relate to that – a grandchild, at least.

Fern@toobusytoTWW

Me too.

Mandi@LusciousLocks

No, my MIL wants a grandson – girls don't really feature in her life. She has already told my friend that she is going to have a boy, and this is at eight weeks pregnant. She makes out she has some way of 'reading' a pregnancy. It's all bullshit – but it's worse than that – it's verging on bribery.

Jane@closetoTWWentyyearsandcounting

That doesn't sit comfortably with me.

Mandi@LusciousLocks

It's old-fashioned, but it's part of our culture. A number of people have moved on from that, at least superficially, but deep down, it still exists. Boys are still considered the superior sex. Giving birth to a boy is seen as an achievement. If I ever do get pregnant and have a girl, my MIL would view her as a mistake.

Jane@closetoTWWentyyearsandcounting

I'm struggling to like the sound of your MIL.

Mandi@LusciousLocks

Join the club.

Fern@toobusytoTWW

You said it's all bribery – how come?

Mandi@LusciousLocks

It all gets very sensitive here and I am sorry about that, but I am not sure my friend is going to want to keep the baby.

Fern@toobusytoTWW

Ouch. Has she told you this?

Mandi@LusciousLocks

No, she hasn't spoken to me about any of it and this really hurts. I've tried calling, but she is blanking my calls. She knows I am trying for a baby, but she's not a very sensitive person, so I don't think she will be holding back cos of that.

Fern@toobusytoTWW

But you think she won't want to keep the baby?

Mandi@LusciousLocks

Pretty certain of it – she is totally NOT ready to have a baby. She smokes, isn't taking any of the right vitamins, is married to her career path and she is neurotic about getting fat.

Jane@closetoTWWentyyearsandcounting

I know a lot of those sort of people who start out convinced they don't want to get pregnant but then become wedded to the idea. I am certain her mummy hormones will kick in, and then she will suddenly be baby-mad.

Mandi@LusciousLocks

I think the reason Gav's brother told his mum about the pregnancy so quickly was so as to trap my friend. Much harder to get rid of a baby when you have my forceful MIL on board.

Fern@toobusytoTWW

WOW.

Mandi@LusciousLocks

Yep!

Anyway, I'm not sure how well I will cope if she does keep the baby. I never thought I would feel jealous of this particular friend. We are so different, but she now has something I want more than anything and I am not sure I will be able to speak to her.

Jane@closetoTWWentyyearsandcounting

You might have to learn to put on a happy smile for someone else's joy. It's painful and I am not convinced very sincere, but I've almost mastered it after twenty years and around three hundred other people's pregnancies.

Fern@toobusytoTWW

Maybe she doesn't want to tell you because you'll try to convince her to keep the baby too?

Mandi@LusciousLocks

What if I don't? What if, because of my own jealousy, I encourage her to get rid of the baby? What a b**ch that would make me, but I am not sure I want her to have it. Not one little bit. Also, just for the pleasure of breaking my MIL's heart.

Becks@desperatemumof1

Now you sound like me. These are the sort of thoughts I have.

Fern@toobusytoTWW

How can you justify ever getting rid of a baby, though?

Mandi@LusciousLocks

I'm not sure my friend has any maternal instinct. She is very self-centred.

Becks@desperatemumof1

She sounds it, allowing herself to get pregnant when she doesn't even want a baby.

Fern@toobusytoTWW

Mistakes do happen, and don't forget, it takes two to tango.

Becks@desperatemumof1

Yeah, but if she was so intent on not wanting one, she should have been more careful.

Star@Gaiababe

I like to avoid the word 'should' when it comes to decision-making. It is a very persuasive word. We all do things for many reasons and often these are unexpected.

Mandi@LusciousLocks

So, Star, you think that maybe deep down she wanted a baby?

Star@Gaiababe

Not at all. I really don't have a clue, but humans are very complex and often we don't know why we do the things we do, or what makes us react when we've done them. My gut feeling is that you need to offer whatever support your friend asks for. By treating her well, you will be inadvertently treating yourself to your own healing balm.

Fern@toobusytoTWW

I'm only just beginning to learn now the complexity of motherhood, after years of denial and pain, and ironically it is just as the point in which I am considering becoming one myself. And so, for once, Star, I think I agree with you.

Loads to discuss on this one, ladies, but GTG, lunch meeting coming up.

Star@Gaiababe

Ditto, work to do… om shanti, dear peeps… Can I just say, I am very happy we found each other. Fern is gone, so I think it is safe to add one more guru quote to reflect on for the remainder of the day:

Life Is Better with True Friends.

Fern@toobusytoTWW

Still here, Star.

Star@Gaiababe

Haha. Thought you might be.

Wednesday 10th February

Day 10 of TWW

"Jane?"

Jane heard the door slam downstairs. *What's Keith doing home in the middle of the day?*

She stayed where she was, curled up on the middle of her bed, and closed her eyes. Sod him. She wasn't going to answer – let him find her.

"Jane?"

Keith entered the bedroom and placed his warm hand on her shoulder. "Look at me."

"No, Keith. Leave me alone." Jane sniffed and theatrically turned her head.

Keith withdrew his hand.

Click. She heard the bedroom door close.

He had gone. Keith never left her alone when she was upset.

"Unreasonable, Jane," she muttered to herself, filled with self-loathing.

She had asked him to leave, but she never expected him to take her at her word. What was happening? She knew from past experience that the TWW was always hard for both of them, but for some reason this TWW was harder than ever. The pressure, sooo intense.

She wasn't even sure her relationship of over twenty years was that secure anymore, and that had never been a concern in the past.

But – how *could* Keith lie to her like that? He was lying. She was certain of it. They had agreed no action to be taken on a puppy until... until a decision was properly and unanimously made. She was totally justified in being unreasonable and hurt. She flipped onto her front and slammed her head into her pillow, muffling a scream of frustration.

"OUCH!"

Quickly onto her back again, eyes wide open.

Jane put both hands on her boobs.

They were really sore.

Shit. In the past she would have rushed to a website, checked for pregnancy symptoms... but she knew what these sore boobs meant now. Her period was coming. As it had, nigh on every month, for the past twenty years.

She pulled the flowery pillow back over her head and wallowed in the hot, snot-filled darkness.

Jane jumped as someone touched her bare belly where her T-shirt had ridden up. She yanked the shirt down to cover herself. She didn't want Keith to touch the squish. To add insult to injury, Jane had been in the kitchen baking like a demon over the past week or so, and comfort-eating the results. Jane was certain that her slim waist was starting to look more sturdy oak tree than lithe and willowy.

Keith gently removed the pillow from her face and put the tea tray down on the bedside table. He sat on the bed, and Jane put her head in his lap.

"Keith..." Jane started, voice muffled in his crotch.

"I know, I know," Keith soothed. "I saw the letter Suz wrote me, open on the kitchen table. I'm not surprised you called me at work in such an annoyed state."

"I'm sorry." Jane sniffed, sitting up. Keith handed over her favourite Emma Bridgewater mug, the one with all the different-coloured dots. She gratefully cupped the warm tea.

"I just felt... so betrayed. I don't know why now, but it felt like such a slap in the face. Like you had given up. You know I didn't want to even think about a puppy until this TWW was up."

"I know. And I'm deeply sorry, Jane. It was just − Suz contacted me, wanting to know if we still wanted the puppy. She had another enquiry. I explained the situation. She was so kind − she said that it sounded like we had been through enough. Suz also said that, although she doesn't normally do this, she would be willing to hold on to the puppy for longer than usual so we could make our decision once... once we knew for certain."

Jane looked at Keith. "She sounds more like a therapist."

"It was comforting having a complete stranger be so understanding."

Thank God she didn't pick up when I called her for a rant, thought Jane. She might have been less inclined to show such generosity.

"I didn't want you to know I had been in contact with her," Keith continued, "because it was going to be a surprise. I was going to let you think that the puppy had gone to another family, and then shoot down to Bristol to pick her up... in case... you know. In case the test didn't turn out the way we wanted it to. I thought that might have taken the sting out of the news a little. I don't want to jinx it by saying it out loud...

but… if we happen to get good news in a few days… then no harm done. The other family could have the puppy, and you would have been none the wiser. "

Jane looked into her teacup. "I'm such a cow," she said. "I automatically thought the worst of you."

Keith took Jane's face in his hands and kissed her nose. "You fool, you know I would never do anything deliberately to hurt you. Why when we have been through so much? All I want is for you to have something to love."

Jane's heart melted. "Er… yep, because I obviously don't love you." She returned Keith's kiss. "You do know I'm really sorry, don't you? I got so upset. I don't know what's come over me. PMT this month is off the scale." Jane glanced at him from under her heavy fringe and wistfully smiled.

"PMT? Are you sure?" Keith looked crestfallen.

Jane picked up his hand and placed it on her left boob.

"Oo, this is unexpected!" Keith's eyes lit up.

Jane quickly batted his massaging hand away. "Careful! Don't squeeze!"

"Why?"

"Just showing you. They are really sore. Like they are every month. Auntie Flo is on her way, I'm really sorry to say."

Keith looked at her and pursed his lips. He rubbed her back in silence, the way he did when she had her period pains.

Jane swung her legs off the bed. "Come on, let's defy the storm clouds and take a picnic to the park. Check it out – see if it will be suitable for Roxy."

"Roxy?" Keith looked puzzled.

"If you think I'm going to call my new puppy Jemima, like a dressed-up walking, talking duck, then you're off your rocker."

"Roxy?" said Keith, trying it out for size. "Rock-zie.

Hmmm… to be discussed!" Keith grabbed Jane and pulled her up off the bed.

"Phew," Jane sighed, as he enveloped her in his arms. Her mood was back to normal again. PMT was a rollercoaster!

Wednesday 10th February

Day 10 of TWW

"Just take a bit of pride! In the house... in YOURSELF, for God's sake!" Mike yelled, as he slammed the front door shut.

Becks stood in the bedroom and closed her eyes against the tears that were threatening to spill. She pulled her dressing gown tighter across her body, surreptitiously sniffed the collar and gagged. There was a distinctly sulphurous scent coming off it. Was that egg down the front? When was the last time she had egg? Two weeks ago??

Becks quickly shrugged the offensive gown off her shoulders and kicked it into the middle of the room with all the other discarded clothes strewn around the floor. She grabbed the plastic wash basket from the corner and started attacking it with garments.

"How fucking dare he?" she muttered. She was raging. This was the final straw.

"Come on, Becks," he was wheedling, clammy hands pawing at her pyjamas.

"You want to have sex? Now? This morning?" Becks asked in exasperation, pulling her PJ top off her head. Becks really wasn't feeling up to it... but was as compliant as always, when Mike wanted sex. He had hinted enough times that he would look elsewhere if she didn't fulfil her wifely duties in the bedroom, and she wasn't quite secure enough to say no. She turned her head away from his boozy fumes. God, stale morning beer breath was the worst.

Mike rolled on top of her. "Yes, I do. Want sex right now. You NEVER want to, so I have to take it when I can," he mumbled into her ear. "You can be a right frigid cow, you know."

Becks froze. She pushed him off. "What are you talking about? I wanted to have sex ten, eleven days ago. I know this for a fact. If I recall correctly... it was YOU who didn't want to."

Mike sighed, placed an arm over his head in that way he thought made him look flexed and manly. "Liar, pants on fire," he drawled childishly. "I'm always up for it. You're the one with the conditions, and times, and... what are you doing?" Mike reached for her again.

Becks was sitting up in bed, pulling her top back on just as quickly as she had taken it off. "HOW DARE YOU?!" she screamed in his face.

"What? Heck, woman, you are all over the place – get a grip!" Mike said in alarm, clutching the duvet. He had never heard her shout so loudly. "Shhh! You will wake up Hector!"

Becks didn't care whether she woke Hector or not. "How dare you call me a liar? Stop gaslighting me! I KNOW I wanted to have sex, like, ten days ago... we had a huge argument about it, remember? I told you that I was ovulating, and you couldn't give two shits. You told me that you were 'tired' and that you didn't want to be treated like a pig stud… an 'inseminator', REMEMBER?"

Becks was hysterical now, thinking back to how furious she had been, when Mike had tried to scupper their plans of trying for another baby because he was 'exhausted' and didn't want to perform to a schedule. Twat. He had just had too much curry and one too many beers.

"You couldn't get it up. Admit it," Becks sneered. She instantly regretted saying this the minute the words left her mouth.

Mike sprung up from bed and snatched a wet towel he had left on the floor to wind around his waist. "I vaguely remember you behaving unreasonably, yes, now you come to mention it," he said coldly. "I stand by what I said then. I am not your performing monkey, Becks, just there to sow my seed when you want it."

Becks was momentarily taken aback. "But… but isn't that what you are doing to me now? Asking me to be your performing monkey?" she asked nastily. "I don't particularly feel like having a sweaty roll around at 6am before a long day with Hector, but you don't see me complaining!"

"Well, actually, I do see you complaining!" Mike stormed round, his face inches from hers. Becks stood her ground, jutting her chin out.

"What are you doing right this minute if it's not whining, and complaining?" Mike hissed. "I work very long hours, Becks. You are just at home, pissing about, pretending your day is really hard… when all you've done is trundled Hector about from nap to playgroup to coffee morning. Well, Jesus wept, sorry if I don't feel sad about your 'loooooooong day with Hector…'"

Mike looked around at the mess in the bedroom.

"You can't even keep the house clean," he bellowed, warming up to his theme.

Becks looked at him, mouth agape.

"And!" Mike continued, jabbing his finger in her chest. "You should be pleased I still want to have sex with you, even if it's not to your agenda..."

"I... I should be pleased you still want to have sex with *me?*" she whispered.

"You're surprised? Look at the state of you, Becks!" Mike stood back and waved his hands down her body like she was an exhibit A.

"When was the last time you had your nails done, or got your legs waxed? You look like an over-ripe pear. And don't even get me started on what's going on down there in your lady garden area. You need an actual mower to sort that mess out. You want to monkey the NCT ladies, but you're nothing like them. I'm sure about that. They are clean for a start, and I bet they're smooth and scented and... most likely..." Mike searched for the word, "vajazzled!"

Becks opened and closed her mouth, lost for words.

Mike was still speaking. "I'm pleased we didn't just have sex. Work would have had to send out a search party to hunt me down in that thicket..."

Mike was clearly pleased with himself, and his insults. He turned on his heel and walked triumphantly into the en-suite to shower.

Becks looked down at the spider legs creeping out of the sides of her greying pants and ran her hands through her lanky hair. She turned to the dressing table and peered in the mirror. There were only a few strands of white hair poking like pubes out of the top of her frizzy fringe.

"Vajazzled?" What was this, like 2010? Since when did anyone vajazzle anymore? Was that the problem? Was Mike gutted because Becks had never been sucked into the whole crazy vajazzling trend? Was that what lay at the root to their dysfunctional marriage?

Silly me. Becks chuckled. *And there I was thinking it was all down to my fallopian tube.*

She plucked one of the offending greys and winced.

I should have just vajazzled.

Becks stormed into the bathroom. Mike was standing in the bath under the shower, covered head to foot in soap. He scrunched his eyes to peer at her though the steam and cupped his manhood in his hands to hide from her accusing gaze.

From his expression it was clear he realised he had overstepped the mark.

"Come on, Becks," nervous chuckle, "don't overreact. God, you used to be a laugh in the old days, you know. Before you became obsessed with the next baby."

Becks softened slightly at the veiled compliment. Yes, she did use to be a laugh. Maybe all of this was her fault. Maybe she could try a bit harder to sort out her appearance. Although, why should she? She was his wife, not his fucking page 3 pin-up. Mike should love her as she was. Who cares about hairy legs? She could feel the rage returning but quickly quashed it. She did not have the strength to argue.

"OK, fine. I admit I have become a bit obsessed with having another child. I'm just trying to create us the perfect family. Is that such a sin?"

"I just don't see why you can't be happy with the child we have. Look after him properly, then maybe you will actually *deserve* a new one," he said, instantaneously ducking as a bar of soap came at him from across the room.

"I'm just saying, Becks," said Mike, hopping out the way. "You just really need to chill out."

"I'll give you chill out," yelled Becks, marching over to Mike in the shower and rotating the dial round to freezing.

Wednesday 10th February

Day 10 of TWW

"So, what are you up to on Sunday? Satin sheets, shags and dildos?" Amelia asked, laughing. She placed a huge glass of wine in front of Fern.

"What? Dildos? What are you going on about now?" Fern asked, distractedly staring at a family with a baby in the corner.

Amelia, Fern's cousin, but more like her older sister. They had been brought up as sisters by Aunt Sadie, after she had taken Fern in. Amelia was Fern's favourite person and closest friend. She had a cutting wit and down to earthiness that kept Fern grounded.

"Valentine's Day! What are you and Jon up to? You have always said he really pushes the boat out – trips away, feather whips, silky gifts."

"Oh! Ha! No. This Valentine's, all I'm likely to get is a high-tech pregnancy kit. Not the most romantic of visions, I grant you. But… if it works out, this will be the best Valentine's ever. If not – well, I don't even want to think about it."

Fern tore her eyes away from the cute baby and looked glumly at the glass of wine. She couldn't drink this. She could even hear Jon's voice in her head telling her to push it away.

"Here, you have it," Fern said. "I want it, but I can't. In case I'm… with child," she added with a wink.

"Don't mind if I do." Amelia took the wine and queued it up next to hers. She poured Fern a glass of water from the jug on the table.

"Cheers!" They clinked glasses.

"OK. So, you find out on Sunday? That's… exciting and shit-scary." Amelia took a long, satisfying sip of wine. "I might be an aunt! Or not! Either's cool. Call me as soon as you take the test."

"Of course." Fern looked around, trying to avert her eyes from the family. "I love this place, you know. It might be the last time I come here. Or at least for a very long time."

"Jesus, Fern. You are trying to get pregnant, not joining a monastery."

"It feels a bit like that! I just can't imagine carrying on with my normal life. You know, after I get pregnant. IF I get pregnant. Maybe this is why I can't have a baby – my body knows I would miss all this too much. The freedom to work, have pub lunches, to do whatever I want." Fern sighed. "Like I told Jon – I think I have to accept I don't have the maternal gene."

"Of course you can do all this! Look at *her*." Amelia turned and waved her hand at the family. Fern pretended to clock them for the first time. She stared at the elegant woman in a chic suit, enjoying a large gin and tonic, totally chilled out with her husband. On the woman's lap was a baby of about nine months, and a pristine toddler was hard at work scribbling on the menu beside her. God, they looked content.

"Yes, but you don't know her story," Fern said. "Maybe all she's ever wanted to do is have a baby, has already got to where she wants to in her career, is now working part time under duress, stressed out, close to jacking it all in. This could be her leaving lunch. You can never tell just by *looking* at people."

"Or she could be celebrating a huge promotion!" Amelia said.

"She could… but my point is, you just can't tell," Fern said.

"No, you can't," said Amelia, thoughtfully. "So, what's your story then?"

"Mine?" Fern said.

"Yes. You're trying to get pregnant. You clearly want a baby, except you talk about it as if it's going to ruin your life. It's a truly complicated message I'm getting here, Fern."

Fern looked at Amelia. Bingo. It was complicated. Why did she want to get pregnant? Because of Jon? Because of societal expectation? Because it was something that had been placed on her to-do list because of her ticking body clock?

"I think you can get why I have tricky thoughts about motherhood? Not the best start in life. Remember? Unwanted? All that. Maybe it's hereditary? Maybe me and baby-rearing don't go hand in hand? And you know I don't like to fail at anything."

"Whaaaat? Girl, you are full of bullsheee-it. Have you forgotten your upbringing? Didn't Sades bring us up to be loving and accepting and responsible?"

"Of course, but she's your mum, not mine."

"She would be super offended if she heard that!" Amelia huffed.

"You know I don't mean it like that. I love her absolutely like she is my mum."

"OK – just saying – she would whoop ya thirty-seven-year-old ass if she hear ya running your mouth about her like that!"

Fern and Amelia laughed.

"Seriously, though. What if... not being maternal is genetic? All I know, is I'm on a forum with all these women, all going through the TWW—"

"The?"

"The two-week wait – it's what you call waiting time between ovulating, when you are meant to be at it like rabbits, and pregnancy testing," Fern explained.

"Oh, OK. Carry on," Amelia said, shrugging and picking up her wine. She drained it and moved on to Fern's.

"They are DESPERATE. Desperate to be pregnant. I... I don't know how I feel. I envy their clarity, their focus. None of them seem to be career women. I just feel my priorities are different to theirs, and that makes it harder."

"Talk to them," Amelia said, and picked up her handbag. "Ask them. They might all have difficult internal conflicts, like you. Might not be the same issues you are facing, but your fears are weird – no offence. I'm sorry, but lunch break over," said Amelia, standing up and blowing a kiss at Fern.

"See what they say. Anyway, you wouldn't be on that damn forum if you didn't feel a bit of yearning – don't diminish your wants just because theirs happens to be more vocal... Hope you got all those wise words, sister," said Amelia knocking back half of Fern's wine and whirling out of the pub in her bold red scarf and striking green boots.

Fern sat quietly after she left, glancing from time to time at the little family again. Having a baby really didn't look too hard or catastrophic. It felt harder to actually *get* pregnant. Maybe she was making this into a mountain. How could Amelia be right? She didn't know the first thing about babies. But she was right. Fine. She would talk to the TWW crew. They might be able to coax her hidden maternal side out from its decades-old hiding place.

Wednesday 10th February
Day 10 of TWW

Fern@toobusytoTWW

Morning everyone.

I have a burning question. We are all on this TWW forum because we want to pass the time/get advice/support from other women trying to get pregnant, right? Sooooo… I guess this is a question for Jane, being the old-timer (soz, Jane, you know what I mean)…

Have you ever had anyone on a TWW forum confess to not feeling sure about having a baby?

Becks@desperatemumof1

Err… what do you mean?? Why would you be on here if you don't want a baby??

Fern@toobusytoTWW

Morning, Becks. Glad to see you are as black and white as always… This is why I need advice. (Jane???)

Of COURSE I want a baby. I just don't seem to be as clear-cut about it as you guys. I feel like I have a lot to lose if I do get pregnant (identity, work, promotion prospects, MONEY) but also a lot to lose if I don't (have a baby!) I'm torn.

Star@Gaiababe

Morning, Fern. Sounds like you need a minute to breathe. Are you having a wobble? I am also finding this the worst day so far. Too early to test, thinking every little thing is a sign that I am pregnant, terrified that I'm not, and excited too, in case I am. In for four, hold for four, out for four...

Fern@toobusytoTWW

Yes, no kidding – I AM having a wobble. Not sure box breathing or whatever you call it is going to help me today.

Star@Gaiababe

Always worth a try.

Fern@toobusytoTWW

OK – let me phrase the question differently:

Everyone is so focused on getting pregnant – have they thought about what it would actually be like to HAVE a child? How they would feel, what they would have to give up? I know this is a TWW forum – I just feel so alone all the time. I thought you fellow waiting-room ladies might be able to help.

Star@Gaiababe

Alone? What about Jon?

Fern@toobusytoTWW

He's great, but he's completely 100% committed to having this baby, as you know. It's less clear for me.

So, I feel alone in everything: in trying to get pregnant,

having no one at work to confide in, and also – now – feeling like I'm the only one with fears about how I will actually cope when the baby comes – if it does! My body and my mind feel at war.

Jane@closetoTWWentyyearsandcounting
Hey, Fern. Sorry, I'm here. This is an interesting one.

No, in answer to your question. All the TWW forum chats I've ever been involved in have been about how we are feeling day by day… Never worrying about whether we GET pregnant. Worries about if it fails (again)… sure.

Fern@toobusytoTWW
I thought as much – I guess people are so preoccupied with their bodies, they can't even think that far ahead into the future.

Jane@closetoTWWentyyearsandcounting
Yep. They don't want to jinx it by imagining themselves with a baby, in case it doesn't happen. Also, if they do let their mind go there, it's normally through an idealised gloss. Like… of course they will be able to cope! Their baby will be the most loved, well-adjusted, wonderful babies! They can't NOT be, as they were so wanted. I hear it time and time again… If mums can get through numerous TWWs, they feel they can cope with anything.

Fern@toobusytoTWW
Hmm. I'm always the odd one out.

Jane@closetoTWWentyyearsandcounting
It's a good topic. Adds a different spin to the usual chats. What exactly is your concern with having a baby? Apart from the ones you listed above. They seem, fairly… superficial…

Fern@toobusytoTWW

Wow. Did not expect that from you, Jane. Superficial? Surely all concerns are valid – what might seem nothing to you… is actually very high on my list of worries…

Jane@closetoTWWentyyearsandcounting

Sorry, that was clumsy of me. My empathy gene is currently malfunctioning. You will be an amazing mother, Fern, in the same way that you are obviously an amazing career woman.

Fern@toobusytoTWW

Well, that's the part that's NOT obvious, actually. The mother part. My birth mother abandoned me when I was a few months old – just gave me to her sister, like I was an old jumper she didn't want. Apparently I was cramping her style. Luckily my aunt already had a baby, so I slotted into their life like I had always been there. It has always made me a bit anxious that I might be like her. My mother.

Apples don't fall far from trees, and all that.

Star@Gaiababe

Wow that's a tough story, Fern. Thank you for sharing. Just because your mum couldn't cope, though, Fern, doesn't mean you won't. You have a loving husband, Jon, and a great career, so you have proved you can stick at things.

Becks@desperatemumof1

Sorry, Fern, but GET A GRIP!!

Star@Gaiababe

WOAH! Chill out, Becks! What's got your goat this morning?

Becks@desperatemumof1

I just can't sit here listening to Fern fretting about whether she's going to be a good mother or not. She didn't even ask me for advice about it, EVEN THOUGH I AM THE ONLY ONE WITH EXPERIENCE OF AN ACTUAL BABY.

Fern@toobusytoTWW

SHOUTING, BECKS!! I'm sorry I didn't ask you – of course you are the one with the experience. I was interested to hear from Jane whether it was a concern people without babies ever had – you know, the fear of not being prepared for one if it came. As you have a child, and tell us how wonderful he is all the time, then… I guess I just assumed you got on with it!

Becks@desperatemumof1

Yes. Well. I have got on with it, I suppose. Sorry, Fern. It was/ is a valid question. Just… bit tetchy this morning. Huge row with Mike again, yawn, but biggest one ever. I wanted to talk about it, and you jumped in with your, "What if I get pregnant? Will I love my baby?" chat. And BTW (more shouting), OF COURSE YOU WILL.

Fern@toobusytoTWW

Just worrying whether I would cope with juggling it all. Who would I be at the end of it? Got the message, though. Won't talk about my worries again, you know – in case it interrupts your time on the forum 'mope' box.

Becks@desperatemumof1

OK, truce.
    I'm at my wits' end. I am thinking of leaving Mike.

Mandi@LusciousLocks

Oh-K. I log on to the forum and world war three is kicking off! What's going on?

Fern – I completely understand where you're coming from. I get that giving up your life as you know it will be scary. But I gave up my life when I married Gav, left work, going out, etc. You just settle in to your new normal. It will all work out fine – you will make it work. I am sure Jon will support you.

Fern@toobusytoTWW

Thanks, Mandi – that's a very mature perspective! And I hadn't considered you have already done the massive life change, being so young. But of course you have. Settling into a 'new normal' sounds like the right attitude. Things will be different, but maybe I need to stop fighting.

Mandi@LusciousLocks

Ha ha, the wise youth of today!!

Now, Becks… Have you lost your mind? You have Hector! With another one possibly on the way? What's wrong?

Becks@desperatemumof1

Mike. He told me I had let myself go. That I was so focused on this baby, I wasn't properly bringing up Hector.

Jane@closetoTWWentyyearsandcounting

...

Mandi@LusciousLocks

...

Fern@toobusytoTWW

...

Becks@desperatemumof1
No wise words of wisdom now? Ladies?

Star@Gaiababe
I'm also quite shocked! BUT.
Leaving him?
That seems like a hasty decision, Becks. How will you cope as a single mum?

Becks@desperatemumof1
How will YOU cope as a single mum, Star?

Star@Gaiababe
Oof… touché.

Thursday 11th February

Day 11 of TWW

Bit shocked.
   Becks!!!
   She has crashed into my karma head on and set things in a spin!

Everyone has always banged on about how mad I am to try and have a baby on my own. I always ignore them, of course. It just doesn't seem a problem. DIDN'T seem a problem.

But now... Becks is considering doing the same... and I think she's MAD!
   I don't think I'M mad.
   But... Why is she any different?

OK – am going to approach this as an Instagram post. What would I say to my followers?

I am not perfect. I have endometriosis. I have been trying for a baby for two years. I want a baby on my own, but I don't know why. *Mummy and Dad have a great marriage and I also want that. But I'm scared I can't match up to that. I've met someone who may very well be the love of my life. I have blocked him, so I hope he can't read this. Endometriosis SUCKS! If this was a male disease there would be a cure by now. I am in pain, sad, lonely. I post mantras to make myself feel better. I am only now seeing that actually those words have power. I just need to FEEL them, rather than just write or say them.*

I don't want to do this on my own, not anymore. FACT!

Thursday 11th February

Day 11 of TWW

"I'm sorry, Star."

Her mum's voice was monotone. She plucked at the white tablecloth over and over to the extent that Star felt a stab of irritation.

"I… I'm ready to tell you. Sorry I couldn't in the cafe the other day. You took me by surprise. You know I hate surprises." Nervous chuckle. "Yes. I had women's troubles. Fibroids. I was told it wasn't hereditary. I didn't mean to keep you in the dark. It just wasn't the sort of thing one discussed, at least in those days."

Star sighed, leant forward and stilled her mother's agitated hands. "But, Mum, you knew I had awful period pains – didn't you think to put two and two together? I thought I was mad! Going from doctor to doctor – it took me nearly nine years to get diagnosed. Nine years! Constant pain, vomiting, thinking I was crazy."

"I'm so sorry, Star. It was so heartless. I just…" Janet sighed. "I suppose I just wanted to be perfect for you, not the harbinger of physiological errors. Seems so, so selfish now and ridiculous. Such pointless pride."

"Who cares about perfect?" *Did I really just say that?* Star wondered, momentarily thrown off course. "Perfect would have been supporting me, not making out I was some kind of freak. You do realise, I might not be able to get pregnant?"

"But you might not have been able to get pregnant anyway," Janet proffered, and then winced. What kind of answer was that?

Star laughed and rolled her eyes. "I've slept with enough men to at least up my chances."

"What? I hope you haven't, young lady!"

Janet looked horrified, and Star relished in teenage delight at still being able to shock her uptight mum. She braced herself for the inevitable lecture on safe sex, but it never came.

"Star, I can only apologise. I love you and, even though I haven't always shown it, I know this now, I have *always* loved you. I had a full hysterectomy after I had you. You were so desperate for a baby brother or sister – I couldn't give you one. I just thought I would pour all my love into you and brush it under the carpet."

Star felt a sudden surge of irrational anger. "Well done, Mum. All that happened was I thought that I was such a handful and a disappointment you couldn't cope with the risk of having another one like me!"

Janet was very quiet.

"You failed me, Mum." Star couldn't help it.

"Don't make me cry, Star, you aren't cruel."

"No, Mum, but I thought you were."

"I'm so sorry." A single tear rolled down Janet's cheek.

Star got up and cuddled her mum. She suddenly realised she was totally lacking the compassion she urged her million followers to show one another.

"No, I'm sorry," Star whispered into her mother's hair. She inhaled the familiar scent of rose soap.

"I support you, Star. If you want a baby on your own, we will help you. Just do what you have to do. And, don't leave it too late like I did."

"I'm doing my best, Mum."

Thursday 11th February

Day 11 of TWW

"Becks?" Mike called out, shutting the front door behind him.

He popped his head around the living-room door. Becks was sitting on the sofa in her (clean) dressing gown, eating a tub of ice cream in front of *EastEnders*.

"Hector in bed?" Mike asked as he came in and took off his tie.

"Mhmhm," Becks replied, licking her spoon.

"Sorry I'm late. Looks different in here... nice," Mike said.

Becks continued staring at the TV and nodded. She had spent all day cleaning and hoovering. There was even a candle flickering on the table, filling the air with the clean scent of fig and roses.

Mike flopped down next to her.

Becks looked at him and glared at his tie, which he hastily picked up from where he had just draped it over the back of the sofa.

"Becks," Mike said, twisting the tie around his fingers.

"Yep," Becks answered coldly, inwardly dreading what words of abuse were about to sprout forth.

"I didn't... mean it. What I said about how you look."

"Don't give me that crap. Words don't just come out of nowhere."

"I know that, but in this case, they did. I genuinely don't know what happened. I was just so angry."

Becks shrugged. "You were a complete shit."

"I know you're not going to forgive me straight off, and I don't expect you to, but I just want you to know that half the stuff I said—"

"Half?"

"OK, everything I said this morning was just bullshit. Raging, madman bullshit."

"Look, Mike, I appreciate that you haven't come in beer-fuelled and alpha and full of cruel abuse, but it doesn't mean it won't happen again, a thousand times and... and I don't know if I can do this anymore," Becks said. She was pumped, warrior-like, brave. She leant forward, picked up the remote and switched off the TV.

"What?"

"I... I want a separation. You clearly find me repulsive," she said.

Silence.

Weird breathing.

Mike crumpled forwards, his back shuddering.

Becks glanced at him out of the side of her eye. What was happening? Was he having a heart attack? Had she just killed him with the shock of her announcement?

"Mike? MIKE?" Becks shook him.

He sat up slowly.

Not dying. But definitely something wrong with his face. Was he... oh God. He was. Mike was... crying!

"MIKE! What's wrong? Was it because I suggested separation? Mike? I... I just don't know what to do. You really, really, REALLY hurt me." Becks was suddenly very anxious about the situation. All courage seeping away. What was Mike doing? He never cried.

"Do you want a beer or something?" Becks put her arm around Mike's heaving shoulders and sprung back as he suddenly sat up. He looked at her intently.

"No. Listen to me, Becks." Mike grabbed her arms. "Things are going to change around here. I... I don't communicate with you properly. I don't know why I said all those things. I can't help myself – it's what I do. When I'm under pressure, I... attack. I just feel... so stressed. I always feel this way, when we're on the two-week wait. Normally I can hold it in, but not this time. It's been building for days."

"We? WE are on the two-week wait?" Becks sat back in surprise. This was the first time he had ever acknowledged that the TWW even registered with him.

"Yes, Becks, WE. This is our baby, remember? I want it to happen as much as you do. I just can't show it like you... I... I think that you would have a nervous breakdown if you felt you were having to cope with my disappointment too."

"You've never shown disappointment! Not once!" Becks said angrily.

Mike took her hands and stroked them. "When I come home, and I see you, lying on the sofa with your hot water bottle – I often take myself away and have a few moments to myself," Mike said quietly. "I just feel so bad for you. For us. For the whole situation."

"I thought you were just distancing yourself from me... because I am a moody cow."

"Well." Mike snorted. "You are a moody cow, that is true—"

"Oi."

"But, that's not why I distance myself."

Becks surveyed Mike's pale face. What was all this? Where did it come from? Was he speaking the truth? Was he on opioids?

"OK, so here's the deal, Becks – we try again, OK? I stop being such a dick and learn to be more open with you. And I do need to learn how to do that, as you know it doesn't come naturally, especially in my job – slaughtered if I show emotion there. And you have to promise to let me know when I need to support you more. I don't do enough I get that. Especially with Hector."

"That's true. I would like a bit more respect. Particularly in front of other people. You make me feel so inadequate."

"I know. I think I'm trying to be funny and messing around, but it's just too sensitive nowadays with the whole baby thing. People change when they have kids."

"That's profound."

"No, I mean, people get so serious and intense. None of the old jokes seem to work anymore."

"I don't think belittling your already insecure wife in front of other women has ever been very funny," said Becks, stiffening.

"I get that. But wasn't it funny once? Not belittling you, but bantering. I would say something to you and you would come back with a witty retort. I am very certain that you are hiding that humorous side, Becks. And I miss it."

"Don't make this about me, Mike. You're the one whose made the belittling mistake."

"I know. I know. It's me. And I will stop. At least for now while we are in this hell hole of waiting."

"And… I promise to dress up a bit more, look like the Becks you fell in love with."

"That would be great. I would love that. But… you don't have to. Really. It's your choice. I'm, er, modern. We could –

SHOULD – go on more date nights," Mike whispered. His hand moved up her leg under the dressing gown.

"Oi!" said Becks but didn't resist.

"Woah, woah woah, what is going on here?" Mike said suddenly, with overexcited energy.

Becks pushed his hand away. "Don't!"

"BECKS!" Mike whipped her dressing gown open and his jaw dropped. "Are those… are those Hector's stickers??"

Becks hastily closed her dressing gown. "They were all I had at home. I wanted to see how it looked… and I wasn't going out to get special 'jazzle' stickers – not sure they even exist anymore…"

"Not bad, Becks. But not necessary. I mean, I liked your bush."

"Liar."

"No, I did. Even thought I was a bit worried Bear Grylls might appear out of the undergrowth."

"I wish."

Mike opened her dressing gown again. "Hmm, but this, yep, I can live with this."

"I didn't do it for you," Becks lied.

"Just as well, because I prefer fire truck stickers to dinosaurs."

Mike stroked Becks' inner thigh. "Although, I give you top marks for being inventive."

Thursday 11th February
Day 11 of TWW

Fern@toobusytoTWW
Quiet today. Everyone hiding?

Jane@closetoTWWentyyearsandcounting
It's a day 11 sort of laying-low type day...
   Excitement mounting, dread mounting... a lot of emotions whirring around...

Becks@desperatemumof1
I'm here... I'm very emotional, but for once I'm distracted from my womb. Something very amazing has happened. I am not sure I want to jinx it, but all I can say is that maybe I am not such an angry, miserable bi**h after all.

Mandi@LusciousLocks
OMG, you're pregnant, aren't you?

Becks@desperatemumof1
Mandi – of course not. Early testing is against the rules.

Fern@toobusytoTWW

Sooo... why so dreamy?

Becks@desperatemumof1

It's Mikey. I really think we might have chance of patching things up.

Fern@toobusytoTWW

That was quick. Your love life is a rollercoaster, Becks. And I say that with pure admiration.

Becks@desperatemumof1

Would love to chat, but I've got a babysitter just arrived. This time we are actually going out for dinner for real. Hang in there, ladies, day 12 tomorrow!

Mandi@LusciousLocks

Wow – I want some of her happy hormones. I eventually spoke to my best friend today. Went around to her salon and asked her straight out to come clean.

Fern@toobusytoTWW

Brave girl. Well done. And?

Mandi@LusciousLocks

She back-footed me by bursting into tears and begging my forgiveness like it was me who got her pregnant. I have NEVER known my friend to cry. She is in a really bad way as she does NOT want to have the baby, but my brother-in-law is insisting. She wants me to talk to Gav and ask him to knock some sense into his brother, but Gav won't do that. He's all for the family seed being spread as far and wide as possible. Anyway, he knows it would break his mum's heart and he would never risk that.

Jane@closetoTWWentyyearsandcounting

Ouch.

Mandi@LusciousLocks

I know. I actually found myself feeling sorry for her. I asked her why she never let on and she told me she was in complete denial. Says she is still in denial except for my MIL calling her every few minutes to make sure she is eating properly and getting plenty of rest. OMG. Something good has come out of this mess. At least I get to have my life back.

Jane@closetoTWWentyyearsandcounting

Poor thing. It sounds terrible for her and I never thought I would say that about someone getting pregnant.

Fern@toobusytoTWW

There is a solution to all this, you realise?

Mandi@LusciousLocks

Don't think I haven't considered it.

Fern@toobusytoTWW

Not sooo bad. I was brought up by my aunt.

Jane@closetoTWWentyyearsandcounting

Woah, woah, woah, hold it right there. This all too much of a moral maze for after dark. Makes my head spin. I'm going to bow out there and see you afresh tomorrow. Sleep well, all.

Fern@toobusytoTWW

I'd love to chat more, but Jon has just appeared with what looks like a bowlful of ocean. Don't stress about it tonight, Mands. Get a good night's sleep. Life always looks rosier in the morning.

Friday 12th February
Day 12 of TWW

Star paced up and down the pavement, deep in contemplation. It was drizzling, but for once she wasn't fixating on the frizz effect it would create on her hair, nor was she fixating on the fact that it was now three o'clock and she had not posted anything on Insta for at least two hours, a world record in Star's book.

Unfortunately, or perhaps, fortunately, she had much bigger matters on her mind than her needy followers. And let's face it, they were needy. Hanging on Star's every word, unable to make a decision for themselves. Star could make decisions. She was a decision-maker and right now, the decision she was on the cusp of deciding upon was vitally important to the rest of her life.

Whoever thought it would be Becks of all people planting the seed in Star's brain? Becks was not the most inspirational person Star had ever come across, yet, based on the impact of her words the last time they chatted on the forum, Star was about to amend her whole life plan.

She was surprised to note that she was nervous. Star could not remember the last time nerves had played any kind of a role in her life. To date, she had always been able to overcome any jitters with deep breathing and positive thinking, but somehow these techniques didn't seem necessary right now. It felt necessary to be nervous. The sensation of nerves made Star feel alive and vulnerable.

And it's not that I don't love him, she said to herself. *What I know of him. I mean, he's kind, gentle, passionate, well toned, funny – in fact, he's perfect.* Star swiped a raindrop off her eyelid. *But most of all, he understands me. I'm sure of that.*

The realisation that she might be able to share her life plan with someone else was an enormous discovery for Star. She had never had to share her life with anyone. Not growing up and not grown up. Life had revolved solely around Star. Star was the centre of her universe.

Until now.

The universe was shifting. Life moves on, and Star was ready to embrace change.

"OK, I can do this," Star said out loud. taking three rapid breaths. "Go Star."

She walked with determination up the short pathway to the front door, rang the bell and stepped back off the doorstep like her mother always told her to do, so as not to overcrowd the doorway.

Standing there, bedraggled but flushed with love, Star couldn't resist picturing how this scene might come across to all her fans. What tagline would she use?

'Love conquers all', 'Committed to love'?

Hearing the approaching footsteps, she stood tall, smacked her cheeks to enhance the blood flow and arranged her face into an 'I'm yours' smile.

"Si?" said a tall, dark, exquisite figure, pulling open the door and staring down at Star through eyelashes long enough to tickle her cheekbones.

"Oh," said Star, heart plunging in her chest. "Hello."

"Si," the woman said again. Her voice was deep, husky and impatient.

"Is, um, Romero here?" Star squeaked, thoughts colliding in her mind.

"Romero. You have woman," called the woman.

"Who is it?" came a voice from inside.

"Who you?" asked the woman.

"I-I'm well, I'm…" Star breathed deep and smiled shallow. "I'm Romero's lover."

The woman looked her up and down and nodded. An enigmatic nod. Disgust? Approval? Star couldn't tell. "She say she's your lo—"

"Star?"

"Romero."

"Star."

Romero appeared at the end of the hall: grey sweatshirt, combat trousers hanging low and speckled with paint. In his hand was a bottle of olive oil. It was the picturesque reunion, bar the imposter.

"I was not expecting you," Romero said, walking down the hallway and taking his place beside the woman.

"Clearly," said Star, aware of the air solidifying. Much to her surprise and annoyance, she felt the sensation of tears prickling her eyeballs.

"Er, Star. This is Maria," said Romero.

"Maria?" said Star, attempting but failing to give a proud nod.

"What? Are you stupid, Romero?" cried Maria suddenly. "Why you introduce me like that? Not just Maria," said the woman, stepping away from Romero. "Maria, his sister."

"Oh, yes, sorry," said Romero, shaking his head out of its befuddlement. "This is Maria, my sister – she's come to visit me from Naples."

"Si, his Napolitano sister," said Maria.

"Oh, your sister," said Star, hesitating to let a small laugh escape her lips. "Of course."

And it was 'of course' – they looked practically identical.

"Si, *older* sister," Maria said. "That is why I am allowed to call him stupid."

Star glanced at Romero, who was busy shrugging and beaming in equal measure.

"So, you wanna come in and make love, or you wanna stay getting wet?" Maria asked, clearly assigning herself the role of hostess.

"Come in," said Romero.

"Er. Come in?" said Star at the same time.

They both laughed.

"She look better in real life," said Maria, eyeing Star up. "Your teeth too white in the photos."

"Thank you, Maria," said Romero. "I can do this by myself, you know."

"You think?"

"I know."

Maria shrugged and shook her head. "I dunno why she like you?" she said, giving Romero a gentle shove and gliding down the hall to the kitchen.

"Sooooo," said Romero, looking at Star, who was busy patting raindrops off her head. "How are you?" He led Star left into the sitting room and closed the door behind him.

Star glanced around the walls covered in paintings.

"Are these all yours?" she asked in surprise.

"Yep," said Romero.

"They... they are excellent!" she said. "You are... actually... really talented!"

"Thank you? I think?" said Romero, laughing at her shock. "These are only a selection. A local gallery have taken the majority of my latest work," Romero added modestly. "Anyway, enough about that. What are you doing here? Last time we spoke – well, you made it very clear you didn't want anything to do with me."

Star sighed. "I know, Rom, and I'm really sorry. Life has been confusing lately, what with coming home from travelling and looking ahead… my head has been all over the place."

"Is that an excuse?"

"Kind of. Not a very good one. But, there's more."

"OK, I'm listening." Romero showed Star to an armchair and sat down on the sofa opposite. Star was momentarily distracted by the perfection of Romero's physique. She had completely forgotten how FIT he was. In Bali, he had seamlessly blended into countless other fit yoga types, but here in the depths of East London, well, he was a different proposition altogether.

"So… I haven't been completely honest with you."

"Oh, OK," said Romero, sitting back and making himself comfortable.

"I'm going to come right out with it," said Star. "I… I am not on the pill."

Romero looked surprised. "Not on the pill? No contraception at all? But you said—"

"I know. I lied." Star shook her head.

Romero ran his fingers through his long hair. "What are you telling me, Star? Are you pregnant?"

"No!" Star said quickly. She picked nervously at a hangnail. "Well. I might be. I am waiting to find out. Don't worry. I don't want anything from you, but I thought I owed it to you to talk about it because there is a possibility."

"Wow," said Romero.

"I know. I'm so sorr—" Star glanced up apologetically to find herself greeted with a huge smile spread across Romero's face.

"A baby? Wow. I'm blown away."

"No... wait. Not a baby. The slim possibility of a baby."

This was an unexpected response. Star was certain that Romero would freak out. She'd met him in Bali, for God's sake, the travel destination of the free spirit, but yet, the excitement radiating from him was, well, endearing.

"Romero, aren't you cross?"

"Cross? Why would I be cross? Babies are wonderful. You are wonderful!" Romero leapt up and flung himself towards her. "I want to tell my sister." Romero went to open the sitting-room door. "Mari—"

"Stop," cried Star, jumping up and grabbing Romero. "There is nothing to celebrate. Not yet at least. Maybe not at all. Ever."

"Wait!" Romero said. If you are pregnant... you... aren't thinking of doing something stupid, are you?" Romero's brow was suddenly knitted with concern.

"Like an abortion? God no! I WANT this baby! I'm desperate for it. The question is – are you?"

Romero sat back on his heels. "You mean, you and me? Back together? Making babies?"

"It had crossed my mind," said Star with a small smile. "Although, we were only together six months – not really a relationship."

"Those were the most important six months of my life," said Romero sincerely. "You... you broke my heart." Romero looked solemn. "I... I can't have it broken again."

"I know," said Star. "I understand."

"If you are pregnant... hold on – when will you know?" said Romero.

"In a couple of days?"

"OK, I don't care what you say, if you are pregnant, I am going to be a part of it. A part of us... that is, if you will have me?"

Star contemplated Romero, staring at her earnestly. She loved a determined man.

"I thought I wanted to go it alone, Romero. I really did. It was nothing personal to you. To us. Just me... being me. But I've changed my mind. I'll have you, if you'll have me."

"Let me think about it," said Romero, glancing at the ceiling. "OK, I've thought. I will have you."

"I'm not as wonderful as you think I am," said Star gratefully. "I can be very spoilt and self-centred and vain and demanding and—"

"Tell me something I don't know," said Romero, pushing Star back onto the sofa and stroking her long, damp hair.

"—and conceited, and did I say vain?" Star giggled as Romero nibbled her ear. "And arrogant and intense and opinionated?" she continued.

"Aha," said Romero. "Well, the good news is, you might be all those things, but I am completely faultless, and so any baby we make will at least be 50% perfect."

"Any more than that and it would be very dull," said Star.

There was a loud knock on the door. "You wanna have lunch or not?"

"Er, thank you, Maria," said Romero. "Be right out."

Maria stuck her head around the door. "And, by the way, don't listen to a word he tells you," she said, looking at Star. "If my brother is perfect, then I'm the Pope's wife."

Friday 12th February
Day 12 of TWW

TWW Forum

Jane@closetoTWWentyyearsandcounting
How is everyone feeling today! Remember – no symptom-spotting! Although – talking about spotting. I think I might be starting my period... definitely saw a spot of blood in my nix this morning. And my boobs are huge and pre-menstrual. Sorry to put a downer on everyone's morning, but looks like I will be getting that puppy after all.

Mandi@LusciousLocks
Oh, bugger, bugger, Jane. I'm so sorry. Could it be the embryo implanting, or something like that?

Jane@closetoTWWentyyearsandcounting
No, sadly not. I don't think, anyway. I feel absolutely nothing, apart from the PMT boobs.

Becks@desperatemumof1
Errr – I definitely classify that as breaking the rules! No symptom-spotting, remember, Jane!

Jane@closetoTWWentyyearsandcounting

Ha, yes, you got me. No symptom-spotting. Won't test until day 14, obviously, but it's obvs it hasn't happened for me again this month. Oh well. It's been fun hanging out with all of you anyway! Always a silver lining. Talking of DRAMAS – Becks? What's going on? Did you have dinner with Mike?

Becks@desperatemumof1

We did!!!!

Jane@closetoTWWentyyearsandcounting

And? (Forgive me if I'm prying – need a bit of good cheer.)

Becks@desperatemumof1

Haha, that's fine. It was lovely actually, and I am NOT just painting a rosy picture (like I might have been prone to do in the past). Thing about Mike is that he really struggles to express himself. He seems to think it a sign of weakness to open up and share how he is feeling. That has caused us soooo many problems.

Jane@closetoTWWentyyearsandcounting

Wow, Becks, that's honest.

Becks@desperatemumof1

I know. How I've changed, huh?! And recently, I have been so self-centred, I stopped listening to his inarticulate attempts at expressing himself. He has had a really hard time at work and then coming home to me, in my permanent misery-guts mode – can't have been easy.

Jane@closetoTWWentyyearsandcounting

You're having a tough time too.

Becks@desperatemumof1

I know, and believe you me, Mike is no saint, but I could see the visible change that came over him last night, simply by opening up about how he was feeling. I know you are going to crucify me for saying this, but sometimes, when all your attention is on a young child (and in my case... obsessing about second child), you forget to notice the person you are with. You get so wrapped up in yourself and day-to-day life.

Jane@closetoTWWentyyearsandcounting

I'm hearing you, Becks. I think I have been very horrible to Keith the last week or so. I'm just struggling with the whole end of the road. I've been equally self-centred.

Becks@desperatemumof1

Keith strikes me as mature enough to be able to handle it, though. Mike, however, has the tendency to revert to immature, childish ways of getting my attention – trying to make me jealous, insulting me, that kind of thing. All he had to do was open up and I (even me) might have found it in me to listen.

Fern@toobusytoTWW

Hold on to my hat. Have I just stepped into a parallel world where Becks is a woman of compassion?

Becks@desperatemumof1

Harsh.

Fern@toobusytoTWW

Sorry, but woah. You are raining wisdom, girl. I'm liking the new Becks.

Becks@desperatemumof1

Fear not, there is still a lot of the miserable, angry bi**h in me. But will bathe in your new-found respect for as long as it lasts.

Fern@toobusytoTWW

I think I've taken on your position as miserable angry bitch now, Becks. As the fourteen-day mark approaches, I am living in fear of the outcome. And not for the same reasons as all of you. I am really worried that I might be pregnant. I know, you can tell me to haul my ass right off, but I am. This last fourteen days has been a shitstorm of emotions for me and I am not sure I am ready for what happens when it's over.

Jane@closetoTWWentyyearsandcounting

From my experience, Fern, nothing happens, so I wouldn't worry too much.

Fern@toobusytoTWW

I know and, sorry to sound like a broken record, but I really don't know what I want anymore. I am so up and down. One minute I want Jon to have everything he dreams of, and the next I am literally packing my bags and running away from the possibility. Sorry, Jane, I read back over today's forum and I know you have most prob got a BFN and I feel for you, I really do. It is a very confusing time.

Becks@desperatemumof1

For someone with a TV show to produce, you're devoting a lot of time to thinking.

Fern@toobusytoTWW

Tell me about it. Sooner or later I'm going to be found out for taking my eye off the ball.

Jane@closetoTWWentyyearsandcounting
As someone who is almost certainly now never going to experience the joy of motherhood, my advice to you, Fern, is just to go with the flow (not Auntie Flo!!). Human beings are the great adaptors and you will figure it out one way or another. That is for sure.

Fern@toobusytoTWW
I know. You're right, Jane. And in the meantime, can I just remind you that this is only day 12? You don't know anything for certain until you test on DAY 14. So stop assuming the worst.

Jane@closetoTWWentyyearsandcounting
Too late for that! Ah well, Roxy will just have to get used to being dressed up in baby clothes.

Mandi@LusciousLocks
Roxy?

Jane@closetoTWWentyyearsandcounting
Woof woof!

Mandi@LusciousLocks
Hahaha.

Friday 12th February

Day 12 of TWW

"I'm happy with whatever you cook, you know that," said Fern down the phone to Jon. "Pie, stew, both fine for me, babe." She probably should have been focusing more on Jon's culinary dilemma, but quite frankly avoiding the puddles on Poland Street was far more of a challenge. Soggy yellow Jimmy Choos was not a look she was going for. "I'm home in twenty minutes – we can discuss everything then?" Fern hung up the phone and swerved an oncoming umbrella. Jon had just been offered a six-month contract in Vancouver but was fixating on the choice of menu for dinner. Fern had to smile. It was so… well, Jon.

It had been a while since Fern was last in Soho. Ever since her production company moved to Clerkenwell, she rarely came to the neighbourhood at all, but she knew it inside out from her year as a runner. It felt nostalgic being back in what used to be her fold. She had once known all the coffee shops and restaurants and offbeat little places suited to the demands of her quirky industry.

Today, though, it was a totally different place. Chain restaurants and tourists.

Arriving on Regent Street, Fern braced herself for the Friday night crowds but it was quieter than normal; most probably because of the rain. It felt like it had been raining non-stop for months – well, the last nine days at least. Even the roads, usually heaving with buses, were progressing at a fair pace. Fern stuck close to the edge of the curb, which she knew from experience was the least congested part of the pavement, and stared ahead in the direct, verging on aggressive, style typical of all Londoners.

There was a small grouping strolling along slowly, just a little way ahead: a mother pushing a pram with two little children on either side; the oldest couldn't have been more than five. Spanish, perhaps, Fern surmised, by the way the mother was dressed. Not that she surmised for long; she was too intent on finding a route to overtake as fast as possible.

Fern was almost on their heels when the younger of the two children, dressed hood to toe in waterproofs, slipped away from the hand of her mother and, without looking left or right, bolted into the road towards the Hamley's beaming lights. The mother screamed and held on to the other child, who was all set to follow. Fern glanced into the traffic. It was all clear on both sides. The child was running towards the middle. In the near distance a motorbike courier clicked into top gear and revved up to speed. It took Fern less than a second to play out in her head how the next few seconds were going to unfurl, and she did not like it. Without pausing to assess, she kicked off her beloved Choos and bounded into the street, oblivious to the water splashing up her tights. The motorbike was fast approaching, taking advantage of an open road, unaware that any second a small child was going to run oblivious across the central reservation and into its path.

Time stood still and sped up at the same time. Fern was vaguely aware of the mother screaming behind her, and of people on the pavement opposite, frozen to the spot, but her eyes were glued to the child. The roar of the bike was so loud, the child momentarily paused. Fern took this as her chance to seize her arm, but she slipped clear and sprinted.

"Nooo," Fern yelled, as child and motorbike converged onto the same square centimetre of tarmac. Lunging forward, Fern grabbed the child and heaved her into her arms, a millisecond before the bike passed with a small swerve and an angry fist from the driver. Fern sat on the wet pavement in the centre of the road, dazedly staring at the bike's rear lights fading into the distance of Piccadilly Circus. She was cradling the young child in her arms as the young child howled for her mother.

Fern didn't bother with putting on her shoes, choosing to walk in just her tights down the remainder of Regent Street to the tube. The sobbing, grateful mother had offered her numerous variations along the theme of wipes and waterproofs, but she waved them off with a simple, "I'm fine." And she was fine. She had simply reacted to what would most likely otherwise have been a tragedy. Anyone would have done the same.

There was nowhere to sit on the tube until past Waterloo when a seat became free and Fern sat. People were looking at her in her bare feet and soaking legs, but she didn't care. The judgement of complete strangers never bothered Fern. The joy of London was that you could be completely anonymous if you wanted to be, as she would never see any of these people again.

It was not until she was home, stuffed full of chicken and mushroom pie, showered, moisturised and clad in her most sloppy pyjamas, that Fern was ready to impart the events of the incident to Jon. That was because she knew that what she had done went waaay deeper than simply removing a child from harm's way. And as soon as she told Jon what had happened, he would know it too.

"I just sensed the danger," she said, as Jon gently massaged the soles of her battered feet.

"Yes, but what I want to know," said Jon, "is would you have reacted in the same way if it was a middle-aged man? Or a woman, for that matter?"

"Course," said Fern defensively.

Jon was looking at her, one eyebrow cocked. "Really?"

"Yes."

"Orrrrr, did you react that way because of it was a young, helpless child, with no sense of safety?"

"What are you getting at, Jon?"

"I think you know."

"Just say it."

Jon grabbed a hold of Fern's ankles and looked at her square on. "Do you think that maybe, just maybe, your deeply embedded, reluctant, shy and ever-so-stubborn mothering instinct might have decided to reveal itself, wake up and tamper with the heartstrings?

"No. Obviously not."

"You said you held the rescued child in your arms?"

"So?"

"So… would you have held a rescued middle-aged man in your arms?"

"No!"

"Hmmm, then I rest my case. There is no point fighting it anymore. You, Fern Abbott, are the ever-so-adverse proprietor of a maternal instinct."

"I can't be." Fern was finding it hard not to smile. She had suspected that this would be the angle Jon would take, but she did not realise it would sound so good.

"I fear to break the news that you are."

"What does this mean?" Fern asked in a small voice.

"I fear it means that you are capable of loving children after all."

"Dang it," said Fern with a contented sigh.

That night, despite being exhausted, Fern couldn't sleep. There was something bothering her, but she couldn't figure out what. She pondered this on and off all night and the next day she did something extraordinary.

"I've decided to take the day off work," she said, rolling over on the bed and prodding Jon in shoulder.

"What, again? You took last Thursday off when we went to the New Forest. Are you ill?" Jon said, sleepy face concerned.

"Nope. I just feel like a day off. And seeing I haven't had an impromptu day off – apart from last Thursday – for about nine years, I think I'm entitled."

"But I've got meetings all day. I won't be here."

That's OK. I'll muddle through."

"Are you traumatised? After yesterday?"

"I'm fine."

"You're traumatised, aren't you?"

"I'm NOT."

Jon hoisted himself up on one elbow. "Well, seeing as you are going to be here all day, I bought you something."

"You didn't know I was going to be here."

"No, but I bought you something anyway."

"What is it?"

Jon climbed out of bed and padded out of the room. When he returned a few moments later he was clutching a paper bag. "Here you go."

"What is it?" Fern stuck her hand into the bag and pulled out the highest-tech pregnancy stick on the market.

"Only the best for you," Jon said. "Well, us."

"But it's day 12," said Fern.

"Look," said Jon, ignoring her and grabbing the box. "It says it can tell you how many weeks pregnant you are."

"Hmmm, so not the Tiffany bracelet I was hoping for."

"No, but this would be a much better present, don't you think?" Jon said, sleepy eyes sparkling.

Fern took the box and examined it. "I thought we made a pact that I wouldn't test until day 14."

"Just do it now," said Jon. "Before that mothering instinct slinks back into the cave of self-doubt."

"Well, that's just it, you see," said Fern, placing the test gently on her bedside table. "Yesterday had an impact on me."

"Yes, you discovered you could be a good mother."

"But something else, Jon."

"What?"

"Hmmm, it sounds much soppier now than it did at 4am."

"I can do soppy."

Fern picked up Jon's hand and enfolded it tightly between her two palms. "Yesterday, when I ran out into the road, I did it without thinking for one second about my own safety."

"I—"

"No let me continue," said Fern firmly. "I'm not saying this to sound all heroic or dramatic or anything, but, thinking about it now, in the cool light of day, I didn't even look left or right. I was prepared to throw myself in front of the motorbike in order to save that child." Fern felt a tear trickling down her cheek. "God, I knew this was going to be soppy."

"Go on…" said Jon.

"And, if I'd died, we would never have had the opportunity to have children of our own. And you would never have had your dream… and my dream… fulfilled. I almost did that to you, Jon. I almost ditched our dreams without ever letting our dreams become a reality and it made me realise how singletrackminded I've been, how scared of stepping out of my comfort zone and taking life in a different direction." Fern paused to grab a tissue. "I've been going on and on about 'not wanting to change for a baby', and 'not being ready', and 'not wanting to give up work', but I've realised all of these are just lame excuses. Yesterday brought home to me the one simple fact I've been dodging all this time and that is that, whatever it takes, I am ready to have our baby and to give our baby all the love and attention it needs."

"And work?"

"Work's important, but so are other things."

"So, let me get this straight. You are prepared to accept that you would like a baby. That there is nothing wrong with you and that you have been going on and on and on—"

"I only said on and on." Fern laughed. "But yes. I think I'm ready to embrace whatever comes our way with open arms."

"My God, you've discovered both motherly and human instincts in the course of twenty-four hours," said Jon. "At the risk of sounding tasteless, are there any more children out there who need saving?"

"But… on the subject of the pregnancy test. I don't want to test yet. We said fourteen days, so let's wait until then. Anyway, I need some time to let my new loving, compassionate, altruistic nature settle in."

Jon put the box away in Fern's bedside drawer and pulled her towards him. "Fine by me. What's done is done. What difference does two days make?"

Saturday 13th February

Day 13 of TWW

Star@Gaiababe
Good morning, babesters, day 13. Hope everyone is as excited as we are to test tomorrow.

Jane@closetoTWWentyyearsandcounting
We?

Star@Gaiababe
You don't miss anything, do you, Jane?

Becks@desperatemumof1
I'm feeling so bloated and I have these strange twinges, familiar, but at the same time, new. Crossing everything for tomorrow.

Jane@closetoTWWentyyearsandcounting
So, come on, Star... who's the 'we'?

Star@Gaiababe
The father of my baby-to-be.

Fern@toobusytoTWW

What?

Star@Gaiababe

Oh, silly me, did I forget to mention that I am no longer going it alone?

Fern@toobusytoTWW

Stop it?

Star@Gaiababe

Aha.

Jane@closetoTWWentyyearsandcounting

Hold on, have you kidnapped the Star who was going to bring up her baby under the stars, running barefoot in the woods like a free-spirited nymph and replaced her with a normal human being?

Star@Gaiababe

Guilty as charged.

Mandi@LusciousLocks

Phew, Star, I'm so relieved for you. TBH, I was terrified on your behalf. Such a responsibility.

Fern@toobusytoTWW

What prompted this about-turn?

Star@Gaiababe

Funnily enough, it was Becks.

Becks@desperatemumof1

Me?

Fern@toobusytoTWW

Becks?

Mandi@LusciousLocks

Becks?

Jane@closetoTWWentyyearsandcounting

Becks?

Becks@desperatemumof1

Alright, everyone, don't sound so surprised.

Star@Gaiababe

Yep, you, Becks. The other day when you announced on here that you were thinking of leaving Mike, I was appalled for you.

Becks@desperatemumof1

Did I admit to that online? OMG, I really do share.

Jane@closetoTWWentyyearsandcounting

Don't worry, Becks, nothing escapes this forum.

Star@Gaiababe

I found myself thinking, NOOOO, don't do it, Becks. Try and work through it with Mike. You obviously once had a good thing with him, which is why you are together. And then I sort of jumped and went, hold on… I had a good thing with Romero. Why throw it away because of a fairy-tale dream of going it alone? Maybe *my* child is going to want a father in its life.

And it was like, bam!!!

Becks@desperatemumof1

God, I'm so inspiring!!!!!

Star@Gaiababe

Totally, Becks, you lit my path.

Becks@desperatemumof1

Aww… Just a shame it was in the context of me ditching my husband!

Fern@toobusytoTWW

But you've turned the corner on that, haven't you, Becks?

Becks@desperatemumof1

Yes, things are definitely looking brighter, not least because I have learned in the course of these last two weeks how to listen. Sometimes you need to listen even when someone isn't speaking.

Star@Gaiababe

Becks, you *are* becoming my guru,

Fern@toobusytoTWW

Woah!! That is deep – respect, Becks!!

Jane@closetoTWWentyyearsandcounting

These two weeks seem to have been cathartic for everyone.

Mandi@LusciousLocks

Hmm, not sure everyone. I feel more confused than ever… like I've been knocked off the very flimsy perch I used to inhabit. I am now a less than complete specimen of a human being. Replaced by my cuckoo best friend, who, incidentally, is going to keep the baby, because she has no choice BUT is not at all happy about it.

Maybe, just maybe when I test tomorrow. Well, all I can say is fingers crossed.

Star@Gaiababe

Be strong, babe. Remember you are a strong, capable, brave young lady and so just be yourself. What's not to love?

Fern@toobusytoTWW

Oh, yes. And I've got news too.

Mandi@LusciousLocks

Pregnant?

Fern@toobusytoTWW

Mandi!!!!!!. Stop it! We've all agreed to wait until day 14, remember? No, I have other news.

Star@Gaiababe

???

Fern@toobusytoTWW

Don't laugh.

Jane@closetoTWWentyyearsandcounting

Would we?

Fern@toobusytoTWW

OK, here goes. I've decided I want a baby.

Becks@desperatemumof1

Er?

Fern@toobusytoTWW

I know it sounds weird. But I've been so worried and unsure and positive that motherhood is not right for me, but all that changed yesterday. I won't go into details, suffice to say, there was an incident between me and a young child nearly getting knocked down on Regent Street last night, and for the first time in my life, I felt maternal feeling gush over me and I thought right, I can do this.

Star@Gaiababe

I was on Regent Street last night. What time were you there?

Fern@toobusytoTWW

Around 7.30.

Star@Gaiababe

Me too. Wait. You weren't the one who ran out into the road to help that child?

Fern@toobusytoTWW

Umm. Yes. That was me.

Star@Gaiababe

Oh my God. I SAW you!!!!!!!!!!!!! I had been in Anthropologie and there was this motorbike and you ran out in the rain in bare feet. I can't BELIEVE that was you. I swear to you, Fern, it was the most beautiful thing I ever saw.

Fern@toobusytoTWW

Er… it wasn't that amazing.

Star@Gaiababe

It was!!! Ladies, I can vouch 100% that Fern is perfect mother material. I had to hold lover boy Romero back from rushing over to hug you (he's really broody BTW). What you did was SOOOOO brave. And you were so cool. You just sort of got up and handed the child back to her sobbing mother like it was all in a day's work to save a child's life.

Jane@closetoTWWentyyearsandcounting

Fern!! SOOOO impressed.

Fern@toobusytoTWW

Anyway… thanks, Star, and I can't believe you were that close by – if only we'd known. That would have been amazing! But, as I was saying, I have now 100% committed to the idea of motherhood, so much so, I have cancelled all thoughts of a second opinion and accepted the fact that maybe there isn't anything wrong with me. We just need to give it time, chill out…

Jane@closetoTWWentyyearsandcounting

Great plan, but oh nooooo, do I feel the 'R' word coming on?

Fern@toobusytoTWW

?

Star@Gaiababe

?

Mandi@LusciousLocks

?

Becks@desperatemumof1

R??

Jane@closetoTWWentyyearsandcounting

Oh, come on, ladies. Have I taught you nothing over the last two weeks?

The R word… RELAX!!!!

Becks@desperatemumof1

Aaarghhh, worst word ever.

Fern@toobusytoTWW

It needs to be banned from the fertility dictionary.

Mandi@LusciousLocks

Wait? There's a fertility dictionary?

Becks@desperatemumof1

Hahahaha.

Jane@closetoTWWentyyearsandcounting

The very best of luck to EVERYONE tomorrow. You already know it's a BFN from me, but I have got everything crossed for the rest of you. And don't forget, if things work out, that I make a very good godmother!!

Fern@toobusytoTWW

Jane! I can't believe someone as wise as you is so utterly determined to think the worst. Ditto everything else Jane said. VERY good luck, everyone. Look forward chatting tomorrow.

Saturday 13th February

Day 13 of TWW

Jane logged off the forum, rounded off the remainder of her cup of tea and checked her handbag for the car keys. It was 11am and she'd told Suz she would be there by 12.30.

It was hard keeping the secret from Keith, especially after everything they had been through on the subject of the puppy, but Jane had made up her mind, and once Jane made up her mind, that was that.

She had come to the decision yesterday morning, after discovering she was spotting. It was devastating seeing the tiny little dot of blood, but Jane was an old hand at dealing with it now. She had learned a long time ago that life had to carry on. She had done rock bottom too many times to count, and it took everything out of her. It was no way to live a life, floundering along the depths of despair. The only way to get through was to have strategies for picking oneself back up. As she closed the front door, behind her, Jane made a mental note to pass on her 'getting over the disappointment' strategies to the girls. They had proved invaluable to Jane over the many years. Star would particularly like the many mantras and positive thinking exercises.

This time, however, Jane was going off-piste. There was no coping strategy entitled 'collect a puppy'.

Jane desperately wished that Keith could be with her as she set off on her adventure to fetch Roxy. It would be so much more fun the two of them, but at the same time this was something Jane needed to do alone. A kind of therapy. 'When one door closes, another one opens' sort of a journey. New beginnings. Also, Jane was certain she would spend a lot of the ride in tears, and crying was so much less complicated when done alone.

Jane started the engine, linked her Spotify playlist of 'reflective' songs on her phone onto the car sound system and drove off into the grey, drizzling rainclouds.

According to the satnav, Bristol was only sixty-three miles away, and the journey was set to take fifty-nine minutes. She was in no rush, though, this was, as Keith had called it, a road trip. 'Trip' being the operative word. Jane was hoping it would be more of a transition where she passed from one state, namely the expectation of motherhood, to another state, namely the realisation that motherhood in the form she hoped, would never be. A sort of sixty-three-mile journey through all five stages of grief, arriving in Bristol at the point of 'acceptance'.

Of course, it was never going to work out like this. She had twenty years of grief all stacked up, which it would take years to work through, but Jane liked all events to have a purpose and so this was a positive focus.

Sinking into the driver's seat, Jane indicated right onto the M5 and set her speed to cruise at a comfortable 50mph down the slow lane. Five miles in, she caught up with a tractor trundling along at 20mph, but she made no attempt to pass, instead she slowed down and imbibed the sickly scent of silage.

At Tewkesbury, she had her first cry. It was not a sad cry, it was triggered by Adele's 'Make You Feel My Love', which always made her cry because it reminded her of the time she and Keith completed their second and final round of IVF. The doctor had been so positive about the likelihood of its success that Jane, even Jane, not known for irrational bursts of optimism, had allowed herself the indulgence of planning ahead. She had even gone so far as to plan buying Christmas presents in late August as it was due to be a Christmas baby, and there was no way she would feel like shopping when she was so close to giving birth. How excited she was. How excited they both were. How naive, and how far the subsequent fall.

Getting her period on that occasion was most probably up there as one of the most wretched moments of her life. She remembered sitting in Keith's arms under a blanket in the garden, all night long, listening to Adele's 'Make You Feel My Love', going around and around on a loop.

So, yes, of course it was going to make her cry, even ten years on. Why else would she have added it to her 'road trip' playlist?

Jane blinked her way through the tears, pleased that she *was* able to cry. On many occasions over the last twenty years, she had felt completely numb. You could have poked her with pins, and she would have felt nothing. Numbness was really hard. One time it lasted so long, it almost led to the end of her marriage to Keith. The problem with numbness is that it cuts you off from everyone else around you, which is an effective form of self-preservation, but Keith needed her as much as she needed him and she refused to let him in. It must have lasted at least two months and during that time, she was like an empty shell: detached, distant, unable to access any sort of emotion. In fact, it was only when her sister introduced her to her new nephew, Benny, that she allowed herself to feel again. Strange that it should have been someone else's child that put her back in touch with the world around her, but somehow holding the baby reminded her that she still had the capacity to love, even if it was not her own child.

Jane shuddered. The thought of going back to those days terrified her. No, without a doubt, crying definitely heals. There was a thread on a TWW forum once, extolling the value of tears, for their stimulation of endorphins and 'feel good' hormones. Everyone was writing, "Bring on the tears," and, "Cry, girls, cry." Jane smiled at the memory.

"Come on, Jane, you can do it – cry, girl, cry," she shouted at the windscreen, and started crying all over again.

At Gloucester, Jane needed the loo. This was highly infuriating as she had been to the loo twice before she left. She kicked herself for having that extra cup of tea, which was not really an 'extra' cup, as she always had two cups in the morning, but clearly it was too much 'extra' for her bladder to cope with.

There was a sign for a service station in 200m. She indicated to turn off, went around a roundabout and pulled into the car park.

The queue for the loo consisted of nine women, whilst there were zero men queuing for the men's. Why were the men's and ladies' toilet facilities the same size? This always irritated Jane. Logic would have it that ladies' toilets were double the size. Jane hopped around on one leg in as ladylike a way as she could muster, reminding herself to sign up to a Pilates class ASAP, to strengthen her defunct pelvic floor.

There was a Waitrose at the service station, which was a pleasant surprise as Jane remembered she needed to pick up some shaving cream for Keith, not to mention food for dinner, dog food, dog collar, dog bed, dog lead – OMG, there was suddenly an enormous list. Her decision to fetch Roxy had come around so quickly she had put no thought into, well, anything to do with anything. Can one even leave the house with a new puppy? What about toys and snacks and toilet training? Jane was immediately overwhelmed with the enormity of the task ahead. She replaced the basket for a trolley and stood still in an attempt to gather her thoughts and organise her brain in a cohesive manner.

OK, so, number one, shaving cream.

Number two... what was it?

Forgotten?

OK, number two, dog food. What does a puppy eat?

Number three? What was number three? Shaving cream. No, I've said that.

What is wrong with my brain?

It was as if Jane's brain had become detached from her head and was floating around just out of reach.

She frowned into the empty trolley, smiled at an elderly lady and attempted a purposeful walk to the toiletries aisle.

One thing Jane was certain of was that shaving cream did not inhabit the same shelf as tampons, sanitary towels and Braun bikini trimmers, but that was where she found herself. She had run out of tampons but previously refused to buy any, not wishing to jinx her TWW, but may as well get some as she was there.

She strode a little further on, past the deodorants and shampoos, past the moisturisers and skincare, the vitamins and showers gels, and arrived at the pregnancy tests. They were hard to miss. There had to be the biggest collection of pregnancy tests she had ever seen. Was there something in the Gloucestershire water that she didn't know about? At least four rows and many brands Jane had never even heard of.

Not for her, though. She already had a pack of five pregnancy tests at home, with three gone – with her track record, it paid to buy in bulk. And anyway, she had agreed not to test until tomorrow even though it was going to be waste of a test.

Jane walked forward with determination, stopped, paused, reversed with determination and stopped. In front of the pregnancy tests.

"What am I doing?" she said, as she raised her hand to hover before a £10 Clearblue digital pregnancy test.

"Jane, what are you doing?" she said, as she lifted the pregnancy test off the shelf and dropped it into the trolley. She was still questioning herself when she walked over to the till, emptied her trolley of its one content and placed it on the conveyor belt.

"Just the one item?" said the cashier with a nosey smile.

"Yes," said Jane. "That's all I need."

Jane ditched the trolley by the exit, walked out of Waitrose and back in through the entrance. There were seven women in line for the ladies'. There were no men in line for the men's. Jane didn't want to wait. Jane shouldn't have to wait. If she was going to make a stand for equality in public toilet formation, what better way to do it than by breaking some rules? She had already behaved in an out-of-character, rash manner, and any second now, her cautious brain might catch up and revert her back to her standard, sensible state. She had to act NOW. Jane ditched the queue for the ladies' and, without a backward glance, pushed opened the door to the men's. There was a young man standing at the urinal with his back to her. To his left were eight empty cubicles. *My point exactly*, thought Jane.

Scuttling into the cubicle closest to the wall, she locked the door and slowly turned around, gearing herself up for what was almost certainly going to present as some form of gut-wrenching filth. Eyes crinkled, nostrils closed... but holy jay cloths, she was blissfully wrong. The toilet seat was spotless and there was still a bleach cube floating in the bowl. *Once again, my point exactly*, thought Jane with a short, matronly nod.

Jane unwrapped the test from its secure plastic casing and balanced it on the toilet roll holder as she prepared herself for the all-too-familiar ritual. Pissing on a pregnancy stick in the men's toilet at a service station was not quite how Jane had envisaged her last and final pregnancy test, most probably EVER, but at least she could cross it off her imaginary list of 'things to do on a road trip': music, cry, stick to the slow lane, piss on a stick, cup of tea. All the essentials.

Hovering over the toilet seat, Jane held the pregnancy stick in between her legs at the necessary downward angle and waited. It had only been fifteen minutes since her last trip to the loo, so it was going to be a case of squeezing out a drop.

Eventually, a small trickle. At last. Jane held the stick and counted just about five seconds. Enough of a trickle to get the tip fully absorbed. She replaced the cap and balanced it back on the toilet roll holder. Her heart was racing, just like it always did post-pregnancy-test wee. Simply a force of habit. Tapping the loo seat cover, Jane let it land loudly on the loo seat and sat down. She picked up the pregnancy test from on top of the toilet roll holder, stole a quick glance to check that there was an hourglass displayed, and that it was flashing, and then concealed it with her hand. She knew the process inside out, upside down:

1. Wee.
2. Wait three minutes.
3. Check display.

She was always bang on when it came to the counting out of the three lots of sixty seconds. No second hand needed. Years of waiting had attuned her to be at one with the passing of time. In another dimension, such accuracy could be considered a gift, but in this world, it was simply evidence of years spent waiting. Outside her cubicle, men were coming in and going out, but they barely registered with Jane. She was lost in her own thin strip of time. As she approached the final ten seconds, Jane slowly lifted her hand. She could see out of the corner of her eye that the flashing had stopped, and the screen was static.

But she couldn't bring herself to look. She wanted to remain in a floating limbo where any possibility existed. Knowing would mean accepting, and she couldn't do it. She just couldn't do it. And anyway, why was she doing this without Keith? They always went through this together. Keith looked first. *I want Keith.* Jane felt a lump germinating in her throat and fought back a sob. "OK, Jane. You can do this," she muttered under her breath. "Just do it. Get the agony over with."

Slowly, ever so slowly, she lowered her head and focused in on the results.

Saturday 13th February

Day 13 of TWW

Gav was late. Mandi had specifically said 11.10am and it was 11.14 and that was why she was tense. In fact, it was not the whole reason she was tense, but it was the one she was focusing on at that precise moment. If Gav dared to do another no-show at the fertility clinic, then that was it; she would pack her bag and move back in with her parents.

Gav knew how important this meeting was, to her at least, and not bothering to show up for a second time would be proof of how little he cared.

Her phone said 11.16. Mandi tried calling, but like the previous four phone calls, it went to answerphone. "WHERE ARE YOU?" she wrote again on WhatsApp and waited for the little grey ticks to turn blue.

Besides anything else, it was embarrassing. They were at the fertility clinic to get the results of Gav's sperm test, and yet, she was here all by herself. Second time around. What kind of message was that? Well, *most probably the true message*, Mandi thought glumly. *It is me who wants the baby, not Gav. It is me who pushed him to have his sperm tested. He thought it was a waste of time.* "Nothing wrong with my machinery." So, it made sense that it was Mandi sitting here by herself to get the results. Except they wouldn't let just her know. Gav had to be here too. It did, after all, concern him.

Sitting in the waiting room waiting, Mandi's thoughts strayed, as inevitably they would, to the remaining source of her tension, the TWW. Day 13 and she did not feel one incy wincy tiny jot different to every other day of her life. No aches, pains or mood swings, no cravings. She was not even bloated. Was this a good thing? Should she be feeling something? Normally she was hyper aware of her PMT, but this time? Had she even got her days right? Yes, of course she had. She knew her menstrual cycle better than she knew her WiFi password. Her hand went instinctively to the tote bag that she was cuddling close to her chest like it needed some kind of security. Which it did, in a sense because in her bag, was the Clear and Simple pregnancy test she had just picked up from Superdrug, at 25% off its standard retail price. £1.25 for six tests. A price even Gav would struggle to gawk at.

Her plan was to test first thing day 14. And by first thing, she meant as soon as Gav had left for work. There was *no way* she was going to do it with him hanging around. For starters, his whole family would know the result before the wee was even cold on the stick and then she would have to endure Agila calling up and offering her patronising 'never mind, dear, try harder next time' speech. Not to mention Gav saying, "Relax," and, "Chill out." And worst of all, his favourite, "Pah, call yourself a wife."

Nope. Gav – house – OUT.

11.21. The bastard. 11.22.

"Mr and Mrs Chadhar?" The small Indian doctor appeared in the doorway of his surgery and looked straight at Mandi.

"Er, just Mrs?" said Mandi, glancing around at the selection of 'couples' looking up from their 'side-by-side' and 'in-this-together' seats. "Held up at work again," Mandi added, with a small laugh and big shrug.

"Come in anyway," said the doctor, a look of sympathy washing over his small, pointy face.

"It's fine. I'm here," called Gav, appearing suddenly at the waiting-room door and walking forcefully over, like a proud lion, purposefully avoiding Mandi's glare.

"Ah, marvellous," said the doctor. "After you." He stood aside to let Gav enter, with Mandi close behind.

"Will it take long?" said Gav, sitting down next to the consulting table and automatically deferring to his phone. Mandi noticed that his hand was shaking and felt a sudden gush of sympathy. Of course, he was nervous. Gav was very protective of the Chadhar family reputation and this was just about the most humiliating event he had most probably ever needed to contend with.

"So, I have the results," said the doctor, ignoring Gav's previous question and shuffling with some notes in an envelope.

"Clearly all is fine, so if you could just confirm, we can be on our way," said Gav.

"Well, actually. Not entirely," said the doctor.

"I'm sorry?" said Gav, his neck turning red.

"Having tested your sample of sperm, Mr Chadhar, by way of assessing the speed in which your sperm move and the quantity of sperm in the specimen, our diagnosis is that you have a condition called hypogonadism."

"Hypo-what?" said Mandi, jaw dropping to her knees.

"It means the testicles are not responding to signals from the brain to produce testosterone and sperm. As a consequence, your sperm count, Mr Chadhar, is extremely low."

"But that is impossible," said Gav, protectively crossing his legs. "Chadhar men have been successfully producing offspring since the beginning of time. My brother has just proved it. You must have diagnosed the wrong specimen."

"My turn to say impossible, I am afraid, Mr Chadhar. There has been no mix-up."

"But how did Gav get this?" said Mandi.

"Our tests predict that it is most likely a congenital condition."

"Born with it?" said Gav.

"That is most likely."

"Impossible," said Gav again, but this time with less vigour. "Chadhar men do—"

"Oh, shut up about Chadhar men, would you?" said Mandi. "This has nothing to do with the Chadhar family tree, Gav, it is about us."

"But..." Gav whimpered.

"What can we do?" asked Mandi, surprised at her assertiveness. "Is there a cure?"

"I wouldn't say a cure, but there are treatments I can recommend which should aid in fertility."

"Yes please," said Mandi.

"It's just not possible," said Gav. "My sperm are perfect."

"I am sure they are perfect, the small number that you have, but there are simply not enough, I am afraid," said the doctor sympathetically. "Your condition is not unusual, Mr Chadhar. And so there are solutions we can offer to ensure you can go on and father a child."

"I don't want children. I just want normal sperm," whined Gav.

"Gav, you're not making any sense," said Mandi, annoyed at Gav's pathetic response. "You're embarrassing yourself."

"Don't worry," said the doctor,. "It often comes as a shock to men."

"So..." said Mandi, twenty-five questions later, "...with the combination of my polycystic ovaries and Gav's hypo-whatever-it-is, do we stand any chance of getting pregnant naturally?"

"There is always a possibility. But the likelihood is greatly reduced."

"But still a possibility?"

"That is correct."

Gav did not go back to work after the trip to the fertility clinic. He blamed it on having a stomachache from something he ate, but Mandi knew it was shock. Truth was, she was shocked. She had always been certain/made to believe it was 100% her with the 'ineffectual baby-making equipment', but it was both of them, in equal measure. How perfectly fair. No more could Gav use her 'lack of womanliness' as an excuse.

Mandi was expecting to feel just a tiny bit triumphant, but instead all she felt was sad. It was going to be SO much harder now. At least when it was just her, she could do whatever it took to create the best possible physical environment for getting pregnant, but if it was Gav as well. He was a nightmare. There was no way he was going to drop off his macho perch and undertake any kind of 'procedures'. It was hard enough getting him to agree to a sperm test, and he only did in the end because he was expecting the doctor to 'oohh' and 'aaahh' at his manliness. Mandi felt immediately helpless. Twenty-one and destined to a childless life. She had strayed so far from her dreams. She felt a sudden pang of jealously (yes, another one) at the thought of Rajul and Naira: so flippant, so disinterested, so superior. It just wasn't fair.

The only good thing to come out of this was that it meant Agila would back off. No more accusing Gav of marrying 'beneath him' or getting into bed with the 'wrong type' or blaming 'incompatibility'. This was a medical problem and if it was congenital, like the doctor said, then, it was all her doing. Haha, Agila.

Digging deep for a drop of compassion, Mandi prepared Gav a round of white, crustless toast smothered with thick strawberry jam and a cup of strong black tea, and carried it to him on a tray into the sitting room. The snooker was on, but the sound was turned down. Gav was on the phone lying on the sofa, back to the door. Normally Mandi would have breezed straight in, as Gav was always on the phone, but for some reason, he was speaking very softly, which immediately pricked Mandi's curiosity. Placing the tray quietly on the table in the hall, Mandi paused in the doorway and listened.

"Not what we expected," she heard him say. "But that's what the doctor said."

Mandi felt her cheeks blushing. Respect to Gav, he was coming right out and telling Agila. Perhaps he was accepting it after all. Mandi crept forward. She wanted to be with Gav when he told his mother, offer him moral support.

"Of course, Mammi," Gav said with a small laugh. "Virile to the core."

Mandi stopped.

"He said I had a higher sperm count than most athletes, almost record-breaking, so nothing wrong with me."

Mandi was frozen to the spot. The coward – the weak, lying, pathetic coward. She walked back into the hall and picked up the tray.

"Yes. The problem is 100% with Mandi. But I will support her... No, I must. She might not be fully woman, but she is my wife. Yes, I love you too. Bye bye, Mammi." Gav thrust his phone into his pocket, picked up the remote control and rested his head on a pillow.

"YOU TOTAL DICK," cried Mandi, coming up behind the sofa and throwing the tray at Gav.

"Mandi, what the fuck?" shouted Gav, jumping up and tearing open the buttons on his shirt. "That tea is burning me."

"You need to call your mother back," said Mandi slowly and authoritatively.

"And what are you expecting me to say?" said Gav, unaware he had a splodge of strawberry jam hanging off his cheek.

"The truth," said Mandi, not bothering to mention the jam.

"The truth will mean nothing to her."

"No, but the test results will."

"She won't even see them," said Gav, wiping his tummy with his rolled-up ball of shirt.

"Oh, she will. In fact, I think she already has because... whoops! I sent her a photo of the sheet of results alongside an explanation of your 'hypogonad' condition. Don't look so shocked. She is your mother, after all. In about thirty seconds, the Chadhar family will know everything there is to know about your weedy little sperm. Poor you, you're not fully man, but you *are* my husband."

Gav's mouth was still hanging open as Mandi turned on her heel and exited the room. She went upstairs to the bedroom, took out the suitcase from the cupboard and began packing her bag. Hearing Gav pacing back and forth downstairs, Mandi felt her blood boil. Really? Was his personal reputation so much more important to him than his marriage and any potential offspring? Was he prepared to let everything go just to maintain his pride? How could I have been so gullible as to believe that Gav would ever put my needs before his own? *Well, let him stew,* thought Mandi, as she dragged the suitcase off the bed and wheeled it down the hallway.

Opening the front door, Mandi heard Gav's voice. He was back on his phone.

"Hallo, Mammi," she heard him say. "I understand Mandi sent you a message about my medical condition."

Hesitating in the doorway, Mandi let out a small, smug smile. How confused Agila would be to receive this phone call.

She could picture her right now, down the end of the line: "What message, my darling? What hypogonad condition? What photograph? I haven't heard anything from Mandi for days!"

"Touché, Gav," whispered Mandi, stepping out into the dusk and pulling the front door behind her.

Saturday 13th February, late

Day 13 of TWW

Star@Gaiababe

Anyone there??

Star@Gaiababe

Just got to share this with all of you...

Saturday 13th February
Day 13 of TWW

It was never easy creeping back into the house late at night, not at fifteen years old or twenty-one or at the grand old age of twenty-nine, but it was a necessity when still living at home. Luckily, years of misspent youth, sneaking out at all hours, meant that Star knew every squeaky floorboard and creaky step and so nimbly manoeuvred herself up onto the hall landing. Romero had wanted her to spend the night at his place, but Star was determined to come home. So much had happened in the last twenty-four hours, that she needed at least a twelve-hour window in the security of her bedroom to reflect upon her new future.

Her bedroom was waiting for her in just the way Janet always prepared it when she was out for the evening: curtains drawn, bedside light on, releasing a warm orange glow, and the top corner of her duvet folded back, all ready for Star to fall into bed. Star smiled. Once a mother, always a mother. She placed her phone and house keys down quietly on her desk and, standing square on, in front of her mirror, looked herself up and down. "So, Stacey-Star," she said. "Are you ready for this? Are you ready for Romero to make an honest woman of you? Is this what you want?"

Star fell backwards onto her bed, landing heavily and causing soft, fluffy cushions to bounce up and down around her. "Of course it's what I want." Star wriggled up the bed towards her pillow. She was so tired, she would, once upon a time, have fallen asleep on the spot, on top of the duvet, fully clothed, but, nowadays, she was too well trained for that. Being an Instagram sensation had shaved off her care-free edge. There were her nightly beauty ablutions to be done. Caked-on make-up was not such a good look in the cold light of a morning.

As Star lay there, she felt something hard under her shoulder. She sat up and pulled back the other corner of her duvet. There was a small object lying on the sheet, wrapped up in flowery paper with a small bow and a greeting tag.

'Dear Star,
Love Mum xxx'

Star tore off the paper and gave a sharp intake of breath. "Oh my God," she said, throwing her hand to her mouth. She looked towards the door just in case her mum was standing there. She wasn't. Wiping away a tear, Star turned the pregnancy test around in her hand. "We've come a long way, Mum," Star said to the empty room. She put the package next to her on the bedside table and padded into her en-suite bathroom to remove her mascara.

Saturday 13th February, late

Day 13 of TWW

TWW Forum (Continued)

Star@Gaiababe

Wow, guys. My mum bought me a gift of a pregnancy test!!
I LOVE my mum!!!!!

Mandi@LusciousLocks

Wow, Star. Your mum sounds amazing!!

Star@Gaiababe

She is, but you know what... I never thought I would say that.

Mandi@LusciousLocks

Gav and I have split up.

Star@Gaiababe

Whaaaaat? OMG, Mandi!! I am SO sorry to hear this.

Mandi@LusciousLocks

I just had to leave him. We found out today that he has a
condition that affects sperm count... he is basically not far

off infertile, BUT, he refused to acknowledge it. But that's not why I've left. I left because he lied to his mum saying he had the sperm of a famous sports star. And therefore… it was ALL ME!

Star@Gaiababe

Ouch. Sounds like he needs serious therapy.

Mandi@LusciousLocks

Maybe. I've moved back in with my parents.

Star@Gaiababe

How long will you stay?

Mandi@LusciousLocks

No idea. This has all come about record fast. I don't even remember how I got home. Bus, maybe? All a whirl.

Star@Gaiababe

Are you OK, babes? You sound like you are in shock. Is there anyone I can call for you?

Mandi@LusciousLocks

I'm OK. It's been a day, that's for sure.

Star@Gaiababe

How are your parents?

Mandi@LusciousLocks

Put it like this: I'm not sure my mum is in the mood to buy *me* a pregnancy test!!!

Star@Gaiababe

No, but there again, can't think of many mothers who might. Believe you me, it has taken many years of dysfunction to get to this point!

Mandi@LusciousLocks

I'll take some comfort in that. So, when will you test?

Star@Gaiababe

When I wake up.

Mandi@LusciousLocks

I'm quite tempted to do it now, considering the way my day has gone. Would actually be quite disastrous if I were pregnant, as I am pretty certain I don't want to be with Gav anymore.

Star@Gaiababe

You've got to trust your instincts, babe.

Mandi@LusciousLocks

I realised today that I have been unhappy for a long time. Good, solid, loving support is worth everything and I never got any of that from Gav or his family.

Star@Gaiababe

Sending you a million virtual hugs.

Mandi@LusciousLocks

Think I need them. I'm petrified. Seem to have lost my best friend and my husband in the course of a couple of days.

Star@Gaiababe

I could sprout out many mantras to try and ease the pain you are in, but they all feel pretty pointless.

Mandi@LusciousLocks

That's OK, Star. At least I know now that the reason we were unable to get pregnant was not all down to me. Sounds mad, but I feel almost relieved that I still stand a chance to follow my dreams of perhaps one day starting a family. Even if not with Gav…

Star@Gaiababe

You sound like you are over him already.

Mandi@LusciousLocks

If only it could be that easy, but rest assured the shit is going to hit the fan.

Star@Gaiababe

You know, I have a feeling you'll be fine, Mands. You're young and stronger than you think.

Mandi@LusciousLocks

I really hope you're right.

Sunday 14th February

Day 14 of TWW

"Wake up, wake up, wake up, wake up, wake up…" came Hector's voice from very close to Becks' ear.

"Oh noooooo. What time is it?" groaned Becks, burying her head under the duvet.

"Wake up, wake up, wake up, wake up, wake up…" came Mike's voice now as Hector let out a loud giggle.

"Mummy's very lazy, isn't she?" said Mike, pulling the duvet down and filling Becks' face with red rose petals.

"Agh, yuck, cold," cried Becks, pushing the bunch of dozen red roses away.

"Do it again, Daddy," said Hector.

"AGAIN?" roared Mike, nuzzling Hector's tummy with his nose. "You want me to be really annoying to Mummy again?"

"Yes… Daddy, more."

"OH MY GOD!" shouted Becks, sitting up, wiping rose water off her cheek. "Can someone please tell me why everyone is awake at 5.59am?"

"Wait… wait… wait one second more… 6am. Time

to get up, lazybones." Mike stripped the duvet right back off the bed, exposing Becks curled up in her fluffy, pink pyjamas.

"Noooo," cried Becks, going to grab the duvet, but Hector and Mike had run off with it. Hector was almost wetting himself with laughter.

"Oh, by the way," Mike said, sticking his head back around the door. "Happy Valentine's Day." He threw the duvet back at Becks.

"Thank God, it's freeeezing," cried Becks.

Two seconds later, Mike and Hector were back in the room, Hector wobbling a balanced tray. "Bought you your mooosli," he said.

"At 6am?" said Becks yawning widely. "Just what I feel like."

"And a coffee," said Mike. "Strong and sweet… Just like you like your—"

"Yeah, alright," said Becks. "My romance detector doesn't kick in until after 8am."

"Spoilsport," said Mike.

"Yeah, spoilyspot," said Hector.

Becks lay back in bed and watched Mike getting dressed for work. Hector had dragged in a knee-high pile of books and was sitting at the end of the bed, engrossed.

"You know what day it is today?" Becks said quietly, as Mike tied his tie.

"Yeah. Do you wanna test now?" said Mike.

"Shall we?"

Mike shrugged. "It makes sense, seeing I'm still here."

"I'm nervous," said Becks.

"Are you still feeling, you know, that feeling?"

"Yeah, I am a bit. Got this weird stomach pain. It won't be anything, though."

"I know," said Mike. "But that's OK, isn't it? We can handle whatever comes our way. Can't we?" he added with a questioning look.

Becks jumped out of bed and grabbed Mike's hand. "Course we can. Come on, let's go do a wee," she whispered.

Sunday 14th February

Day 14 of TWW

"That's OK," said Jon, sitting down next to Fern on the edge of the bath and putting his arm around her shoulder. "We weren't really thinking it would be this time around."

"No," said Fern. "It would have been pretty incredible after all the soul-searching of the last couple of weeks."

Jon took the test out of Fern's hand and examined it. "I guess the reading is right," he said.

"Seeing it's the classiest pregnancy test we've ever had I would hope so."

"Hmm, but there again, might be all fur coat, no knickers. Sometimes there's a lot to be said for your bog-standard Boots Essential."

"Is that right?" said Fern. "Oh, master of the home pregnancy testing kit."

"It comes with the territory," said Jon. "Most neurotic father-to-be."

"That's the only test we have," said Fern. "Happy to pick one up later on."

"See how you feel," said Jon.

"I know how I feel, but I have a feeling you won't be satisfied until we've done the standard five tests and a sixth for luck."

"We only test six times? How very remiss." Jon was putting on a brave face, but Fern was feeling his pain. She was feeling her own pain too. But they had to stay positive, for one another. It was only a matter of time. That was what the doctor said. There was nothing wrong with either of them. It was just time, time, time.

"Fine. I'll buy one of every brand on my way home from work," said Fern. "And that is our fun evening all planned."

"Can't wait," said Jon, getting up and throwing the pregnancy stick in the bin. "In the meantime, green tea with a natural yoghurt shake?"

"Hmmm, I think I'll have a coffee," said Fern. "And a hot bacon roll."

Sunday 14th February

Day 14 of TWW

"Where are you going?" whined Nina, Mandi's sister, rolling over on her bed.

"Sshhh, go back to sleep."

"I'm trying, but you're just so restless. It's like sharing a room with a washing machine."

"I'm sorry, I've got a lot on my mind. I'm going to go downstairs." Mandi climbed out of bed and wrapped herself in a blanket.

"Do you want me to come?"

"No, you're fine. You need all the beauty sleep you can get."

"In that case, you must be insomniac," said Nina.

"Haha… shhhh, I'm opening the door. I don't want Dad coming out."

"They will hear you, you know that. Mum has ears like an owl."

"She's most probably awake already, worrying about me," said Mandi with a pang.

She crept out of the room and down the stairs, shivering in the cold dead of night. There was a grey tinge to downstairs, as if the moon was in two minds about whether or not to shine. It was just bright enough for Mandi to see where she was going. Not that she needed any light for this. She was back in her childhood home. She knew every nook, cranny and dark corner. She pattered across the warm carpet and into the downstairs loo.

The pregnancy test was all ready to go. She had unwrapped it in her bedroom, and left the box and instructions hidden in her handbag. She was a married – well, in theory – woman, and so naturally kids were on the cards, but at the same time, pregnancy testing at home with her parents sleeping in the room above felt rebellious.

This was the first time Mandi could remember doing a pregnancy test without fumbling fingers. Normally, she was so nervous that attempting to align the stick with the stream of urine left her in a wee-splattered mess. Today, though, she was calm. Strangely calm. She was just going through the motions, almost indifferent to the results. Agila was not going to call in less than three hours and demand to know if there was a grandson on its way, because, well, Agila wouldn't dare. Not anymore. That is assuming Gav told her the whole truth, which was questionable. He was bound to have found some way of squirming the blame back onto Mandi.

As she positioned herself on the loo, Mandi wondered how she could have been so blind.

She must have known that Gav was a lying, slithering wimp, but somehow, it had always been her fault. Perhaps it was her lack of confidence that made her take the blame for his every undermining act. The fact that it was Mandi versus the entire Chadhar clan, not only in the present day, but dating back practically to the Mogul empire.

Being pregnant with Gav's child would mean having to remain bound to the entire family for the rest of her life. Even if she produced seven strapping sons, the success, in Agila's eyes, would be all Gav's. She was and always would be, nothing to them.

Just the thought of all the above, made Mandi's skin crawl. It was as if she had woken up after a hundred-year sleep and discovered that the frog was not budging.

As she completed her wee, and shook the stick, she was begging not to be pregnant. *I've made a mistake*, thought Mandi. *I have no idea how I am going to get out of the 'till death us do part' mistake, but OMG, I will. I'm going to release myself from this stranglehold and reconnect with the true me.*

That is so long… please, so long as I'm not pregnant.

Mandi cast a look at the pregnancy stick display, inhaled, counted to five and exhaled.

Sunday 14th February

Day 14 of TWW

"Before you ask, no, I haven't used it, not yet," said Star, striding into the kitchen and wrapping her arms around Janet.

"I wasn't going to ask," said Janet, trying but struggling to relax in Star's embrace.

"I know, I was joking... as if you'd ask. But, thank you, Mum, for the gesture."

"So, I got the day right?"

"Bang on. Day 14 and I am teetering on the edge of nauseous, migrainous and a bloat so severe I look like a speed hump."

"You don't, you look lovely," said Janet, scarpering to the other side of the kitchen and rewashing a plate.

"I know I'm about to come on, any second," said Star. "And so not sure I should waste the pregnancy test."

"Or..." Janet said, spinning around to look at Star with moist eyes. "Maybe you're feeling like this because... you're pregnant?"

"Mum? Since when did you become the optimist?"

Janet shrugged. "There's a lot about me you don't know."

"Clearly," said Star. "But I really don't *feel* pregnant."

"And you know how it feels?"

"Well, no, but I do know how periods feel and this is PMT."

"Tell you what, why don't you go and test in the upstairs loo, while I'll make you a celery, apple and mint goddess."

"You remembered."

"Of course."

"Don't forget, it has lime as well. To neutralise the acid."

"Be gone, girl," said Janet, chasing Star out of the room with a celery stick.

Star ran out with a playful giggle.

"But please don't go getting your hopes up, Mum," she said, turning in the doorway. "You do know that it's not going to be."

"With the soundproofing in this house, I could think of nothing worse than having a newborn," said Janet.

"Liar," said Star.

Sunday 14th February

Day 14 of TWW

Becks@desperatemumof1

Soooooooooo?

Becks@desperatemumof1

Anyone?

Becks@desperatemumof1

Well, just for the record. I got a BFN – boooo hoooooo. Devastated. Been crying for last twenty minutes. Did get a bunch of Valentine's roses from Mike, though. He wants to test again, bless. Not sure, might do, just to appease him. I really thought that this time… it was a maybe. OK, back on the TWW bandwagon.

Becks@desperatemumof1

Anyone else? Oh, God. Please don't tell me you're all pregnant and I'm the only one who's not. You know how sensitive I am…

Becks@desperatemumof1

Starting to freak me out now.

Mandi@LusciousLocks

Hallloooooooo, I'm here... I got a BFN too, Becks. Thank God. I was really worried I might be pregnant.

Becks@desperatemumof1

Er, hello. Confused.com.

Mandi@LusciousLocks

I know... about-turn. Check out yesterday's forum. Gav and I broke up. I was actually starting to have nightmares that I was pregnant and would have to go back to him. A lot to say there, Becks, but won't burden you. Really sorry to hear about your BFN.

Becks@desperatemumof1

I know. Gutted. Might test one more time. Just for added disappointment.

Mandi@LusciousLocks

Might be worth it... Superdrug are running a discount on pregnancy tests.

Becks@desperatemumof1

I am thinking you just said you broke up with Gav, or did I imagine it?

Mandi@LusciousLocks

Read yesterday's forum, that's all I can say on the subject.

Becks@desperatemumof1

Fuck, Mandi!

Mandi@LusciousLocks

It's alright. Plenty of fish in the supermarket.

Star@Gaiababe

Hi, babes. We tried, we did not conquer, not this time around.

Quote for the day: "There is a positive side to everything; it just takes a positive mind to see it."

Becks@desperatemumof1

I bet you had that one all lined up ready to reel off today.

Star@Gaiababe

You know me too well now, Becks.

Becks@desperatemumof1

What's concerning is that I am beginning to find comfort in your positive thinking.

Star@Gaiababe

And that is why I have committed my life to imparting wise advice.

Mandi@LusciousLocks

Any positive words to say about the nightmare I have plunged into?

Star@Gaiababe

Most probably loads, but I am not sure any of them will help where you are right now. This is going to be a tough day for all of us, but for you it sounds like it is just the beginning.

Becks@desperatemumof1

Jane? Fern? Where are they???

Star@Gaiababe

Mysteriously quiet...

Mandi@LusciousLocks

Maybe they know something we don't know...???

Fern@toobusytoTWW

I'm here. Sorry, was just arguing with the director who wants to add five new shots... Grrrrr, why??? Anyway... yes I am part of the BFN crew too, girls. Jon is mortified. I almost found myself saying the R word to him this morning... Jane would be livid!!

Star@Gaiababe

And are you mortified?

Fern@toobusytoTWW

Yep. Totally. Properly. Not a nice feeling, girls. Give me tough ass, feelingless bitch any day.

Star@Gaiababe

Being human hurts!

Fern@toobusytoTWW

Beautiful!!!

Star@Gaiababe

Ouch!!!

Fern@toobusytoTWW

Not taking the piss, Star. That 'ouch' was genuine. Discovering my maternal side has been like unzipping a bulging sack of pent-up emotions. And it does HURT!!! Particularly today. I hope we all have something planned for getting us through??

Mandi@LusciousLocks

I am spending my day getting under my mum's feet, annoying my sister and dodging phone calls from Gav… oh wait, phone calls to date this morning – ZERO!

Becks@desperatemumof1

Mike suggested we go for a pub dinner at the Duck and Hound, which was really touching until he added the bit about 'sitting near the screen for the rugby'.

Star@Gaiababe

Aaahh, kind of…

Becks@desperatemumof1

Baby steps, ladies – and I'm talking about Mike.

Star@Gaiababe

I'm going to go and calm down Romero, who is certain that he is about to become a father. Whoops, I might have over-egged his expectations.

Mandi@LusciousLocks

Did you say anything to your mum about her kind gift?

Star@Gaiababe

My mum is the coolest chick on the block – and I never thought I'd say that. She is more upset than me about the baby. Bit of an added new pressure having her come along with me on this 'journey', but at least we have found some common ground to bond over. That and smoothies.

Becks@desperatemumof1

Anyone going to test again?

Fern@toobusytoTWW

That is what Jon has got planned for tonight: wall-to-wall weeing on a stick.

Becks@desperatemumof1

Haha. Lucky you! I think we might test again, but not expecting anything new…

Mandi@LusciousLocks

OMG, I'm suddenly feeling emotional. Is this the end… of us?

Fern@toobusytoTWW

But where's Jane?

Mandi@LusciousLocks

I hope she's OK… She was so certain about the BFN. Do you think she even tested?

Saturday 13th February
Day 13 of TWW

"Don't move," said Keith. "I'm taking an Uber."

"But it's forty miles."

"I don't care," said Keith. "Just stay there."

Jane had no intention of moving. Well, she had every intention of hauling herself out of the men's loo, as there was a rapidly emanating reek of stale wee, but she was not budging from the service station.

She could not trust herself to drive.

Clutching on to the pregnancy stick as if her life depended on it, which it did to a degree, she unlocked the men's loo, shook her hair into some sort of style beyond that of the 'glued-to-forehead-with-sweat' look and strode out.

There were a few men now lined up at the urinals at various stages of urination; some tapping, others shaking, one or two stuck firmly to the spot, legs apart and going with the flow. Jane might have been staring at them, she might not; she didn't know what she was doing, as she was in a daze.

She was vaguely aware of colliding with a beefy lorry driver, aware enough to note that he had tattoos for cheeks, long hair and pierced eyebrows and that he said, "Wrong toilet, lass."

And that she said, "I'm sorry," and added, "I'm pregnant."

And he said, "Aye up."

And she said, "Er, thank you," and added, "My first baby."

And he said, "Ladies' next door."

To which Jane rounded off the conversation with: "Got the pregnancy stick to prove it," before gliding out of the toilet and into to the throng of travelling public.

On finding herself back in Waitrose, Jane came to, enough to realise that sometime earlier in the day, at least thirty minutes before everything in her life turned upside down, she had to buy a puppy collar, and puppy bed and lead and food and… shaving cream and…

Oh my God, I'm pregnant. Jane wanted to skip and dance, but she kept her feet firmly on the ground and paced over to the pregnancy tests. She had to be sure. One test might not be accurate.

She didn't have a basket or a trolley, so she carried the three different tests back to the same cashier.

"Just the three items?" asked the cashier with a nosy and curious smile.

"Yes," said Jane, and added, "I'm pregnant." She was going to wave the 'positive' pregnancy stick under the cashier's nose to prove it, but common sense kicked in. What were the supermarket hygiene rules when it came to waving wee on a stick?

"Do you want a 5p bag for those?"

"No, I can manage them," said Jane.

The queue for the ladies' loo was four women deep, but Jane could wait. She had waited twenty years – what was ten more minutes?

The lady in front of Jane was pregnant. *What are the chances of that?* thought Jane. *Both of us pregnant together.*

"How many months?" Jane asked, beaming.

"Seven," the lady replied.

"How exciting," said Jane. "I'm pregnant too," she added.

The lady smiled wearily, her eye straying to the packages in Jane's hand.

"Well, just confirming," Jane added. "Need to be sure."

"I've always sworn by the Clearblue myself," said the lady.

"They are the most reliable, aren't they?" said Jane. She really had no idea what she was talking about, but God, it did feel good to be part of the 'pregnancy chat' gang.

"Good luck then," said the woman. "That is, assuming you *want* to be pregnant."

"Ohhhh, yes," said Jane. "I'm thrilled."

By the time Keith arrived fifty minutes later, Jane had completed four pregnancy tests and each one of them had the same results. PREGNANT!

"I just can't believe it," said Keith, tears pouring down his face. "I just can't believe it. I just can't believe it!"

"So, you can't believe it?" said Jane, hugging Keith in the car park.

"I want to shout it from the rooftops. MY WIFE IS PREGNANT."

"Oh, don't worry, I'm not sure there is anyone left in a hundred-mile radius who hasn't heard."

"I just can't believe it." Keith was shaking his head, wiping away tears, smiling, laughing, hugging...

"It was the threat of Roxy that did it."

"You would have loved a puppy."

"I know. Poor Roxy. We could have given her a lovely home."

"Don't worry, I spoke to Suz and she says she has called the other family about adopting Roxy, and they are thrilled."

"OK, phew! So no guilty Roxy thoughts."

"None whatsoever," said Keith. He stared around at the depressing red-brick service station, made all the more gloomy in the pervading drizzle. "You know that for the rest of our lives, this service station is going to mean something to us."

"I can live with that," said Jane. "As far as I'm concerned, right here is the happiest place on earth. Particularly the men's toilets."

"Sooo, do you want to hang out here a bit more then?"

"God no, let's go home."

"Well, that was quite some road trip," said Jane, as Keith parked up outside the house. "I left as one woman and came back as a whole new one."

"Whole plus one," said Keith, stroking Jane's tummy.

"Can you feel it kicking?"

"Haha," said Keith. "Something tells me this nine months is going to last a very long time."

"I'm going to be counting every single second," said Jane.

It was not until later that afternoon, as Jane walked into the bathroom, that she remembered what was number one on her shopping list.

"Oh, darn it," she called out to Keith, "I forgot to buy you shaving cream."

"And there I was thinking I had everything I needed in life."

Sunday 14th February

Day 14 of TWW

Jane@closetoTWWentyyearsandcounting

Can I just say... to all of you newbies who have not yet been waiting 7,300 days to get pregnant, your time will come. I am delighted to announce the very happy news that... I AM PREGNANT!!! Miracles occur!!!!

Sorry, I know this is a very hard subject for everyone, particularly today, but I like to think that after all these years we've waited, our success can bring hope to you all.

Fern@toobusytoTWW

Jane!!!!!! The biggest, hugest, most expansive congratulations to you both. This is simply the happiest outcome (sorry, ladies), but you've done your time, Jane, and you deserve every bit of this.

Star@Gaiababe

Wahoooo!! Agreed!! Jane, I am literally spinning virtual somersaults for you and Keith. SO happy for you.

Becks@desperatemumof1

Never thought I would feel joy for someone else's happy pregnancy news, but I am sprouting tears (God, I'm hormonal). Jane, you bring hope to us all. I really did not think that it would happen to you. You seemed so certain of your BFN, but, well, congratulations and have a big virgin cocktail on me. xxxx

Mandi@LusciousLocks

Jane. Thank you for being there for all of us. This could not have happened to a kinder, more generous person and I am so so happy for you. All the very best to you and Keith and everything that is to come.

My God, I am really going to miss you all.

Star@Gaiababe

You don't have to miss me, I will be back in two weeks' time to begin the TWW!!!!

Fern@toobusytoTWW

Me too.

Becks@desperatemumof1

Sigh… me too.

Jane@closetoTWWentyyearsandcounting

I'm here for all of you. I might not have mentioned that I have twenty years' worth of experience to share so… don't think you're shot of me that fast.

Star@Gaiababe

Ladies. It's been real and if I may just sign out with a guru quote: "The only time goodbye is painful is when you know you'll never say hello again."

See you in two weeks, and Jane. You look after that beautiful, nurturing body of yours. That baby is lucky to have you.

Fern@toobusytoTWW

See you in two weeks xxx

Becks@desperatemumof1

See you in two weeks xxx

Mandi@LusciousLocks

Two weeks, my friends, by which time I will either be running free or bound by my ankles (and I don't mean in a good way). Goodbye and thank you. I am all the richer and stronger for your love xxx

Monday 15th February

Day 15 of TWW

* * * * * * * * * * * *

Anyone out there?
   Hello?
   Forum friends?
   Ladies…

You're not going to believe this…

I've just done another test and OMG… I'm pregnant.

Acknowledgements

There are a few people I would like to thank for this book, because without any of you, I cannot function, let alone write a book...

Charles, Heidi and George – without you, I would be lost. You make every day wonderful.

To my girls who keep me going... Sophie, Kate, Amy and Maxine (and Steven!) I love you.

A big thank you to my friends Abby and Hannah for 'O- A -O' and giving me to courage to go for it.

To all the amazing women that have reached out to me and shared their stories.

To my Instagram followers, who never fail to amaze me, with your support for others and your bravery.

And finally to all the people who are giving fertility issues and the couples struggling to conceive, a voice.

Writer, mother and passionate supporter of women on their fertility journey, Lucy is a holistic fertility and wellness coach working alongside women, offering them therapies, support, motivation and inspiration.

When seeking advice about fertility and the gift that is pregnancy, we're overly faced with medical jargon and unsolicited advice. Whether it's from well-meaning doctors or misunderstanding friends, the comments that we absorb during this time are ones that have really staying power. Lucy helps women to positively reframe their fertility journey in a way that feels safe and supported, without jargon and confusion, to help you manage the emotions, talk about the choices and develop a mindset that prevents you from becoming totally overwhelmed.

Join her community to find ways, through personalised one-to-one coaching, workshops, therapies and retreats to support you during your wait, no matter how long that may be...

Online at: www.thetwoweekwait.com